Petals of the Soul

God's Love vs. Satan's Deceit

Cathy BeDell Ritter

Seventy-nine short stories that show God's love and Satan's influence in almost every situation in our lives.

PublishAmerica
Baltimore

First printing

Cover photography by Rachel BeDell.

Comments? Contact the author at:
cathyritter@publishedauthors.net

ISBN: 1-4241-9400-8
PUBLISHED BY PUBLISHAMERICA, LLLP
www.publishamerica.com
Baltimore

Printed in the United States of America

7/8/08

Dedicated to the glory of God for nudging me to write this book!

Benny & Ashley,

To my favorite "adopted" son. May you find happiness in life and in hopes that God will be an important part towards that happiness!

Know that He loves you dearly!

Love,

Mom Ritter

Special Recognition to...

My husband, who has been a great provider for my family, making it possible for me to be able to write this book. To my daughters Cassie and Robyn and best friend Debbie Jones for editing the book. To my son Jake and friend Sherry Waddell who kept encouraging me to finish the book. To my dad, who exemplified writing for me as I was growing up. To my mom who inspired to make *The Promise*. Most of all, to all those who don't believe. May this book create a desire in you to know Christ.

Contents

Foreword

God calls upon each of us for certain tasks during our lifetime. Unfortunately, we may not always recognize that call and therefore don't respond to it. God has nudged me to do many things during my life. Some of His calls were heard clearly and acted on diligently. Others were just passing thoughts that were soon forgotten. This book is the response to one of those calls. This call was unmistakable in that the burning desire to write it would not go away. I did put it away for a year or so but then He reminded me again and I got back to work.

I don't claim to have any college or seminary degrees that make me a qualified theologian or a religion expert. I'm just your average, everyday "Peter" who has made many mistakes and has experienced many situations with the knowledge that God always was an important part of those experiences.

Important themes throughout the book are a need for God, service to others, loving others, mistakes made, negative thinking, acceptance, and forgiveness. Although I wrote the stories and suggest the way we should live according to the Bible, that doesn't mean that I have mastered these principles myself. In fact, most of the themes I write about I struggle with on a daily basis. Thank goodness we have a loving and forgiving Lord!

The stories in *Petals of the Soul: God's Love vs. Satan's Deceit* are stories that show how God is with us everyday and in all circumstances, yet there is another influential force that is also always beckoning us; Satan. The *God's Love* stories show God's unending love is seen in every aspect of our life. The *Satan's Deceit* stories show some type of temptation, failure, flaw, or sin that we all experience and struggle with. However, you can still feel God's presence in all the stories. I wasn't able to leave God's love out of any of the situations. When Satan is tempting, God is often close by encouraging you to be strong and still showering His love on you.

The feeling you get from reading a *God's Love* story and then a *Satan's Deceit* story is the feeling you would get as your emotions are being pulled as to whether to make good choices with God's help or bad choices with Satan's temptations. With each different petal, or story, you feel God's love and Satan's lure in a bouquet of emotions. In the end, it is my hope that you will feel God's love so strongly that making the right choices becomes easier.

The Bible verses chosen for each story were picked with great deliberation and are very important for setting the mood for the particular story. Please be sure to read these and take in God's word as if it were a breath of fresh air in a world that becomes very stale without it. Some verses are used over again for different stories to reaffirm the significance of the verse and hopefully allow you to internalize it better.

Each story ends with a prayer to ask for guidance related to the theme. Prayer is a very important part of our relationship with God. It is too often that we just go to God in desperation while asking for a need. Make your prayer life one of a conversation with God, sharing both your joys and concerns as you would a dear friend.

Enjoy!

Chapter 1
The Promise

"I establish my covenant with you: Never again will all life be cut off by the waters of a flood; never again will there be a flood to destroy the earth."

Genesis 9:11

God's covenant with Abram:

"I will make you into a great nation and I will bless you; I will make your name great, and you will be a blessing. I will bless those who bless you, and whoever curses you I will curse; and all peoples on earth will be blessed through you."

Genesis 12:2-3

"Praise awaits you, O God, in Zion; to you our vows will be fulfilled. O you who hear prayer, to you all men will come. You answer us with awesome deeds of righteousness."

Psalm 65:1-2, 5

"When a man makes a vow to the Lord or takes an oath to obligate himself by a pledge, he must not break his word but must do everything he said."

Numbers 30:2

"Let her live and I will do whatever you require."

Me

I remember the day well…my parents had taken my brothers and me out to lunch after church as had become the tradition. This time however, was extra special because we were told the good news that we were going to have another baby. This was especially exciting to me because I loved to babysit and maybe I would get a sister this time.

The big day finally came and my dad took my mom to the hospital while we stayed home with a neighbor. It was time to go to bed, but there was no news of the new arrival yet. However, our sitter told us she'd wake us up when there was any news. I was so excited I could hardly sleep.

Later that night my dad woke us up. He had a very solemn look on his face and his eyes were swollen from crying. I wondered, *What could be wrong, having a baby isn't that big of a deal?* He took my older brother and me into the kitchen to tell us our mother was in serious condition. It turned out that something had gone terribly wrong during the delivery called an amniotic embolism that was fairly rare. Somehow the amniotic fluid burst and got into her bloodstream, poisoning her whole body. Shortly after she delivered my brother, she went into a coma. There had only been fifty-four cases of this reported in the United States, and only a handful had been known to survive.

My mother's doctor was a man named Dr. Hughes, who was a very caring and dedicated doctor that many women had grown to love and admire. He stayed up with her for three days and nights trying to save her life. All of the blood in her body had to be completely drained, then replaced with new blood. She had to be revived several times to bring her back to life. After around the clock care for three days, she finally came out of the coma. As she was beginning to regain her senses from the near loss of her life, she noticed a sense of sullenness along with the joy that she had survived in the faces of the nurses and hospital staff. She soon came to realize that Dr. Hughes had died from a heart attack shortly after she had come out of the coma. Everyone was happy that it looked like she would survive, but devastated at the great loss of this wonderful man.

I remember when I went back to bed after my dad told us the news that night, I never felt panicked, but prayed to God to please let her live. If He would, I promised I would do whatever He required of me.

God has never let me forget that promise. He has nudged and pushed me in several directions during my life to do His work. Not only have I been nudged to do His work, but I've also been called a "pusher." In order to accomplish

His work requires using many people. Sometimes I wonder if people feel like running when they see me in fear that I'm going to ask them to do something else again. When God puts something in your mind that needs to be done, there's no turning back. It's full force ahead. If a door closes to get the job done, a window will open.

As a chosen people that are blessed, once touched by Christ, there becomes a sense of urgency to help those in need and to bring others to Him. The need can be either physical or spiritual. People say, "You do so much for the church." How can you not? I try to make it a goal to make a difference in someone's life every day. You need to open your heart and eyes to be aware of needs around you. It is so much easier to give than receive. Hopefully, others will be able to see and feel God's love through me in at least a small way.

You don't need a dramatic event such as my mother's near death to be moved to reach out to others. Once you accept Christ, His Spirit will lead you. Are you ready to take on this challenge? He has made many great promises to us; as in the promise of the rainbow to not destroy the earth with water again; and the promise to make a great nation out of Abram and his descendants. What promise can you make to Him to make a small difference in the world? (Told you I was a pusher.)

Prayer: *God, You have blessed us in so many ways. Help us turn those blessings for ourselves into blessings for others. Keep us ever mindful that it is only through You that these things can be accomplished. Let them be done to glorify You alone Lord. You are such a merciful and gracious God. I am willing to promise this to You today Lord... (make your own promise).*
Amen

Chapter 2
Make Them Love You, Lord

"There was a rich man who was dressed in purple and fine linen and lived in luxury every day. At his gate was a beggar named Lazarus covered with sores and longing to eat what fell from the rich man's table. Even the dogs came and licked his sores.

The time came when the beggar died and the angels carried him to Abraham's side. The rich man also died and was buried. In Hell, where he was in torment, he looked up and saw Abraham far away with Lazarus by his side. So he called to him, 'Father Abraham, have pity on me and send Lazarus to dip the tip of his finger in water and cool my tongue, because I am in agony in this fire.'

But Abraham replied, 'Son, remember that in your lifetime you received your good things, while Lazarus received bad things, but now he is comforted here and you are in agony. And besides all this, between us and you a great chasm has been fixed, so that those who want to go from here to you cannot, nor can anyone cross over from there to us.'

He answered, 'Then I beg you, Father, send Lazarus to my father's house, for I have five brothers. Let him warn them, so that they will not also come to this place of torment.'

Abraham replied, 'They have Moses and the Prophets; let them listen to them.'

'No, Father Abraham,' he said, 'but if someone from the dead goes to them, they will repent.' He said to him, 'If they do not listen to Moses and the Prophets, they will not be convinced even if someone rises from the dead.'"

Luke 16: 19-31

Can you make somebody love you? I remember in my early years when I had a crush on someone—I'd use the attention grabbing tricks we've all used. When I knew I was going to see "him," I'd make extra efforts to look nice. If I could muster up the courage to actually talk to him, I'd talk about things that I knew were of interest to him or would try to be funny (at the risk of making a fool of myself). Sometimes my efforts would spark some attention, but there was always someone else more popular or prettier and I just became someone that was a friend. My self-esteem in the boy department wasn't very good. I was beginning to think I would certainly be an old maid and live by myself the rest of my life. Now, with a husband of thirty some years and three grown children, I am a living testament that there is hope for everybody.

In the same way that we seek someone out that we are attracted to and try to start a friendship—God also offers His friendship to us. Just as badly as we want to know that "special person," God wants to know us. Talk about rejection! It's a good thing God doesn't have an ego problem since so many people reject Him on a daily basis.

Sometimes I wish that God would make people close to me want to love Him, but He doesn't operate that way. Just like someone who desperately wants someone to love them may try many approaches to get the other person's attention, God also uses many approaches to reach us. It may be by bringing a special person into our life to teach us an important life lesson or by putting someone in our path to see how we will react to a need. It may be through healing us when we are very ill or by showing us a beautiful sunset. It may be by bringing us down when we think we are better than we are so that we don't become too self-centered. It may be by giving us a sense of peace when we think the world has forgotten us and we are so low we don't think we can make it another day. It may be by sending you that special soul mate that was meant only for you because together you are a force to be reckoned with.

You may have heard the story about the man that was in a flood and refused help from a boat, helicopter, and a life jacket from people who tried to save him. His reply to his rescuers was that God would save him. He died as a result, and when he got to Heaven he asked God why He didn't save him. God told him, "I tried to—I sent you a boat, helicopter and life jacket." We are so much like that. God sends us all kinds of opportunities and we can't even open our hearts enough to realize what He has done and continues to do for us.

Try as you may, it is very rare when you can change someone's opinion through your words. You can talk until you're blue in the face, but unless someone comes to Christ on his or her own terms, it's not going to make a difference. They may see that you have something they don't have in your walk with Christ and may start to wonder what it's all about, but until they are ready—it's got to be their decision. God didn't create us to be robots to do and act as He says, but has given us a free will to make our own decisions, including loving Him.

My desire is somewhat selfish on my part because I want my loved ones to spend eternity with me. It also scares me to think what the alternative is...the story about Lazarus portrays this so well. If we go to Hell, will we want to come back and tell our friends and family to repent and come to Christ so they won't experience this agony?

With death comes wisdom. We will then know the mysteries of life and death and wonder—why didn't I get that then? Fortunately, God gives us until the last minute to accept His love, but what a better life we have when we accept it earlier.

Do you love God? I mean really love Him with your whole heart—or is your relationship one that's mediocre or lukewarm? Do you think He's satisfied with your relationship? Do you show your love for Him through service to others? Do you want to know Him intimately, but are afraid it will put a dent in your lifestyle? There will be a change in your life, but it will be a loving, peaceful, satisfied feeling that you may have been searching for all along. I can't make you, but you can do it today...love God.

Prayer: *God, You show Your love for us every day in so many ways, and yet we still don't know You. Since You are a God of love, You don't force Your love on us. You have given us that stubborn trait of free will. In so doing, it can be used to choose or reject You. Thank you for not giving up on us and for continuing to try to reach us in many ways. Those who finally come to You will one day know that:*

"No eye has seen, no ear has heard, no mind conceived what Christ has prepared for those who love Him."

1 Corinthians 2:9

Chapter 3
Sharing Joy

"Moreover, when God gives any man wealth and possessions, and enables him to enjoy them, to accept his lot and be happy in his work—this is a gift of God. He seldom reflects on the days of his life, because God keeps him occupied with gladness of heart."

Ecclesiastes 5: 19-20

"Lord, you have assigned me my portion and my cup; you have made my lot secure. The boundary lines have fallen for me in pleasant places; surely I have a delightful inheritance."

Psalm 16: 5-6

"Then Jesus told them this parable: 'Suppose one of you has a hundred sheep and loses one of them. Does he not leave the ninety-nine in the open country and go after the lost sheep until he finds it? And when he finds it, he joyfully puts it on his shoulders and goes home. Then he calls his friends and neighbors together and says, 'Rejoice with me; I have found my lost sheep.' I tell you that in the same way there will be more rejoicing in Heaven over one sinner who repents than over ninety-nine righteous persons who do not need to repent."

Luke 15: 3-7

*****

As I am writing this story, we are preparing to leave for the beach at Nags Head, North Carolina in two days. This is our usual vacation spot, as we have been going there since I was a child.

It is an ideal family vacation choice because the island is very narrow, making it possible to go to the beach side one minute and a few minutes later you can be on the sound side. Since we are fortunate enough to own a small boat, the sound side is our favorite because we can go out on fishing excursions and explore the many small islands.

It is especially exciting to go out after it rains. I'm sure this is where they get the saying, "The calm after the storm" (actually I think it's before the storm, but oh well) because following a storm the sound is very calm. This is a prime time to go dolphin hunting. If we time it just right, we can find a school of dolphins swimming together. This is so special because they will swim right next to your boat as if you are a dolphin yourself. When you hold your hand out they will even jump up to touch you. This is just one example of the beauty that God has given us in this world that causes great joy. After experiencing something like this you want to go get everybody you know and bring them along so they can share the same experience.

When we go on vacation it seems we have a caravan of people that want to go along: Nieces, nephews, friends of my children, brothers-in-law. This year there will be fifteen people staying at our house. In addition, my parents will have another house across the street with nine people staying there. There have been times when I thought, *This is going to be chaos.* However, it always turns out fine and everyone does their share of chores and shopping so the work and expenses are shared evenly. Everyone also does their own thing, giving each other needed space in such a crowded house. One reason I like bringing so many people is that I'm able to share the joy I get from our vacation. If it weren't for all of us going together, many of those that do go would not be able to afford a vacation. It also gives us a chance to bond with family members we don't get to see real often. It makes me happy to see other people happy.

In the same way, I have a strong desire for those around me to know the joy of Christ. If those who have been struggling all their lives in search of happiness would just open their hearts to Him, they could experience this joy also.

Although I've experienced the death of some close friends, I have been fortunate to not have lost an immediate family member yet. I know this will be a very difficult time no matter what, but I could handle it much better if I knew they were with Christ when they left this world. Thank goodness Christ allows room for everyone, even if they don't choose Him until they are on their deathbed. However, those who choose him at the last minute are taking a big chance. Their death may be so sudden—they may not have time to ask Christ into their hearts. If only they could feel the joy throughout their lives rather than waiting.

I can understand the joy of the shepherd in Luke 15, where he has so much joy when he finds the one lost sheep. All of us have had times where we've lost something and have made ourselves crazy looking for it. When/if we find it, we are so happy we usually let out a hoot or smile with delight. It's this kind of joy that God experiences when one of His lost sheep comes to Him. The ironic part is that He was there all along and not hard to find.

Are you one of the fortunate people that have had many blessings bestowed upon you? Are you so grateful to be so blessed that you want to share these blessings with others? Let the joy of God's love flow through you to others so that they too will want to know what this joy is all about. Don't keep them waiting! Tell them your story today.

Prayer: *God, thank You for accepting us at whatever stage we are at in our lives. Just like the father of the prodigal son, You are always waiting for us with open arms and are ready to throw a grand party for each of us wanderers that returns to You. May all those who are close to us or those we don't know; strangers on the street; friends; family members; and those in faraway countries know what this joy is all about.*

Chapter 4
God's Voice

"While he was still speaking, a bright cloud enveloped them, and a voice from the cloud said, "This is my Son, whom I love; with him I am well pleased. Listen to him!"

Matthew 17:5

"As he neared Damascus on his journey, suddenly a light from Heaven flashed around him. He fell to the ground and heard a voice say to him, 'Saul, Saul, why do you persecute me?'"

Acts 9:3-4

"So, as the Holy Spirit says: 'Today, if you hear his voice, do not harden your hearts as you did in the rebellion, during the time of testing in the desert, where your fathers tested and tried me and for forty years saw what I did. That is why I was angry with that generation, and I said,' 'Their hearts are always going astray, and they have not known my ways.'"

Hebrews 3:7-10

"The Lord said, 'Go out and stand on the mountain in the presence of the Lord, for the Lord is about to pass by.' Then a great and powerful wind tore the mountain apart and shattered the rocks before the Lord, but the Lord was not in the wind. After the wind there was an earthquake, but the Lord was not in the earthquake. After the earthquake came fire, but the Lord was not in the fire. And after the fire came a gentle whisper.

When Elijah heard it he pulled his cloak over his face and went out and stood in the mouth of the cave."

1 Kings 19:11-13

I wonder when Elijah was experiencing all these great acts of God; wind, earthquake, and fire, if he just stood there and watched without fear or if he trembled with uncertainty, not knowing what would happen next. (1 Kings 19:11-13) The verse does tell us that just hearing God's whisper caused him to "cover his face" as he stood at the mouth of the cave.

Some of us have experienced natural disasters such as hurricanes, earthquakes, tornadoes and fire. After witnessing any one of these, it helps us to realize how great God's power really is. If even after experiencing all these, and then it was only God's whisper that made Elijah retreat—can you imagine how powerful God's voice must be?

Have you ever heard God's voice? I used to think that you could only hear His voice if you reached a certain level of "holiness." For me, His voice came at times of disobedience. The first time was when I was around thirteen years old. It was during the summer when a friend's parents were at work and we often congregated at her house when we could get away with it. With a mixture of boys and girls we came up with the idea to play a game of spin the bottle with a twist—to take off clothing items instead of kissing when the bottle pointed toward you. When it got to where several people were getting down to just a few clothes—I heard God's voice loud and clear. He simply said, "SIS," very loud. (That's what my close friends and family call me.)

Well, I don't know if anyone else heard it, but I jumped up, screamed, and ran out of the room with the few clothes I had removed and put them on very quickly. I don't know if it was just my reaction or if everyone else heard their names too, but they all ran screaming too.

Another time I was acting like I thought I was pretty wonderful, but I was on a wrong path. I heard Him loud and clear again. This time He said, (in the same loud, thunderous voice I heard many years earlier) "It is finished!" This put me in a state of shock for several minutes and it took my breath away. It wasn't until I heard His voice the second time that I knew it was God's voice the first time too. I guess I thought it was my conscience, or it actually sounded like my own father's voice the first time. Just like Elijah's response was to cover his face, it immediately makes you realize your shame and unworthiness to be in God's presence.

I am so thankful that God cares enough about me to speak to me, especially when I need it most. Wouldn't it be great if everyone heard His voice so loudly that it would bring him or her to their knees when they were getting ready to sin? Just imagine—bank robbers dropping their loot and running out of banks, adulterers grabbing their clothes and running for cover when they are getting ready to commit adultery, murderers throwing down their guns and hiding in shame when they are getting ready to kill someone. The reason that some of us may feel this way when a wrong is about to be or is committed, is because when we have accepted Christ, His Spirit encourages us not to do wrong. And if we do, we have such strong feelings of remorse; we feel we will die without His forgiveness.

God has continued to nudge me through my life with smaller infractions, many times with guilt feelings because of an unkind word or for not helping someone in need. When He speaks, it's not always in words. It may be by an acquaintance that helps you see things differently; someone or something that just happens to be at the right place at the right time; a message from a sermon about an issue that had been bothering you; or just the majesty of the beauty of this world He's given us to let us know how awesome He really is. I'm glad God continues to work in my life when I need Him most. If you listen very closely you'll hear Him talk to you in many different ways throughout your life. Can you hear His whisper? Listen a little harder. Yes, He is there-whispering, nudging, encouraging.

Prayer: *God, we never cease to be amazed at Your awesome power and majesty. Continue to reach out, yell, or whisper to us when we need to hear You the most. Keep us ever mindful of our sinfulness and Your constant presence.*

Chapter 5
Love Ya, No I Don't!

"Search me, O God, and know my heart; test me and know my anxious thoughts. See if there is any offensive way in me, and lead me to the way everlasting."

Psalm 139:23-24

"We all stumble in many ways. If anyone is never at fault in what he says, he is a perfect man, able to keep his whole body in check."

James 3: 2

"Or take ships as an example. Although they are so large and are driven by strong winds, they are steered by a very small rudder wherever the pilot wants to go. Likewise the tongue is a small part of the body, but it makes great boasts. Consider what a great forest is set on fire by a small spark. The tongue also is a fire, a world of evil among the parts of the body."

James 3: 4-6

*****

Okay. I admit it; I'm a quiltoholic. I love to sew, and especially make quilts. My quilt making experiences began when I became involved with auctions for our church to raise funds for missions, the building fund, and a fifteen-passenger van our church wanted to purchase.

The quilt I was the most proud of, was one that I titled the "Blessings Quilt." It had hand prints of many members of the church embroidered on it with favorite Bible verses on each block. As I made this quilt, I prayed every time I worked on it that whoever received it would be truly blessed—in hopes that it would bring them comfort in times of need. I also felt God's Spirit and a great sense of passion as I quilted. My mother and another quilting friend helped, which made the project even more fun to share with others. When it was finally finished, after nine months of hard work, it was displayed to help promote the upcoming auction it would be sold at. It went for a pretty decent price and I was happy for the person that received it.

Several months later, during a sermon, as an example on gifted people and how they sometimes flaunt their talents, my quilt was given as an example. The fact that it was displayed was said to "show people how wonderful I was." I felt like someone had punched me in the stomach. It took every bit of strength I had to not completely fall apart and run out during the rest of the service crying. For several weeks afterward, it was all I could think about. I had high regard for the person that had said it, so I kept re-examining my motives. Could it be that he was right? I don't remember feeling or thinking that way at all. This bothered me so much I considered leaving the church. I don't say this lightly since I had come to love my church and the people that had become my church family. I prayed asking God for guidance as to what to do.

A few weeks later I made a phone call to a man who had left an organization that I'm very involved in. I had only met him once, but was very impressed with his dedication to this very important ministry. I wanted to call to tell him how disappointed I was to hear he was no longer a part of the program.

Well, right before this, I had talked to my two daughters on the phone and ended the conversation with "Love ya" like I usually do. When I called my friend, he wasn't home so I left a message on his answering machine. You guessed it, at the end of the message I unconsciously said, "Love ya." Realizing as soon as I said it and not knowing how to fix it, I quickly said, "No I don't!" and hung up. Afterward, I paced the house thinking, "Oh my Lord, he's going to think I'm an idiot! What if his wife hears it and thinks he's having an affair with me?"

After fretting about this for several days, a thought came to me. Maybe this was God's humorous way of teaching me that sometimes people say things that they don't mean. Also, I was reminded how I had misjudged another person recently and even made a remark as to my judgment. Through this, I was finally able to forgive the person who said what he did about the quilt and move on with my life. I also realized how wrong I was to have judged someone else wrongly and how deeply people could be hurt by our words. I pray I have never hurt anyone like this. If so, I am so very sorry!

I have read many verses that describe hardships we experience such as these and lessons learned from them. If you are a somewhat intelligent person, the best you can hope for is to learn your lesson and never repeat it again. Just like the Israelites in the desert that continued to sin over and over again, there have been times I continued to say hurtful things. (Usually not realizing it until later.) Another area brought to light after this experience is the people whose actions I've misjudged many times. Judgment is a very dangerous thing, but many of us need to learn the hard way. If everyone learned from his or her mistakes, I should be a very smart person by now.

Although it hurt very deeply, this was one of life's lessons I've learned best. Do you have lessons that need to be learned the hard way? Have you been hurt deeply? Turn it around and consider if it's possible that you've hurt someone else as deeply. As scripture says, *"Do unto others as you would have them do unto you."* It is my prayer that I will never hurt others again. Look at everyone with love and give him or her some slack, even if their heart isn't in the right place. They will come along in God's time just as you and I did.

Prayer: *God, even though You sometimes use drastic measures that can really hurt to show us our sin, in the end we can learn so much from them if we are willing to let go of our pride and see where we fail. Help us to keep a tight reign on our tongues and to use them only for praise and good works. Like our mamas said when we were children, "Sometimes it's best to keep your thoughts to yourself." Help us to only have good thoughts, O God.*

P.S. The lady who got the quilt lost her best friend to suicide a year later. The mother of the lady who committed suicide got an "Ecclesiastes" quilt I made from another auction. I pray that the verses on the quilts have brought them comfort. The man that I said "Love ya" to never contacted me again.

Chapter 6
Let's Make a Deal

"One day the angels came to present themselves before the Lord, and Satan also came with them. The Lord said to Satan, 'Where have you come from?'

Satan answered the Lord, 'From roaming through the earth and going back and forth in it.'

Then the Lord said to Satan, 'Have you considered my servant Job? There is no one on earth like him; he is blameless and upright, a man who fears God and shuns evil.'

'Does Job fear God for nothing?' Satan replied. 'Have you not put a hedge around him and his household and everything he has? You have blessed the works of his hands, so that his flocks and herds are spread throughout the land. But stretch out your hand and strike everything he has, and he will surely curse you to your face.'

The Lord said to Satan, 'Very well then, everything he has is in your hands, but on the man himself do not lay a finger.'"

Job 1:6-12

Bargaining between God and Abraham when God wants to destroy Sodom because it has become so wicked:

"Then the Lord said, 'The outcry against Sodom and Gomorrah is so great and their sin so grievous that I will go down and see if what they have done is as bad as the outcry that has reached me. If not, I will know.'

Then Abraham approached him and said, 'Will you sweep away the righteous with the wicked? What if there are fifty righteous people in the city? Will you sweep away the righteous with the wicked? Far be it from you to do such a thing—to kill the righteous with the wicked, treating the righteous and the wicked alike. Far be it from you! Will not the Judge of all the earth do right?'

The Lord said, 'If I find fifty righteous people in the city of Sodom, I will spare the whole place for their sake.'"

Genesis 18:20-26

This conversation goes on until Abraham convinces God that the city should be spared even if only ten righteous people are found. God agrees. but ten are not found.

*****

Being raised Catholic, I had never received much Bible education and had not even read the Bible until I left the Catholic Church and attended an adult Bible study at the Methodist Church I now attend.

The class I attended was studying Job at the time. What a shock this chapter was to me. First, because of how it describes God and Satan having a casual conversation after Satan had "Roamed the earth and went back and forth." I had always imagined God in Heaven and Satan in Hell. I never thought that they got together to talk, let alone have a conversation like this.

Then I was surprised at the fact that God was bragging, *"Have you considered my servant Job? There is no one on earth like him. He is blameless and upright: a man who fears God and shuns evil."* I know some men are known for their bragging, but I never thought God would do it.

Lastly, I was mystified that God would make a deal with Satan and allow so many bad things to happen to a person just to prove a point. (His family dies, he loses all his livestock, his house is destroyed, he gets boils all over his body, and his friends condemn him) What would have happened if Job had not remained faithful? I don't think this book would have been in the Bible.

Again, I find it interesting in the story of Sodom and Gomorrah that Abraham has such a close relationship with God that he brings the fact to God's attention that it wouldn't be fair to destroy a city if fifty righteous people are found there. And then he keeps on dealing with God until if only ten people are found (which they aren't).

Do these stories prove that God can be bargained with? I have always put God on such a high pedestal that I never imagined being able to talk to Him like this. Now that I have read the entire Bible and have a closer relationship with Him, I realize that the story of Job is important for anyone who is going through trials in their life. It helps us to understand that from God's prospective, there is probably a lot more going on than we will ever know.

The point is to remain faithful no matter how hard the "going gets tough." If we prevail until the end, God will be there for us and our reward will be well worth the wait. God is all-knowing and all-powerful; however, these stories indicate that He is willing to talk—if our relationship is right with Him.

Many of us haven't experienced tragedies such as Job had to suffer. However, if we do suffer the tragic death of a loved one, or have had a serious illness, or the many misfortunes of Job, I wonder how many of us would remain faithful? I know of some who have experienced such things, and they do go through a period of much questioning and anger. I feel certain that God is okay with our questioning and uncertainties. You won't go to Hell for wondering why.

Even though God was willing to make a deal (be reasoned with) in both of these stories, He did end up being right in both cases; Job did remained loyal and not even ten righteous people were found in Sodom.

No one's sure if this story actually happened, or if it was just written to prove a point. Either way, it shows how much of a role God plays in our lives. The misfortunes of Job wouldn't be wished on anyone; however, we will all go through difficult times in our lives. It may seem like you're going it alone, but in the end you'll realize God was there with you all the way.

If you are dealing with a tragic situation in your life, God is open for questions and wants you to come to Him with them. It may take some time, but you will eventually get an answer and hopefully find peace in whatever you're dealing with. May the peace that can only be found in Christ be with you in your time of trial. With Him on your side—you will always end up a winner.

Prayer: *God, even though we don't always understand trials we experience, we do know that You have a perfect plan for us all. That doesn't mean that we will lead a trouble free life, but that You will in some way turn these bad experiences into something that we can learn and grow from. Sometimes You have to use drastic measures to help us come to our full potential and realize that plan. With Your help in this "game of life" we know we will always make the right choices.*

Chapter 7
Does God Have a Sense of Humor?

"A cheerful look brings joy to the heart and good news gives health to the bones."

Proverbs 15:30

Sarah said, *"God has brought me laughter and everyone who hears about this will laugh with me. Who would have said to Abraham that Sarah would nurse children? Yet I have born him a son in his old age."*
Genesis 21:6-7

"Then the Lord opened the donkey's mouth, and she said to Balaam, 'What have I done to you to make you beat me these three times?'
Balaam answered the donkey, 'You have made a fool of me! If I had a sword in my hand, I would kill you right now.'
The donkey said to Balaam, 'Am I not your own donkey, which you have always ridden to this day? Have I been in the habit of doing this to you?'"

Numbers 22:28

"The Lord provided a great fish to swallow Jonah, and Jonah was inside the fish three days and three nights."

Jonah 1:17

"From inside the fish Jonah prayed to the Lord his God."

Jonah 2:1

"The Lord commanded the fish, and it vomited Jonah onto dry land."
Jonah 2:10

"There's a time to weep and a time to laugh."

Ecclesiastes 3:4

*****

Most of us are goofy at times and like to sing silly songs. Two of my favorites silly songs are one by Janis Joplin called, "Lord, Won't You Buy Me a Mercedes Benz?" and another called "Plastic Jesus" sung by Erie Mars. In case you don't know the lyrics, I'll share the chorus:

Mercedes Benz: *Lord, won't you buy me a Mercedes Benz? My friends all have Porsches. I must make amends. Worked hard all my lifetime, no help from my friends, So Lord, won't you buy me a Mercedes Benz?*

Plastic Jesus: *I don't care if it rains or freezes, long as I've got my plastic Jesus, sitting on the dashboard of my car. He don't slip and he don't slide, because his feet are magnetized, sitting on the dashboard of my car.*

"Plastic Jesus" has special meaning to me because my grandmother was a devote Catholic who had an old Falcon car that had a metal dashboard with a plastic Jesus (and Mary) sitting on it. "Mercedes Benz" is just a play on people's attitudes and on people praying for worldly things.

This past year I was in an intensive Bible study call Disciple IV. Our assignment was to rewrite a Bible verse using different styles. My group chose to do it as a rap song. I rapped while a friend made noises (you know, those weird sputtering noises) for the background. Now I usually don't like rap, but we had so much fun putting this passage into a modern form. A few of the older people in the group sat and stared as if we were committing a sin, while most of the others laughed. My friend and I agreed that we hoped God has a sense of humor or we were in trouble.

After reading the Bible stories that include a talking donkey; a man-swallowing whale; and Sarah conceiving a child in her very old age—you know God must have a sense of humor. What's amazing to me is how Balaam talks back to the donkey as if it's natural, or as if it's not unusual for a whale to swallow a man and then "vomit him out on dry land." (That's a nasty visual) I often wonder if these stories are tales made up to make a point as Jesus often did in his parables. Sometimes the best way to get someone's attention is by using humor. There's no better way to ease a tense situation or to bring change then by making someone see how foolish he or she may be acting or making light of a situation that's not going well.

In looking through the New Testament, I found it hard to find humorous passages. As Ecclesiastes 3:4 tells us, *"There is a time to weep and a time to laugh."* I would like to imagine the disciples and Jesus sitting around the campfire telling jokes or trying to make light of their situation. Possibly the mission Jesus was sent here to accomplish was so urgent there wasn't room for humor.

People that I have known in my life who have made the biggest impression on me are ones that could make light of many situations and make people laugh. I like to make people laugh and feel good about themselves. In fact, I feel uncomfortable if there isn't some humor in most things I'm involved in. When I give someone a hard time about something silly, it's my way of saying I feel comfortable enough with them to kid around. In effect, showing them I like them. What's important though, is to never use humor to put people down or make fun of an unfortunate situation. No one should find humor at another person's expense. If what you're saying is hurting them, humiliating them, or making them feel uncomfortable, then you've gone too far. It's no longer funny.

I know God smiles down on many of us as we do His work. He's especially happy if we can do His work with a joyful attitude. Humor makes the heart lighter. Don't be a stick in the mud. Laugh some and love much. This is a new commandment according to Cathy!

Prayer: *God, help us to be able to look at life and all the joy it brings us: Innocent statements of a child, fun found in friendships, being able to laugh at ourselves when we make stupid mistakes. Help us to remember to laugh some and love much. Joy is a wonderful thing. Thanks for giving this gift of humor and laughter. What a boring world it would be without it.*

Chapter 8
Many Religions, Many Rooms

"Do not let your hearts be troubled. Trust in God; trust also in me. In my Father's house are many rooms; if it were not so I would have told you. I am going there to prepare a place for you. And if I go and prepare a place for you I will come back and take you to be with me that you may also be where I am. Thomas said to him, 'Lord, we don't know where you are going, so how can we know the way?' Jesus answered, 'I am the way and the truth and the light. No one comes to the Father except through me.'"

John 14: 1-6

"If anyone considers himself religious and yet does not keep a tight rein on his tongue, he deceives himself and his religion is worthless. Religion that God our Father accepts as pure and faultless is this: to look after orphans and widows in their distress and to keep oneself from being polluted by the world."

James 1: 26-27

*****

After September 11th we seem to be more aware of other religions and how they differ from ours. My response was, "How can they hate us so much? We are a good people."

Recently I bought a book on world religions to try to make sense of it all. It showed the percentage of world religions as follows:

Christianity: 33%: *(Includes Catholics, Protestants, Eastern Orthodox Jews, Pentecost, Mormon, and Jehovah's Witnesses. Every group that upholds Jesus in some way.)*

Islam: 22%
Hinduism: 15%
Chinese Religions: 4%
Primal & Indigenous: 3%
Others: 3%[1]

This means that 47% of the religions are not Christian or Jewish. As Jesus tells us in John 14:

"I am the way, the truth and the life. No one comes to the Father except through me." At the same time, the Islam Koran tells them: "He that chooses a religion over Islam, it will not be accepted from him and in the world to come he will be one of the lost."

Qur an 3:86[2]

Both religions are taught these beliefs from birth and are as real to each as the sunrise—so who is right?

Nothing can cause a heated argument more than a discussion on religion. Why is that? I would say because it's something so personal to us and means so much—that if you criticize it or try to tell us any different, you are tearing at our hearts as well. It would be the same if someone told us our mother was ugly or our father was worthless, or tried to harm our child. We would immediately be up in arms and ready to fight. There is also an underlying fear that another religion would be more powerful and infringe on our right to believe as we do. The real problem arises when somebody branches off from a particular faith, adding beliefs of their own to make it fit their ideas.

Islam is characterized by "accepting the doctrine of submission to God and that Mohammed is the chief and last prophet of God."

A Muslim is a follower of Islam. Most Muslim's do not agree with Osama bin Laden's claim to "jihad" or a holy war. They point out that "jihad," according to Mohammad, is "the challenge of living one's daily life is the greatest struggle." They say that jihad has "intellectual, spiritual and moral dimensions."[3]

However, for those that follow "Islam," as they interpret it, to the point that they are willing to commit suicide bombings, they must feel very strongly about what they believe. Those that go to these extremes to protect their religion and it's beliefs must feel their religion is being threatened and they are losing control of it in this world unless they commit this act. In addition, they are told that they will have many virgins and be fed grapes like a king.

Look at us as a Christian nation—how we get in such an uproar over religious issues, sometimes to the point to kill or die for something we strongly believe in. Are we that much different? I can understand strong sentiments about a religion, but once it starts getting violent, people are losing their perspective. The main emphasis of the God of all of our religions is love, unity and peace.

There are many people who don't even want to get involved with religion because of the killing and fighting it has caused in many nations. I can understand their position, but at the same time I encourage them to have a personal relationship with Christ and let God take care of all that other stuff. Once you have a close relationship with Christ, you understand how much it hurts Him too. Can you imagine how it hurts a loving God to see the killing and bloodshed that takes place in His name?

It does bother me to think that only Christians can go to Heaven. Those raised in other religions are also convinced that their religion is the only one that will go to Heaven.

In the verse from John 14, Jesus tells us *"In His Father's house there are many rooms."* Although He goes on to tell us the only way to the Father is through Him, maybe there are other "rooms" allowed for other religions that stress love and fellowship. Maybe it is in the other "rooms" where they can experience Jesus' love and come to know Him.

All I am sure of is that the God I know is a God of love. When you are pure love and you see violence done in defense of that, it must hurt deeply. It would be the same feeling you would have if your own child killed someone.

Please don't let the confusion of the world turn you away from God. He's got big shoulders and arms open wide hoping to comfort you and show you the way to His love.

Prayer: *God, You have blessed us with such a beautiful world and country; and at the same time there are many things wrong with it that man has done. Not by Your doing God, but by men's hearts that are led astray by the evil one. One so cunning, that we can easily be lead astray to believe things that aren't true. In the end we know that only love will prevail. Make Your rooms ready Lord! We look forward to the day that we will come to Your house.*

Chapter 9
Sacrifices

"Now Abel kept flocks, and Cain worked the soil. In the course of time Cain brought some of the fruits of the soil as an offering to the Lord. But Abel brought fat portions from some of the first born of his flock. The Lord looked with favor on Abel and his offering, but on Cain and his offering he did not look with favor."

Genesis 4: 3-5

"Will the Lord be pleased with thousands of rams, with ten thousand rivers of oil? Shall I offer my first born for my transgression, the fruit of my body for the sin of my soul?

He has shown you, O man, what is good. And what does the Lord require of you? To act justly and to love mercy and to walk humbly with your God."

Micah 6: 7-8

"Our offering to God is this: We are the sweet smell of Christ among those who are being saved and among those who are being lost."

2 Corinthians 2:15

"My life is being given as an offering to God, and the time has come for me to leave this life. I have fought the good fight, I have finished the race, and I have kept the faith. Now, a crown is being held for me—a crown for being right with God."

2 Timothy 4: 6-8

When I first began studying the Bible, the part that bewildered me the most was animal sacrifice. How could God require His people to kill the best of their animals? And then the fact that the smell of their burning bodies could be a "pleasing aroma" to God was beyond me.

The thinking of Bible time people and the Old Testament God is foreign to modern people. We read with amazement their actions in those days and what God required of them and it doesn't make sense to us.

The first time sacrifice is mentioned in the Bible is when Adam's sons, Cain and Abel, presented offerings to God. Cain's was a grain offering, Abel's an animal offering. God was pleased with Abel's, but not with Cain's. Thus came the first feelings of rejection and jealousy, which eventually lead to the first murder.

A commentary in my Bible tries to explain sacrifice. It describes how sacrifices were offered to atone for sins. The costs for sacrifices were high. The more you owned, the higher the sacrifice. The sacrifice couldn't be blemished; it had to be the best of what they had. This is the reason it is believed that Cain's offering wasn't pleasing. It was given either with a wrong attitude or wasn't the best.[4]

There were three types of offerings: Guilt and sin offerings which cleansed you of sin; burnt offerings which expressed complete dedication to God and a fellowship offering in which a family meal was shared in the presence of God. The sequence of the offerings shows that fellowship with God is their goal: Forgiveness, dedication, and fellowship. When explained in this way, you can begin to understand their thinking: To gain closeness to God you first need to rid yourself of sin by asking for forgiveness. You need to prove your dedication to Him by following His commands and then after these, you can seek fellowship with Him.[5]

What God seems to be stressing about obtaining fellowship with Him is the importance of attitude. Don't try to approach Him carelessly thinking you can fool Him. He knows your thoughts, sometimes better than you do.

Then comes the final, ultimate sacrifice of His Son that He offers to us. Now the tables are turned, He is offering the sacrifice. He allows His only Son to die for our sins. And it wasn't a quick painless death. (Believe me, I just came from the movie *The Passion* which depicts it very realistically.) God realized that the sacrifices were just becoming a ritual without meaning. Killing animals and burnt offering are no longer necessary. All we need to do is believe in His

Son now. When we do—all the other things fall in place naturally out of love for Him. It sounds so easy, but why do so many people have such a hard time with this? Could it be because Satan is a force to be reckoned with? Yes, he's there crouching at your door convincing you otherwise, especially the closer you get to God. He was there—tempting Jesus. Here was the Son of God, tempted to the utmost by Satan and He didn't waver—even as He was dying on the cross. What does He say? *"Forgive them for they know not what they do."* Wow, what kind of love is that! What earthly person could ever love that much?

What kind of sacrifice have you made lately? Do you think God was pleased with it? Was it a sacrifice out of plenty or did it hurt to give? Did you do it in private or did others know you did it? Was it a sacrifice of money or your time? Possibly by offering the best piece of meat of your dinner to your spouse or children; Maybe by staying up late at night taking care of your sick child or even giving up a job to care for a loved one; Maybe you sacrificed by going on a mission trip rather than taking a vacation this year.

Yes, I still see sacrifices being made to God each day. I'm sure He is delighting in the pleasant aroma of love and dedication that is rising to Him daily. Make your sacrifice today—ask for forgiveness, show Him you love Him by loving others and following His Word, and seek fellowship with Him with a right mind on a daily basis.

Prayer: *God, although we will never completely understand Your ways, we know everything You do is to help bring us closer to You. God, I offer my best to You. The best of what I do at home and at my job, the love of my family and neighbor, and tithing my income to do Your work. Most importantly, fellowship with You as I read Your word and offer prayers to You daily. Such small sacrifices compared to You giving Your Son to die on the cross for us.*

Chapter 10
Idols/Holy Places

"Who may ascend to the hill of the Lord? Who may stand in His holy place? He who has clean hands and a pure heart, who does not lift his soul to an idol or swear by what is false.

He will receive blessing from the Lord and vindication from God his savior. Such is the generation of those who seek Him, who seek your face God of Jacob."

Psalm 24: 3-6

"Where then are the gods you made for yourselves? Let them come if they can save you when you are in trouble! For you have as many gods as you have towns, O Judah."

Jeremiah 2: 28

"We know that an idol is nothing at all in the world and that there is no God but one. For even if there are so-called gods whether in Heaven or on earth (as indeed there are many 'gods' and many 'lords'), yet for us there is but one God, the Father, from whom all things came and for whom we live; and there is but one Lord, Jesus Christ, through whom all things came and through whom we live."

1 Corinthians 8: 4-6

"You know the way you lived before you were believers. You let yourselves be influenced and led away to worship idols—things that could not speak."

1 Corinthians 12: 2

I can remember going to church as a child, and, like most children, it was difficult to pay attention to the sermon and the message of the service. Since I was Catholic at the time, there were many other things for me to focus my attention on. The Stations of the Cross (a depiction of the actions that lead to Christ's death), the statues of Mary and Jesus, the stained glass windows, the cross with Jesus hanging from it, and especially the huge painting on the ceiling that showed Christ in the clouds surrounded by Cherubim. If I remember correctly, His hand was outstretched and the angels were coming toward Him to touch and attend to Him. Simply put, you can tell they seek to be near Him.

Although I didn't learn many stories from the Bible as a Catholic, I can remember the sense of awe and sacredness that these symbols created in me. As Christians, the fact that they are symbols is important. It is important that we worship what they represent not the item itself.

As the Psalms 24:3 tell us, we are not to worship idols. You may think of an idol as a golden calf or Buddha-type figure. Modern day idols are much more subtle. Do you have any item in your life that you put such a high priority on that it is more important than your relationship with Christ? If so, then you have idols in your life.

I know many people who wash their cars daily and freak out at the possibility of a scratch or dent. Then there are those who want beautiful houses and spend all their time cleaning them and buying more things to make them impressive; those who buy more and more clothes and are never satisfied with what they have (that's me); those who spend more time watching sporting events and admiring sports figures and teams much more than they spend with Christ; people who become so caught up in politics that it becomes the focus of their life; the list goes on. We are all guilty of some of these or other behaviors to some degree. For me it is the clothes. Although I buy them cheap, I can't seem to get enough. Also, I try to make my house a showplace at times, but eventually give up in frustration or run out of money. Most of what we do in moderation is okay, but once it takes precedence over our relationship with Christ, it becomes wrong.

In Bible days, idols were of great importance. So much so that they were treated as gods themselves. This sounds ridiculous to us today, but don't we do the same thing when we place a high priority in all the things we have in our life?

These symbols I saw as a child and still see in churches today are good ways to constantly remind us of the Christian story. However, we must never lose sight of Christ in all the clutter. If it causes us a humbling feeling and desire to be close to Christ, it is serving a good purpose. If the item itself becomes of such great importance that you'd be devastated at it absence, you may have gotten off course.

Many wear the cross as a constant reminder that Christ died for us. They may be made of gold, silver or diamonds. Even this can become an idol if what it is made of becomes the focus rather than Christ's death and resurrection for us.

My favorite symbol from that church as a child was the painting on the ceiling. If only we could all be as focused on seeking Christ as those angels were! It doesn't matter what religion you are, if you truly search for a relationship with Him—your life will be complete.

Where is your holy place? At your church, in your home, at your favorite hangout, the local bar? Let it be in your heart with God in the center.

Prayer: *God, thank You that I have found You in the innocence of a child, in the beauty of a sunset, in a breeze on a hot day, in the change of the leaves in the fall, when someone was there when I needed them most. Your holiness doesn't need to be found in a church. It can be seen and felt all around us. It cannot be found in material things but in the love and beauty You have provided us with and in seeking Your Son.*

Chapter 11
Beauty and the Beast

"I the Lord search the heart and examine the mind, to reward a man according to his conduct, according to what his deeds deserve."

Jeremiah 17:10

"A beautiful woman without good sense is like a gold ring in a pig's snout."

Proverbs 11:22

"Your beauty should not come from outward adornment, such as braided hair and the wearing of gold jewelry and fine clothes. Instead, it should be that of your inner self, the unfading beauty of a gentle and quiet spirit, which is of great worth in God's sight."

1 Peter 3:3-4

"All flesh is not the same: Men have one kind of flesh, animals have another, birds another and fish another. There are also heavenly bodies and there are earthly bodies, but the splendor of the heavenly bodies is one kind, and the splendor of the earthly bodies is another. The sun has one kind of splendor, the moon another and the stars another; and star differs from star in splendor. So will it be with the resurrection of the dead. The body that is sown is perishable, it is raised imperishable; it is sown in dishonor, it is raised in glory; it is sown in weakness, it is raised in power; it is sown a natural body, it is raised a spiritual body."

1 Corinthians 15:39-44

Two of the most popular stories of all time, especially for girls, are *Beauty and the Beast* and *Cinderella*. The theme behind both of these stories is that outward appearances aren't what are important. It's what's on the inside that counts.

The "beast" in *Beauty and the Beast* resembles most of us a lot of the time—irritable with a chip on our shoulder, begrudged because of things that have happened to us in our lives. But after beauty keeps showing him love and kindness over and over again you begin to see a transformation take place. We even begin to like him once we see his soft, more personable side. He even likes himself now.

Then, of course, in *Cinderella* we can relate because we've all had an ugly "stepmother" in our life: Someone who hasn't treated us right, someone unloving and uncaring, someone who favors someone else over us. We cheer for Cinderella when she is chosen by the prince because we are all for the underdog—because we've all been the underdog at one time or another. Through it all, Cinderella continues to be a good hearted, loving, caring person and is rewarded for it in the end.

I've met people that were beautiful or handsome by worldly standards, but have a greedy, self-centered or mean spirit. Once I realize this, I don't see them as attractive anymore. On the other hand, I've met people who weren't very attractive physically, but have a loving; caring spirit, then I begin to see them as beautiful.

Society places so much emphasis on outward beauty and appearances that we are all brainwashed to think we have to have a perfect body, perfect features, and the best of clothes to be of any value. Styles and name brands are of high importance to be accepted by many groups, especially teenagers.

If I could give my children one trait, it would be a loving and caring spirit. I'm proud of all the accomplishments they've made and can understand their desire to look good, but what's inside is of greater importance. Even if they achieve high status in society and make lots of money, this wouldn't mean as much to me if they didn't have a good spirit.

Two of my children are in their mid twenties and don't have a significant other yet, and the other is married. I pray every day that when they find a mate it will be someone that will be their soul mate, someone that genuinely cares and will be of good character. Choosing a mate is so important because they can make you either a better or worse person. It's also important that we choose close friends by their character and not by their social status or attractiveness. It is so easy to let other people's values have an influence on us when we are surrounded by them every day.

We need to look beyond the facade of people's bodies and see the real person underneath for what they are worth. I can usually tell by someone's eyes and their actions what they are really like. Even if someone has a mean demeanor or a chip on their shoulder, if you look close enough, you can find good in them. It's so touching to see a transformation in a person that may have been mean spirited but then begins to show a loving attitude. Most people just need to feel unconditional love for themselves in order to be able to give it to others.

Christ offers unconditional love. He knows that His Father doesn't make junk and there is a beautiful person inside each of us; a beauty that is beyond human understanding—if we could just reach down deep enough to find it.

When you get ready for your day today, remember to shave off the grudge you have against your neighbor, put on the makeup of love and kindness, put on the fresh aroma of forgiveness. Then look in the mirror and see what a beautiful person you are.

Prayer: *God, help us to find the beautiful person that is inside each of us and everyone else we meet today. Help us to realize that what's on the inside is what really counts and not all the clothes, makeup, or hair products in the world can make us truly beautiful.*

Yes, we can make ourselves look good, but You know our hearts, Lord. Let me love and be loved as only You can show us how. I'm glad You don't make junk. Thanks for loving me today and every day whether I'm a "beauty" or a "beast!"

Chapter 12
Yeah, I'm Cool

"One man pretends to be rich, yet has nothing; another pretends to be poor, yet has great wealth."

Proverbs 13:7

"All man's ways seem innocent to him, but motives are weighed by the Lord."

Proverbs 16:2

"A good name is more desirable than great riches; to be esteemed is better than silver or gold."

Proverbs 22:1

"Four things on earth are small, yet they are extremely wise: Ants are creatures of little strength, yet they store up their food in the summer; Coney's are creatures of little power, yet they make their homes in the crags; locusts have no king, yet they advance in ranks; a lizard can be caught with the hand, yet it is found in the King's palace."

Proverbs 30:24-28

"I am afraid that when I come, you will not be what I want you to be, and I will not be what you want me to be. I am afraid that among you there may be arguing, jealousy, and confusion."

2 Corinthians 12:20

Most of us have probably done something in our lifetime to try to impress somebody or a group of people in hopes of being accepted or fitting in. If these acts of impressing worked...then I would be a very popular person.

The first time I remember trying my "coolness" was when myself and a several other kids in my neighborhood were doing flips and cartwheels in my yard. One of the bigger kids had the idea of someone getting on their hands and knees while the rest of us did flips over them. This was okay until it was his turn—nobody wanted to be under this 160 pound 5th grader. But being the cool person I was, I said, "I will." It was such a cool thing to do that he landed on top of me instead of going over me, breaking my collarbone. My mother didn't have very much sympathy for me for doing such a stupid thing.

Another time some boys were jumping off of a huge cliff into the Shenandoah River where we used to go boating. Only a couple had gone and some of them were even scared. I thought, *If I do this they'll think I'm really cool, especially since I'm a girl.* As I was getting ready to jump, knowing there could be rocks under the water and fearing for my life, my father drove up in the boat very fast yelling, "Don't you jump from there!" What a relief! Now, it wasn't because I was scared, but because my Dad told me not to. By the way, thanks, Dad!

There were other times at the city pool when I tried doing a 1 ½ flip from the high dive and landed on my face and stomach, knocking me senseless; I swam to the bottom thinking it was the top, then barely made it back to the top. To add pain to misery, the fall knocked my bathing suit top off. (I certainly didn't have anything I wanted anybody to see.) If people didn't think I was cool by now, they never would.

Why do we do things to gain approval from other people? It's all that underlying need we all have; to feel loved and accepted. Siblings in families may fight even into adulthood out of jealousy—feeling another is valued more than they are. Out of peer pressure teens drink, smoke, get anything and everything pierced, or try to be funny and may go to whatever extremes necessary to be liked.

The most admirable people are those that are self confident enough that they can be themselves and not care what other people think. This can be very difficult for kids and teens, especially because they can be very cruel to each other at that age.

My hope for my children has always been that they would have a good enough self-esteem that they wouldn't have to put on pretenses. However, even with the best child rearing efforts, children may struggle to find their identity and make bad choices to fit in. Nothing breaks a parent's heart more than to see their child rejected by their peers. Although you know in the back of your mind that these may be some of the best life lessons learned, there's still a part of you that wants to trade places with them so they won't feel the pain.

There's only one person we should be concerned about impressing and trying to please—God. If we could only realize the strength gained from knowing His love, we wouldn't go to these extremes and make all the mistakes we make growing up to feel accepted. God accepts and loves us unconditionally, mistakes and all.

Prayer: *God, even though we go through life convincing ourselves that our actions are justified and may go to great lengths to impress others, it's only You we need to impress. Help us to only strive for Your approval. In the end we will know, it is Your love that matters most. Do you think I'm cool God? (It was a good belly flop!)*

Chapter 13
Gifts and Talents

"May the favor of the Lord our God rest upon us; establish the work of our hands for us—yes, establish the work of our hands."

Psalms 90:17

"We have different gifts, according to the grace given us. If a man's gift is prophesying, let him use it in proportion to his faith. If it is serving, let him serve; if it is teaching, let him teach; if it is encouraging, let him encourage; if it is contributing to the needs of other, let him give generously; if it is leadership, let him govern diligently; if it is showing mercy, let him do it cheerfully."

Romans 12:6-8

"Each one should use whatever gift he has received to serve others, faithfully administering God's grace in its various forms."

1 Peter 4:10

"And in the church God has appointed first of all apostles, second prophets, third teachers, then workers of miracles, also those having gifts of healing, those able to help others, those with gifts of administration, and those speaking in different kinds of tongues."

1 Corinthians 12:28

*****

Recently I have been drawn to the works of Michelangelo and Leonardo da Vinci. I am particularly interested in the *frescoes* that Michelangelo painted on the ceiling of the Sistine Chapel and *The Last Judgment* scene painted behind the wall of the altar at the same location. He painted the ceiling with pictures depicting the creation, sin and redemption of mankind. Hundreds of over-life-size figures are shown of prophets, athletes, and children who are united with the figures of God and Adam and Eve.[6]

Leonardo da Vinci's, *The Last Supper* is also dramatic in portraying this important event of the Christian church. Of special interest to many art specialists and theologians is the fact that it appears that Mary Magdalene is included, sitting next to Jesus. A television documentary I watched even suggests that Mary and Jesus were possibly married, although there is no proof of this. (That would get some people stirred up, wouldn't it?)

When you see these dramatically lifelike pictures, you know that artists such as these have certainly been given a special gift. What makes their gift especially profound is that it was used to depict God and other special biblical figures to help make them more real to us.

God-given talents can often be seen early in life as children begin to show an interest in a particular area and display extraordinary talent. However, for others the talent might not be discovered until later in life.

In the book *The Purpose Driven Life,* the author describes how "once you've found your purpose in life, and then focus on it, it can be compared to light. Diffused light is spread out and has little power. However, light that is focused, such as with a magnifying glass or laser, becomes very powerful."[7] Once you have an interest and begin to focus on it, you can become very good at it. If God has given you a special talent in an area and you begin to recognize it and respond to it, the results are what we see with the works of da Vinci and Michelangelo.

In Romans 12:6-8 it tells how spiritual gifts of prophesying, serving, teaching, encouraging, helping those in need, and leadership are gifts of grace and it tells us to use them in proportion to our faith. If faith is a big part of your life, you can "move mountains" using these gifts.

Have you discovered your gift or purpose yet? We all have one you know. If it is singing, use it to sing praises; if it is writing, write of God's grace and glory; if it is painting, use it to glorify God; if it is carpentry, use it to help people; if it is teaching or prophesying, help teach others about Christ.

Michelangelo was so passionate about painting the murals of the Sistine Chapel that he painted on his back for hours upon hours, day after day, and month after month. Once the Spirit is leading you in your gift—you will work passionately to complete it with seemingly endless energy.

Discover your talent and use it wisely. God has great plans to accomplish through you and your works.

Prayer: *God, You have given us each a special gift. Help us to find the gift You have planned for us. Help us also to remember to use those gifts for Your kingdom and to not let them make us proud. God, continue to give us gifts that You know are best for us. P.S. I've always wanted to be a singer, God.*

Chapter 14
Misunderstood

"Everything is boring, so boring that you don't even want to talk about it. Words come again and again to our ears, but we never hear enough, nor can we ever really see all we want to see."

Ecclesiastes 1: 8

"In the past, God spoke to our forefathers through the prophets at many times and in various ways, but in these last days he has spoken to us by his Son, whom he appointed heir of all things, and through whom he made the universe."

Hebrews 1: 1-2

Referring to those that don't understand that Jesus is "The High Priest" and God's Son:

"We have much to say about this, but it is hard to explain because you are slow to learn. In fact, though by this time you ought to be teachers, you need someone to teach you the elementary truths of God's word all over again. You need milk, not solid food!"

Hebrews 5: 11-12

"Jesus said to them, 'I tell you the truth, unless you eat the flesh of the Son of Man and drink his blood, you have no life in you. Whoever eats my flesh and drinks my blood has eternal life, and I will raise him up on the last day.'"

John 6:53-54

When I first read John 6:53-54 where Jesus talks about eating His flesh and drinking His blood, I literally laughed out loud realizing how this must have sounded to the Jews of that day who didn't know what we know now. To them it must have sounded as if Jesus was encouraging cannibalism. I can only imagine the expression on their faces. In fact, Jesus lost many disciples that day because His words were too difficult for them to understand.

How many times in our lives have relationships been strained or lost because of a misunderstanding? Two incidences come to mind for me concerning my teenage son:

Once he was singing a song (you have to realize our family is not known for our singing ability). He was listening to rap music at the time, and I thought he was singing a rap song. Irritated because I didn't like that kind of music, I said, "Would you quit singing that crap (sorry)." He looked at me in disgust and said, "Mom I was singing 'Lord of the Dance.'" (A Christian song he learned at church)

Another time, more recently, when I was doing my devotions I thought he said, "Only pansies read the Bible." I felt like screaming at him, but kept my cool and replied, "Well, I guess I'm a pansy then and I'm proud of it." He looked at me with a perplexed look on his face wondering what I was talking about. As it turns out he asked," How many pages are in the Bible?" After I apologized for both incidences, we all had a good laugh from both blunders on my part and I felt pretty foolish.

Since my hearing is not real good, and I now realize it is easy to misinterpret people's actions and words, I try to give people the benefit of the doubt—thinking I probably misunderstood them. Even those we think we know best can be misunderstood.

In some cases, as we get to know someone well, especially a mate, we come to know what they're thinking and how they feel about many circumstances. As Christians, we can also have such a relationship with God. If we become very familiar with His Word, and go to Him in prayer on a daily basis, knowing how He wants us to react to everyday situations in a Christ like manner is much easier. In the end we are closer to Christ, resulting in less misunderstandings and bad judgments made.

As the verses in Hebrews 1:1-2 and 5:11-12 tell us, in the past God spoke through the prophets. Most people at this time were inaccessible to speak to and hear God themselves. Then Jesus came and opened the door for us. This was very difficult for the teachers of that day to understand. Verse 12 in chapter 5 says it well when it says, *"You need someone to teach you the elementary truths of God's word all over again. You need milk, not solid food!"* If you don't understand, start from the beginning. Begin a relationship in which you truly understand how God, or anyone close to you, really feels. As a result misunderstandings will be fewer and farther between. Think about it...who are the people you can trust to tell your deepest thoughts to? Aren't they the ones that know you the best, the ones you know will still care about you even if they know your faults and flaws? Is there is someone like this in your life? Know that a relationship with Christ can far outweigh any human bond you can have. Begin to know Him today! He understands you better than even a best friend.

Prayer: *God, help me to know and understand You (and others) better. Let me give people the benefit of the doubt, even if their intentions are hurtful. Help me to continue to show love even to the unlovable. Before Your death, You were cursed, spit at and beaten, yet You continued to love them and ask, "Father forgive them, they know not what they do." Let us live by Your example Lord.*

Chapter 15
Keep Them Safe

"But let all who take refuge in you be glad; let them ever sing for joy. Spread your protection over them that those who love your name may rejoice in you. For surely, O Lord, you bless the righteous; you surround them with your favor as with a shield."

Psalm 5:11

"For He will command His angels concerning you; to guard you in all your ways; they will lift you up in their hands, so that you will not strike your foot against a stone."

Psalm 91:11-12

"Are not all angels ministering spirits sent to serve those who will inherit salvation?"

Hebrews 1:14

"You are my hiding place; you will protect me from trouble and surround me with songs of deliverance."

Psalm 32:7

The verse from Psalm 91:11, along with a guardian angel, is inscribed on a pewter key chain I gave my daughter Robyn when she first started driving. When children start to drive, it creates a fear in us parents—different than most others we've had to face as our children were growing up. In driving, they are now required to make very grown up decisions—and we hope and pray they make the right ones. (Example: When to pull out in front of a car, using rearview and side view mirrors, close attention to speed limits, and not taking your eyes off the road to put in a CD or to answer a cell phone.)

When children are young, we have more control and responsibility for keeping them safe. By commands or actions we teach them: Don't play in the streets, don't touch hot things, we keep medicines and poisons out of their reach, put safety locks on our cabinets, I'm sure you can add a hundred others. Then, as they become adults, we have to start letting go of that control or protectiveness. At this point we need to pray that they will make good choices and ask God to watch over them. No matter how much harping we've done, they are now in charge of their decision-making and a small mistake could be a life-threatening one. Like most parents, I pray for my children's safety on a daily basis and rightfully so.

When my children were young, like all parents I dealt with emergencies such as bloody mouths, bumps from falls, serious illnesses, and broken or nearly broken bones—and somehow survived. At this time, all three of my children are in their twenties, but all have had experiences that could very well have turned into life-threatening situations.

My daughter Cassie had her car break down on an interstate between Arlington, Virginia and our home in northern Virginia. A man picked her up to give her a ride. Although she's been taught to never ride with strangers, she felt like he looked safe and this was her only option since she didn't have a phone. In an effort to make her feel "comfortable," he let her hold the gun he kept in a case in his car. (It didn't make her feel better) However, he did get her help and she got home safely. Praise the Lord!

When Robyn went to college at Coastal Carolina in South Carolina, she would make several trips home a year. One time she couldn't leave to come home until late in the afternoon, which would make her getting home at 3:00 in the morning. I asked her to call me along the way so I would know she was okay. At 1:00 a.m. she called to say how far away she was and she was calling from a phone booth at a gas station that was closed. Suddenly, she quickly said, "I've got to go! A car of strange looking guys just pulled up next to me." and hung up. I stood there with my mouth wide open, just staring at the phone. She did get home safely two hours later. (After much praying and pacing on my part.) They both have cell phones now.

My son Jake has been in several minor car accidents, but the worst one occurred when he flipped his Jeep Cherokee one Thanksgiving morning. After seeing the car, I realized how lucky he and his friend were. The top was completely smashed in and all the windows were popped out. They had to climb out of the back window. They did have their seatbelts on and, miraculously, didn't even get a scratch. Another answered prayer.

There are many other occasions where I know they have been kept safe. I know that God has been there for them and continues to keep them safe. No matter how old your children are, continue to pray for their safety. Pray that the angels will watch over them. God provides plenty of guardian angels to go around. Hopefully theirs won't have to work overtime as my children's angels have. Thank you God!

Prayer: *God, I know You have been there many times for my family and myself. Please continue to be with us and those we love. Thank You for angels that guard and protect us in times of need. At the same time, let us be there for anyone else who may be in need of a guardian angel. You can accomplish Your work through us as well as the angels. At the same time God, we know that for whatever reasons, some of Your children have come home to You. Please hold these in Your loving arms until the day we can hold them again ourselves.*

Chapter 16
Graduation

"So Jacob said to his family and to all who were with him, 'Put away all the foreign gods you have and make yourselves clean, and change your clothes."

Genesis 35:2

"One thing God has spoken, two things have I heard: that you, O God, are strong, and that you, O Lord, are loving. Surely you will reward each person according to what he has done."

Psalm 62:11-12

"My heart took delight in all my work, and this was the reward for all my labor."

Ecclesiastes 2:10

"O great and powerful God, whose name is the Lord Almighty, great are your purposes and mighty are your deeds. Your eyes are open to all the ways of men; you reward everyone according to his conduct and as his deeds deserve."

Jeremiah 32:19

"If anyone belongs to Christ, there is a new creation. The old things have gone; everything is made new! All this is from God."

2 Corinthians 5:17

Most of us have experienced graduations for many people throughout our lives. First, our own graduations and then our children's from preschool, high school, and some from college. Then there are nieces and nephews, and friends.

As a preschool director for twelve years, I have personally graduated approximately 700 children. I would say I'm pretty experienced in graduations. Graduations can be hot, boring, inspirational, emotional, crowded, and unusual.

With your own children, each graduation represents a different stepping stone in their lives—making you reflect on what they've accomplished already and what lies ahead.

For me, my children's high school graduations brought the most tears—both of joy and sadness. Joy that together you have accomplished so much—all those hours of homework, trips to sporting events, piano and other types of lessons, learning to drive, broken bones, healed hurts and struggles as to what they can and can't do. And then the sadness of knowing they will be leaving home and learning to live life on their own—without you to tell them what to do and how to do it in an effort to prepare them for life. As we prepare to release them to the world, we worry—did I teach them well? Will they be safe? Will they make good choices?

Recently I attended a graduation that was different from any I had been to before. When you entered the facility, you walked through a twelve-foot high fence with razor wire at the top and bottom. You then entered a room where you had to take off your jacket, shoes, and put any items from your pockets into a tray that was closely inspected and then you were frisked and walked through a metal detector.

This was for my nephew's graduation for his GED while he was in prison. The inmates were able to wear caps and gowns and there was a small celebration with cake and drinks afterward.

The school in this prison was operated by a separate organization that also taught mechanics, carpentry, computers, and plumbing. The principal was an amazing and caring woman who truly cared about the young men that had achieved this accomplishment. I was especially touched by the story she told of one young man that had taken the GED test many times over the past three years and now had finally passed it. The pride in his face as he received that award was beyond words. I cried tears of joy for him and I didn't even know him.

As I sat there and looked at all the faces of these young men that had made many bad choices in their life, I was so grateful that the prison system didn't just treat them like dirt, but gave them opportunities to make a better life for themselves and put their mistakes behind them.

The speaker for the day was an ex-inmate who had served nine years in prison. During that time he attended every class he could go to in order to learn as much as he could. His specialty was mechanics, and after his release he was able to obtain a good job as an auto mechanic. He now has a family and had just purchased his first home. He told how all the things he learned while in prison had not only helped him get a job, but also helped him become self sufficient in fixing things around the house and was able to help other people. His message was one of great hope for the others that would be released in the near future.

Many people feel that those who have committed crimes should just be locked up, given bad food to eat and have all privileges taken away; basically, treated like animals. Thank goodness God doesn't feel that way about us when we make mistakes. Just like these prisoners—we are given chances to redeem ourselves and become worthwhile citizens and members of His family.

One of the things Christ urges us to do is visit the sick and those in prison. I asked my nephew what he misses the most—his answer was freedom. As Americans we don't know how much we take our freedom from granted. However, even as a free nation, it is known that you can't live a dishonest or lawless life. In so doing, you will lose your freedom. It is my hope and prayer that after seeing the consequences of losing this freedom, he will make better choices when he is released.

Throughout history and in other countries even today, people are put in prison for simply thinking differently than their leaders, for standing up for what they believe in and may even be accused falsely of a crime. Many important people of the Bible went to prison, including Joseph and many of the Disciples. Although in prison unjustifiably, they made the best of their situation and Joseph was even able to move all the way to second in power next to the King because of his special talent of interpreting dreams.

As fair as we try to be in proving people guilty beyond a shadow of a doubt, our system is not foolproof and some are still sentenced unfairly. Thanks to DNA testing these cases are becoming fewer and fewer.

Those who are in prison still need to know and feel love. If they can experience God for the first time while they are there, their life can be changed forever. The message God wants us to learn is to not give up on people that make mistakes. Give them examples of unconditional love and friendship. Through your perseverance they may then be able to graduate to a better place; a place in the Kingdom beside you and me. The best graduation of all!

Prayer: *God, We know You've been with us for each accomplishment and failure we've made in our lives. Thanks for not giving up on us when we've made mistakes. Continue to be with us as we grow in our faith and get closer to the grandest graduation day of all—when we see You face to face.*

Chapter 17
You're Not Dotting Your I's and Crossing Your T's

"God does speak—sometimes one way and sometimes another—even though people may not understand it. He speaks in a dream or a vision of the night when people are in a deep sleep, lying on their beds. He speaks in their ears and frightens them with warnings to turn them away from doing wrong and to keep them from being proud."

Job 33: 14-17

"What then shall we say, brothers? When you come together, everyone has a hymn, or a word of instruction, a revelation, a tongue or an interpretation. All of these must be done to strengthen the church. If anyone speaks in a tongue, two—or at the most three—should speak, one at a time, and someone should interpret. If there is no interpreter, the speaker should keep quiet in the church and speak to himself and God."

I Corinthians 14:26-28

"If we say we have no sin, we are fooling ourselves, and the truth is not in us. But if we confess our sins, he will forgive our sins, because we can trust God to do what is right. He will cleanse us from all the wrongs we have done. If we say we have not sinned, we make God a liar, and we do not accept God's teaching."

1 John 1: 8-10

When we go on vacation, I enjoy going to different churches and even experiencing other denominations. One summer that I will never forget, we tried a neat looking church in the shape of Noah's Ark in Nags Head, North Carolina. I had attended there one other time and liked it because they had contemporary music and a relaxed friendly atmosphere. This service went well as before, then at the end the pastor/preacher asked everyone to come up front. Suddenly he began speaking in tongues. It was a strange language that was spoken very quickly and sounded like gibberish. I had read about speaking in tongues in the Bible before, but had never experienced it. The preacher went from person to person touching each of them on the forehead as he spoke. As he was getting closer and closer to me I was feeling strange and thought, *How can that possibly mean anything? This guy is really weird.*

When he got to me, as soon as he touched me I understood him clearly. He simply said, "You're not dotting your I's and crossing your T's." I felt as if lightning had hit me and I looked at my daughter and brother-in-law as if to say, "Did you hear that?"

The whole experience left both of them very uncomfortable and they wanted to leave as soon as we went back to our seats. I just followed, still numb from what I had just experienced. I wondered, *Did God actually speak to me through this man, or had he just changed from speaking gibberish to English the moment he touched me?* When we got to the car I asked my daughter and brother-in-law if they had understood anything he had said. "No way!" they said. "That whole thing was weird." Since they didn't experience what I did, I just kept silent, not ready to tell anyone about what had happened. It wasn't until a year later that I was able to tell anyone about the experience.

I often wondered what he meant by his statement, "You're not dotting your I's or crossing your T's." I tried writing it out on paper without dotting the I and crossing the T. The conclusion I came to is that it means that I have the general idea about following Christ, but don't have it completely right yet. Doesn't that speak to most of us? Do we ever get it completely right when it comes to knowing and following God? Even Paul tell us in Philippians 3: 12-14 that he doesn't have it right yet, but keeps "straining toward the goal." Ecclesiastes 7:20 reminds us *"that no man (or woman) is without sin."* We are incapable of not sinning. Only with God's help can we strive for it. And most of the time we don't want His help. It's easier to keep sinning.

It's interesting how the verse from I Corinthians 14:26-28 stresses the importance of being able to interpret, or have someone there to interpret, what is being said in tongues. If not, it shouldn't be done. I can understand why some people thought those who were filled with the Holy Spirit at Pentecost (Acts 2:1-13) were drunk when they began speaking in tongues. If you don't understand what is being said, it seems like a very strange thing.

My experience with tongues has made me more aware of the Spirit. It has become real to me rather than something I have just read about in the Bible. Before, I thought that the people that claimed these things were religious fanatics that got so caught up in their religion that they were imagining things. I can see how it would be scary or seem so strange to a newcomer of the church. Especially if no one is interpreting and those there do not understand what is being said. Even if someone did interpret it, there is so much skepticism in the world about religion; some may believe it's a hoax. Had I not experienced this, I don't know if I would have believed. God never ceases to amaze me at how powerful and all knowing and caring He is. It's amazing for me to think that He has spoken to me, a plain everyday sinner. How blessed I am that He is a part of my life.

Instances such as these have created an insatiable thirst in me to know more about God and to become closer to Him. Hopefully, one day I will get to the point that I am truly dotting my I's and crossing my T's.

Prayer: *God, we acknowledge we are not capable of being without sin. However, because of Your blessed grace we will be saved anyway. Thank You for Your "Counselor" that makes us aware of the sins we need to confess for. Help those who have ears to hear the special message You have for them from Your Helper, The Holy Spirit.*

Amen

Chapter 18
One of These Days You're Going to Like Me

"Having loved his own who were in the world, he now showed them the full extent of his love."

"He got up from the meal, took off his outer clothing and wrapped a towel around his waist. After that, he poured water into a basin and began to wash his disciples' feet, drying them with the towel that was wrapped around him."

John 13: 1, 4-5

"This is how we know what love is: Jesus Christ laid down his life for us. And we ought to lay down our lives for our brothers. If anyone has material possessions and sees his brother in need, but has no pity on him, how can the love of God be in him? Dear children, let us not love with words or tongue but with actions and in truth."

1 John 3: 16-18

"Therefore, as God's chosen people; holy and dearly loved, clothe yourself with compassion, kindness, humility, gentleness and patience. Bear with each other and forgive whatever grievance you may have against each other. Forgive as the Lord forgave you. And over all these virtues put on love, which binds them all together in perfect unity."

Colossians 3: 12-14

*****

It was obvious that a lady that worked in the building where I worked didn't like me. I would say "*Hi*" as we passed and she wouldn't respond. If I asked her a question, it was a very cool, one word answer, or as few words as possible. I just overlooked it thinking, *One of these days you're going to like me*.

Then it got worse. Another lady came to work there and she didn't like me either. (I thought I was a likable person?) They teamed up against me and I wasn't sure if I could take it any longer. They constantly answered me with sharp cool answers, rolled eyes, and shook their heads in disgust at requests or simple statements made. I am a very friendly and outgoing person and I just couldn't understand this. How I reacted to them often depended on how I was feeling about myself that day.

During this time I was going through a period of depression and lack of self-esteem. Although I put on a front that I was happy-go-lucky, I would come home exhausted from acting as if everything was okay. With a low self-esteem, their dislike for me was reinforcing my negative view of myself.

I remembered how Christ calls us to remind people of their sins privately first, then with a witness. I wrote one of the women a letter explaining how she made me feel. She called me, kind of apologizing, saying that was just her personality and she couldn't help it. As it turns out she ended up moving so that ended the dealings with her.

After some time, the other lady began to warm up to me once we were in a Bible study together. I remember seeing her smile for the first time. I had known her for two years and never had seen her smile. I thought, *She looks so pretty when she smiles.*

Then I saw her cry at a funeral. I thought, *She does have feelings!* Then I heard that she played a practical joke on somebody. I was amazed!

Now, on many occasions, seven years later, she is starting to act like she likes me. This makes me happy. There are times when she still gives me that stern cold look or rolls her eyes, but they are becoming less and less and actually we are becoming pretty good friends.

Sometimes my first response when people act like this is to avoid them and not talk to them. *That will teach them!* I will think. But this only lasts for a few days and then I want to be their friend again. It really bothers me when somebody doesn't like me. In the same way, it really bothers God when people don't love Him.

God never gives up on us. If He were to return (again) in a human body, I imagine Him as someone doing a menial job, that's always friendly, willing to talk, and doesn't get hurt when people constantly reject Him and put Him down. These are attributes I always admire in people and wish I could possess.

It takes a lot of self-confidence and humbleness to be able to live with a constant forgiving heart. A trait most of us are lacking.

Now when people act like this, I try to see their good qualities and pray for them. As the above verse says, *"Bear with each other and forgive whatever grievance you may have against each other."* In doing this, I have gained many friendships that otherwise may have been lost. It's amazing how prayer can really change people.

Two great movies that portray a loving and forgiving heart are *What About Bob?* and *Forrest Gump*. Both of the main characters have a childlike attitude and don't take offenses to heart and, in addition, are able to turn them around to make something good out of them. Isn't that what Christ did on the cross? This example gives me more strength to endure and overlook unkindness from other people. Thank goodness God was willing to send His Son to teach us this lesson. What a loving God we have!

Try liking someone who is unlikable and see what happens. What a great feeling when they start liking you back. Yes, the next time someone is rude or mean to you, take the attitude that—"One of these days you're gonna like me." Guess what! One day they probably will.

Prayer: *For today's prayer I'd like to use the lyrics to Tim McGraw's song* "One of These Days You're Going to Love Me"*: (I felt love was too strong for the story so used "like" in it.)*

> *One of these days you're gonna love me*
> *You'll sit down by yourself and think*
> *About the times you pushed and shoved me*
> *And what good friends we might have been*
> *And then you're gonna sigh a little*
> *Maybe even cry a little*
> *One of these days you're gonna love me.*

Chapter 19
Are You Ripe Yet?

"He will be like a tree planted by the water that sends out its roots by the stream. It does not fear when heat comes; its leaves are always green. It has no worries in a year of drought and never fails to bear fruit."

Jeremiah 17:8

"Make a tree good and its fruit will be good, or make a tree bad and its fruit will be bad, for a tree is recognized by its fruit."

Matthew 12: 33-34

"You don't know where the wind will blow and you don't know how a baby grows inside the mother. In the same way, you don't know what God is doing, or how he created everything. Plant early in the morning, and work until evening, because you don't know if this or that will succeed."

Ecclesiastes 11: 5-6

"I do not mean that I am already as God wants me to be. I have not yet reached that goal, but I continue trying to reach it and to make it mine. Christ wants me to do that, which is the reason he made me his."

Philippians 3: 12

"We pray that you will also have great wisdom and understanding in spiritual things so that you will live the kind of life that honors and pleases the Lord in every way. You will produce fruit in every good work and grow in the knowledge of God."

Colossians 1: 9-10

Have you ever eaten fruit that wasn't completely ripe yet? You know, like the big shiny delicious looking apples that are polished to give them an extra tempting look. I recently ate one of these beauties and, to my disappointment, when I took a bite it had a chalky taste that lingered in my mouth and made my teeth feel weird for quite awhile. The problem was that it wasn't ripe yet.

Just like the seemingly delicious apple, we can look good and appealing on the outside, but it's what's on the inside that counts. Apple growers know the secret to selling apples is to pick it at just the right time to give his customers a pleasing product.

As we grow and mature, we go through many stages in our life. Some are good and some not so good. It is very common for young people to make mistakes and try different ways of thinking before they become a mature adult.

As people growing in faith, we also go through similar stages. We may dress up and go to church every week, but are we where God wants us to be at this point in our faith journey? Does your life have order, is your family your number one priority after God, do you do your best at whatever you do, do you care about others?

One Sunday I asked my Senior High Sunday School students if they felt giving God one day a week was enough for them. A couple honestly responded yes. I went on to tell them that God wants us to have as close of a relationship with Him as they would anyone else they cared deeply about. The way you would when you can't wait to see that person again and want to be with them every day and every moment.

Have you ever gone to school, work, or an event that you were in charge of when you were unprepared? There is no scarier feeling. It will leave you with bad dreams for years to come.

When I was a senior at the University of Arizona, I was pregnant with my first child. My husband and I got married in my junior year and we couldn't wait to start a family. He joined the Air Force and I was out of school for a year. Thankfully he got stationed in Tucson, Arizona, which worked out well so I could finish my education. I was pregnant and doing my student teaching. Our advisor had told us that it usually wasn't a good idea to take extra classes during student teaching because it was so time consuming and demanding. I really wanted to take a class on child guidance and it wouldn't cost any extra, so thought I'd try it anyway.

As our advisor had warned us, it was a very demanding semester, especially for a pregnant student. One day I had to miss one of the child guidance classes for a doctor appointment. When I returned at the next class, there was a test lying on our desks. My heart sank to my stomach and I felt like I was going to get sick. I failed the test miserably and, as a result, ended up dropping the class.

There have also been times where I have put a lot of time into preparing for an event or big occasion. Even with all the planning I still forgot something important that I needed. After beating myself up and swearing I would do better next time it would happen again. Feelings from these instances were so strong that I continued to have dreams about not being ready for something for many years. No matter how hard I try in the dream, I can't get to where I'm going or just can't get ready because other things keep preventing me from doing what I need to do. I wake with a very uneasy feeling and am left with an anxious feeling all day because of the dream.

Are you ready for Christ to return? Would He be satisfied with the life you have lived and the relationship you have with Him? Just as someone who goes into the ministry has to do much Bible study and begins a closer walk with Christ before they can preach the Word, we also must prepare ourselves to face the world as Christians. Could you imagine getting in front of a congregation to preach and not knowing what you're going to talk about? (Talk about bad dreams)

Will your fruit be on the tree of life and will it be pleasing on the inside and outside when Christ comes for the harvest? Start sowing your seeds now. You know not the day or the hour when He will return. Don't procrastinate any longer. Be ready for the picking!

Prayer: *God, help me to be prepared for the day that I will meet You. I know You're not interested in clothes and looks, but more concerned about our hearts. Help me to be ripened just the way You want me to be. Not too sour, not too sweet, but just right so that I am pleasing to You alone.*

Chapter 20
Goodbyes

"Now I am going to Him who sent me, yet none of you asks me, "Where are you going?" Because I have said these things, you are filled with grief. But I tell you the truth: It is for your good that I am going away. Unless I go away, the Counselor will not come to you; but if I go, I will send Him to you."

John 16:5-7

"While he was blessing them, he left them and was taken into Heaven. Then they worshiped him and returned to Jerusalem with great joy. And they stayed continually at the temple praising God."

Luke 24: 50-53

"'Lord, first let me go and bury my father.' But Jesus told him, 'Follow me, and let the dead bury their own dead.'"

Matthew 8: 21

"I taught you to remember the words Jesus said: 'It is more blessed to give than to receive.' When Paul had said this, he knelt down with all of them and prayed. And they all cried because Paul had said they would never see him again."

Acts 20:35-36

Paul's final farewell:

"For I am already being poured out like a drink offering, and the time has come for my departure. I have fought the good fight, I have finished the race, I have kept the faith."

2 Timothy 4: 6-7

It is encouraging to see in Luke's version of Jesus' ascension that the disciples were filled with "great joy" as he was ascending. What a contrast this was to the sadness and pain of Jesus' first departure when he died on the cross. They now knew that this isn't really the end, but the beginning of a new life for all that will die in Christ. They knew that one day they would see Him again.

Goodbyes are very difficult for me. Especially since all my children are living at different places away from home. I will usually see them anywhere between a month to three months, but the joy of being with them when they come to visit turns to sadness the day they leave. How does that saying go? "If you love someone you've got to let them go." Letting go can be hard.

One of my favorite country songs is one sung by Trace Adkins called "Then They Do." He sings about the stages of children's lives and how when they are younger and have a lot of demands on you, you can't wait till they get older; and "Then They Do." But then they leave and now it's a different story, there's a part of you that wants them to stay young forever.

Then there is Patty Loveless' song, "How Can I Help You Say Goodbye." What a tear-jerker. First she experiences the pain of saying goodbye to a good friend when she moves away. Then her and her husband gets a divorce and she expresses the pain this causes. In both cases her mom is there to help her through it all. Then the hardest part of all—her mom dies (I'm getting teary-eyed just writing about it) and she has to tell her goodbye.

When you finally get used to saying goodbye to your kids, then grandkids come along and it starts all over again. But there is also joy in looking forward to the time when you will see them again.

The hardest goodbye of all is with the loss of a loved one. It may be a parent, spouse, or a best friend that you always called or talked to share your joys and sorrows with. The emptiness this brings can hurt deeply.

I recently attended a funeral like one I had never seen before. The man that died was in his early forties and died as a result of drinking and driving. During the funeral at the gravesite, his mother was crying uncontrollably and passing out. After she was taken away a sister started to pass out while another sister was in the background screaming as she was crying, then began screaming at the deceased man's young wife blaming her for his death. The funeral director and the attending pastor were in shock as were many attending.

This is the reaction you may get from a family who doesn't know God. Without God death is not only sad but also nearly unbearable. When you know

God you know His peace that transcends all understanding when you lose someone you love dearly.

Live each day as if it's going to be your last. If you live life this way, you will have no regrets. Don't let an argument go too long without rectifying it; be sure to tell those you love how you feel about them on a regular basis; don't put off the help you wanted to give someone until you have more time; make time for those you love now.

Prayer: *God, Satan loves for us to think that death is the end. Because of Your willingness to let Your only Son die for us, we know this isn't true. He has gone to prepare a place for us in hopes that we will come to Him and accept Your love. Lord, if only everyone could know this love so they won't have to suffer a lifetime of pain. With You, goodbyes become "Welcome, dear child. I have been waiting for you."*

Chapter 21
Does Meek Mean Weak?

"Blessed are the meek, for they will inherit the earth."

Matthew 5:5

"Two things I ask of you, Lord; do not refuse me before I die. Keep falsehood and lies far from me; give me neither poverty nor riches, but give me only daily bread. Otherwise, I may have too much and disown you and say, 'Who is the Lord?' Or I may become poor and steal, and so dishonor the name of my God."

Proverbs 30: 7-9

"Then Pilate asked him, 'Don't you hear the testimony they are bringing against you?' But Jesus made no reply, not even a single charge—to the great amazement of the governor."

Matthew 27: 13-14

"Bless those who persecute you; bless and do not curse. Rejoice with those who rejoice; mourn with those who mourn. Live in harmony with one another. Do not be proud, but be willing to associate with people of low position. Do not be conceited."

Romans 12:14-16

Webster's Dictionary definition for meek and weak:
Meek: *soft; gentle; mild of temper; refrain from; forbearing; humble; submissive; yielding; obedient; compliant; unpretending character.*
Weak: *Not strong; feeble; infirm; frail; silly; wanting moral courage; ineffective.*

I never quite understood the line from *The Beatitudes* where Jesus said, "The meek will inherit the earth." I've always thought of someone who is meek as shy and backward and afraid to speak up. However, the words used to describe meek from the dictionary describe it as someone having self-control, someone who is humble and submissive. When used in reference to God—meekness is definitely a good attribute.

When meekness is used for God's purpose, we are able to keep quiet, even when we are falsely accused of wrongdoing. We are able to give up control of our lives and let God take control; we learn to not take credit for things we've accomplished when God was the one working through us to accomplish a goal. Yes, put in this light I can see the benefits of being meek. It actually takes great strength and faith to be a truly meek person.

When you have a lot of pride you always want to be in charge, like to argue, always want things done your way. If this describes you, you are about as far from meek as you can get. These attributes describe many people I know…including myself. I am especially likely to fly off the handle if someone accuses me of something I didn't do.

Jesus gives us the perfect example of meekness when Pilate asks him to speak concerning the charges against Him. Knowing that everything that is taking place was planned to happen by his Father, Jesus remains quiet and doesn't speak. There are many times when Jesus did speak up against injustices, but when it comes to this situation He knows it's necessary for these things to take place for God's plan to unfold.

The key to meekness is knowing when and when not to react, then when you do, you do it in such a way that it leaves people wondering, "what just happened?" The meek can make a big statement in a quiet way.

Mother Teresa was the perfect example of meekness. She simply went about serving those in need. Along the way, she was able to be an example of a loving spirit that spoke louder than any proclamation made by man. Those who she served felt it, others that watched her saw it.

On one of the mission trips I went to in Appalachia, we did a meaningful activity that either touched people or made them mad. We were all divided into groups representing the different populations of the world. One group was given much food, another group was given a little food with no utensils, and the last group was given a spoonful of rice with no utensils. The ones that were given more felt so uncomfortable about having more than the others that they shared their food with everyone else. It also touched those who had the least and received more because most of us had never had to receive anything from anyone in such a way before.

For some it was not accepted well because we had already put in a hard day's work and they felt we should all be fed well. Others, especially those who hadn't had a close relationship with Christ were touched and it opened their eyes to the needs in the world that they had never noticed before. With everyone in the same room it was easy to see the need, but when the hunger is on the other side of the world or in a different part of the country, it's easy to ignore. Many of us had a lesson in meekness that day.

The meek know how God wants them to react and they do so in an obedient, humble, submissive way, rather than the irrational, aggressive, "I will be heard!" way—the way most of us naturally react.

If you're not a meek person, don't feel guilty, very few of us are. But, oh how I admire someone who is. We can strive for these attributes, but we can't do it alone. Only with God's help can we obtain this. Or it may be that meekness isn't the plan that God has for you. He didn't mean for everyone to be meek. These are gifts He's given to a chosen few. He gives each of us the gift He feels is best suited for us and that He is able to use to accomplish His work the best. Is meekness your gift?

Prayer: *God, You have given us many gifts. Some people have been able to obtain meekness while the rest of us are searching for the gift You have especially chosen for each and everyone. Help us to realize that gift and how to best use it for Your purposes.*

Chapter 22
Please Be Patient, God Isn't Finished with Me Yet!

"I tell you the truth; Jesus answered, 'This very night before the rooster crows, you will disown me three times.' But Peter declared, 'Even if I have to die with you, I will never disown you.' And all the other disciples said the same.

Matthew 26: 34-35

After Peter's third denial of Jesus:

"Then he began to call down curses on himself and he swore to them, 'I do not know the man!' Immediately a rooster crowed."

Matthew 26: 74

"Therefore, as God's chosen people, holy and dearly loved, clothe yourself with compassion, kindness, humility, gentleness and patience. Bear with each other and forgive whatever grievance you may have against one another. Forgive as the Lord forgave you. And over all these virtues put on love, which binds them all together in perfect unity."

Colossians 3:12-14

"When I was a child, I talked like a child, I thought like a child, I reasoned like a child. When I became a man, I put childish ways behind me. Now we see but a poor reflection as in a mirror; then we shall see face to face. Now I know in part; then I shall know fully, even as I am fully known."

1 Corinthians 13: 11-12

Many people relate well to Peter because most of us have messed up over and over again as he did on several occasions. The beauty of it all is that Jesus didn't give up on Peter and kick him out of the "disciple society" and condemn him to Hell. No, rather than disown him, Peter was given many chances as he learned from his mistakes.

How about you? If someone makes a mistake, do you immediately give up on them or are you able to look past their mistake and still see their potential? Many people tend to build a wall of perfection around them, expecting their children or close friends and family to follow a regimented, high standard of living that they have created in their mind. In this mindset, there is no room for mistakes. If someone does slip up, family ties are then severed and in some cases never reconciled again. How sad for a family that has thrown a child out of the home when they were simply testing the waters, trying to find their way in life.

There is no better lesson learned than one made from a mistake. In learning to do many things, we often use trial and error until we get it right. Some of us may read directions first or will listen to advice given on how to do something, but lessons learned from mistakes are worth more than a thousand lectures.

As parents, we harp at our children about not doing this or attempt to tell them how to do that. When they don't "listen" to us, we often get angry or frustrated and can't help but say, "I told you so" or "Why didn't you listen to me?" It isn't until they actually experience mistakes themselves that the message sinks in. However, through mistakes and all, we continue to love them. (I hope)

This must be how God feels about us. He sent His only Son to be an example and die for us, perform many miracles, and has given us His Word, yet we continue to try to do things our own way. Thank goodness He is patient with us. I love that picture of a child with the disheveled hair and dirty clothes with the quote, "Please be patient, God isn't finished with me yet." I think this applies to all of us.

After Peter denied Jesus the third time, Jesus later reinstates him by asking him three times if he loves Him. At first Peter is agitated with Jesus for asking him so many times; however, it is this act that frees Peter of the guilt he had felt so heavily from the denial. After this, Peter goes on to become "The Rock," one of the most influential and powerful leaders to spread Christianity. Thank goodness he didn't get so down from his mistake that he may have committed suicide as Judas did after turning Jesus over to the authorities. If only we could learn from our mistakes as well as Peter.

How many friendships have you lost because of your rejection of those who don't think as you do, irritate you, or who have made mistakes that you won't forgive? Christ calls us to give grace to others as He gives it to us. We have done nothing to earn it; He just continues to love us, just as we continue to love our children unconditionally. Knowing they are loved helps them grow a deep love for us, which also becomes unconditional.

In the movie *Groundhog Day* the main character played by Bill Murray, is a self-centered guy who goes about life with a grumpy, don't care about people attitude. Every day is the same, day after day, as he continues to make the same mistakes over and over again. Finally, one day he "gets it" and starts to care about people and do nice things for them. The transformation that he goes through is refreshing.

Jesus has told us that loving only the people that love us isn't enough; we are called to continue loving and forgiving people that may irritate, hurt or even mistreat us. (This doesn't mean staying in an abusive situation.) If we can hang on long enough to see a transformation take place in their lives, the rewards are beyond words. It would be similar to the joy the father must have felt with the return of his prodigal son.

In Terry Clark's song "I Just Want to Be Mad for Awhile" she describes how she will continue to love her mate unconditionally and won't leave him, but sometimes she just needs to get away for awhile when he messes up. Eventually she will get over it, she just asks for some time. If that is you, just make sure your "awhile" isn't too long.

Allow the people in your life room for mistakes. Do this knowing they will learn from them and with prayers and patience, they will develop into the person God has planned them to be.

Prayer: *God, thank You for having patience with us when we continue to mess up. Open our eyes so we can see the mistakes we've made and learn from them. Help us to continue to love and show kindness to people who may need to make lots of mistakes to learn life's lessons. Let them be able to feel your unconditional love. We are continually tempted to ignore, ridicule, and dislike people who are different from us. Fill us with Your Spirit to strengthen us with patience and kindness Lord.*

Chapter 23
Simple Things

"Do not deceive yourselves. If any one of you thinks he is wise by the standards of this age, he should become a "fool" so that he may become wise. For the wisdom of this world is foolishness in God's sight."

1 Corinthians 3: 18-19

"We know that we all possess knowledge. Knowledge puffs up, but love builds up. The man who thinks he knows something does not know as he ought to know. But the man that loves God is known by God."

1 Corinthians 8: 1-3

"When they saw the courage of Peter and John and realized that they were unschooled, ordinary men, they were astonished and they took note that these men had been with Jesus."

Acts 4: 13

"When he was alone, the Twelve and the others around him asked him about the parables. He told them, 'The secret of the kingdom of God has been given to you. But to those on the outside everything is said in parables so that, 'they may be ever seeing but never perceiving, and ever hearing but never understanding; otherwise they might turn and be forgiven!''"

Mark 4: 10-12

*****

You probably already know that one of my passions in my life is a mission we do at our church called the Appalachia Service Project (ASP). We take teams of youth and adults to the mountains of Appalachia to rebuild homes for those who cannot afford to do so themselves. What used to be thriving coal-mining towns are now areas with high poverty levels due to the lower demand for coal and the fact that most industries don't want to develop in these areas because of the difficulty of transporting products.

When you first decide to go on this mission trip, you think, "I'm going to help people and make a difference in their life." Most of us usually discover we are the ones that are helped or changed through the experience. New relationships are built and many lessons are learned.

The people of Appalachia are much more laid back than most other Americans. They may not have the luxuries most of us have, but their simplicity of life is much more of a valued treasure.

We spend much of our time rushing from place to place, trying to improve our lives with more education, always searching for better paying jobs and a higher social status. Much time is spent rushing our children from one social or athletic event to another. If we have time, and it fits into our schedule, we go to church and may even get involved. Most people think, "I can't fit that in my schedule. Let someone else do it."

In Appalachia, people spend much of their time on front porches talking. Most days are spent with family and friends. Church, in many cases, is the focal point of their social life. They don't have the nice houses and cars we have, but are happy and content with what they do have. Of course, they do desire a functioning vehicle to get them to work, and a safe, warm, dry home, which is where the ASP volunteers come in.

The people of Appalachia have the beauty of the mountains surrounding them every day, the song of the whippoorwill and the bobwhite to entertain them and a light show put on during the summer evenings by thousands of lightning bugs. Most importantly, many have an understanding of God and spirituality that most of us spend a lifetime trying to obtain. Perhaps by doing without and being in need creates more of a dependency on God. This is what God desires from us.

Sometimes I think knowledge is a dangerous thing. Just like the Pharisees and Scribes of Jesus' day, we are seeking to know more and more, but don't allow the mystery of God's plan and His love into our hearts. The most intelligent person on earth cannot even begin to fathom the omniscient knowledge of God. Some things aren't for us to understand in God's plan; we are to just believe. This is faith! God sees the whole picture. We need to become like a child and not over analyze every situation and simply believe.

How simple is your life? Do you run around trying to keep up with the Joneses? Are you and your children involved in so many activities you don't have the minutes to spend quality time with each other? At what point do you draw a line and decide that this activity or that meeting isn't really that important. Take time to smell the roses and see the beauty that God has given us as a gift to enjoy. It's doesn't even cost anything.

It is good to be educated, but don't let what you learn take you from God. As 1 Corinthians 8:1 says, "Knowledge puffs up, but love builds up." Acts 4: 13 reminds us that Peter and John were just "unschooled, ordinary men" and yet they had a courage and knowledge that was hard for the even the very educated to understand.

Strive to keep your life simple enough that you don't overextend yourself. Make God and the beauty of His world the focus of your life and you will be much happier. Do some front porch sitting, some family talking, and lightning bug watching and a simple more happier life will open up to you.

Prayer: *God, when we constantly strive for things of this world, we become burned out and frustrated. Thank You for the example You give us in the people of Appalachia. Let us be able to hear and see the simple things in life that many of us have lost. There's no more pleasing sound than the rush of a stream, the song of a whippoorwill, the orchestra of crickets and frogs in the spring. Help us to not get so educated and caught up with the noises of this world that we lose sight of You and the world You have created for us. The best part of it all is that they are all free yet so invaluable.*

Chapter 24
Depression

"The Lord reached down from above and took me; he pulled me from the deep water. He saved me from my powerful enemies, from those who hated me, because they were too strong for me."

2 Samuel 22:17-18

"The righteous cry out, and the Lord hears them; He delivers them from all their troubles. The Lord is close to the brokenhearted and saves those who are crushed in spirit."

Psalm 34:17-18

"Why are you downcast, O my soul? Why so disturbed within me? Put your hope in God, for I will yet praise him, my savior and my God."

Psalm 42:5

"For my soul is full of trouble and my life draws near the grave. I am counted among those who go down to the pit: I am like a man without strength."

Psalm 87:3-4

"Why, O Lord do you reject me and hide your face from me?"

Psalm 87:14

*****

These verses, especially Psalms, convince me that David, the author, truly knew what it was like to be depressed. Words David uses such as "crushed in spirit," "downcast my soul," "rejected," "hidden from God's face," are good terms to describe the feelings associated with depression.

I have dealt with three bouts of depression in my lifetime. The first happened when all my children were small and I was trying to start a preschool at our church. As the term goes, "I was burning the candle at both ends," and it finally burned out. Meeting the demands of three small children between the ages of two-five years is in itself very demanding, let alone trying to start a new organization from scratch. In trying to accomplish this and in an effort to keep things running as smoothly as possible at home too, I was soon on a downward spiral. It didn't take long until any decision-making became very difficult for me. I felt as if I were walking on a moving boat being tossed around, and was completely and totally exhausted, but couldn't stop with three small children to care for. The breaking point came when I was getting everyone's drink for dinner one evening and accidentally gave my husband one of the children's small drinks. He looked at me like as if I was crazy and I started to laugh hysterically. Then a few minutes later I started to cry hysterically. (He knew something was wrong.)

I eventually went to the doctor who is the one who told me "I was burning the candle at both ends," and he said I needed to slow down. It was the beginning of summer, so I was able to get away from the preschool and at least not let that wear me down as much. It took me several months to recover from this episode, but I never received any medication.

The second and third time seemed to have run together since I never really got over the second when the third one hit. I believe these were triggered by troubles I was having with my teenage children and the thoughts that they were getting older and that my oldest would be leaving for college soon.

The first time it affected me more physically, this time it affected me more mentally. Thoughts about how I had failed as a mother began to overtake me. Every mistake I had ever made in my life came back to haunt me. I had an overwhelming feeling of worthlessness and hopelessness. At first I prayed daily for God to take this from me. Then I felt like a failure as a Christian. I thought, *If I was strong in my faith I wouldn't be having these feelings. Even God finds me disgusting.*

If there were anything that resembles a person having a demon posses them, depression would be the best description I could find. It's as if there is another being inside of you, telling you that everyone hates you and that you are worthless and causing pain to those closest to you. Now I began to pray daily, "God, *please* let me die." I would try to think of my children, but then this voice would convince me that they would be better off without me—I was making them miserable also. I knew I couldn't take my own life, but would drive down the road and wish another car would run into me or wish that I had a brain tumor and would die suddenly.

This went on for possibly two to three years. I was able to put on a front around people, but when I got home I was completely drained mentally. I wanted to be alone, but realized the more I was, the easier it was to convince myself these thoughts were true. Although being around people was exhausting, it kept me grounded in reality.

I will never forget the first day I felt the depression was beginning to lift. I felt like Saul before he became Paul on the road to Damascus. (Acts 9) In pursuit of persecuting the Christians, God blinded him. It was as if his eyes were covered with scales. I could feel the "scales" starting to go away and was able to see beauty again. When depressed, your mind feels very heavy and dark, and no matter how hard you try, you can't see beauty or good in the world. The better I got, the more I appreciated the majesty that God had created: the sunset, the sky and clouds, the ocean, the changing of leaves in the fall, smells, and all the things I hadn't been able to see for years. Although, not completely better, I would also get a sense of sadness that I would lose the ability to see this beauty again and cry often.

As it turned out, I finally admitted to my doctor that I needed something for depression when it started to come back the third time. She looked at me and said, "Maybe we should do a thyroid test first." I was so happy when the test showed I had hypothyroidism. It took being on medication for a month before I started to feel better. This little pill "fixed" many symptoms; complete exhaustion, female problems, sleeplessness, susceptibility to infections, the depression, the feeling of being cold, etc.

Going through this experience has caused me to be more sensitive to people whom may be experiencing depression themselves and helps me understand why they may react to situations the way they do. It has also helped me purge the negative feelings I had about myself and has brought me closer to God. I can really understand how Saul must have felt when the scales fell from his eyes and why he became so passionate about spreading Christianity after his experience.

There is something to be said for brokenness. It helps you to realize your deep need for God. I now know what the scripture means when it says, "Do not hide your face from me, O Lord." When you can't feel God, you have a sense of desperation and realize you can't live without Him.

If you are "broken," seek the help you need first (physical or medical), then let God come into your life. With Him, you will experience a strength and peace that you never thought possible.

Prayer: *God, thank You for carrying us through the dark times in our lives. Thank You also for physicians and medicines that make us well again.*

Lord, there are so many people that don't have a happy ending when it comes to mental and physical problems. Please be with anyone who suffers from this terrible disease called depression. Lift the scales from their soul and let them be able to feel You again. Thank You for our life and not answering horrible prayers we sometimes pray. Let us put our lives in Your hands with the confidence that Your love and understanding is all we need.

Chapter 25
The Big Picture

"For my thoughts are not your thoughts, neither are your ways my ways, declares the Lord. As the heavens are higher than the earth, so are my ways higher than your ways and my thoughts than your thoughts."

Isaiah 55: 8-9

"Bear with me a little longer and I will show you that there is more to be said in God's behalf. I get my knowledge from afar; I will ascribe justice to my Maker. Be assured that my words are not false; one perfect in knowledge is with you."

Job 36: 1-4

"From that time on Jesus began to explain to his disciples that he must go to Jerusalem and suffer many things at the hands of the elders, chief priests and teachers of the law, and that he must be killed and on the third day be raised to life.

Peter took him aside and began to rebuke him. 'Never, Lord!' he said. 'This shall never happen to you!'

Jesus turned and said to Peter, 'Get behind me, Satan! You are a stumbling block to me; you do not have in mind the things of God, but the things of men.'"

Matthew 16: 21-23

*****

Recently, our dog Bailey had to go through some testing for a bad limp. Since he had to be given anesthesia for the procedure, he wasn't allowed to eat or drink past eight o'clock the night before. It was hard not to give him what he wanted, especially since he didn't understand why. If it had been one of my children, I could have at least explained it to them so they would understand.

Many things happen during our lives that we don't understand why they happened. We may wonder, "Why did God let this happen to me?" Just as when God explained to Job in the verse above where Job questioned the terrible things that happened to him, "Your thoughts are not my thoughts, and your ways are not my ways." God can see the big picture and knows what needs to happen for your best interest. Just as I knew giving my dog something to eat or drink would have made him very ill during the anesthesia, God knows that things that we think we want may not be good for us.

Many times we think we know what path we are to take, but have a hard time discerning if it is God's plan or ours. (Hint; if you choose a path and it's rocky, it probably is not the right one.)

Recently I was looking for a job in the paper for my son, since he was home from college for the summer. Suddenly a description for a job popped out at me that listed many areas I had a lot of experience in. I was presently unemployed, so I thought, *God must be telling me to apply for this.* I applied and was interviewed. I was excited because it looked like a good place to work and the pay was better than I had ever received. I prayed and decided that I would leave it up to God if I should get the job or not and asked him to give me peace if I did not.

As it turned out I didn't get the job. The first few days I was really bummed out and kept wondering, "What did I do or say wrong? I was so sure this was God's plan for me." This made me question how do I really know what God wants me to do.

God wants us to come to Him in prayer and faithfulness, knowing that He will choose the right path for us. Like my dog, we might not understand when we can't have what we want, but need to trust God to make the right decisions. We also need to accept that decision with peace in our hearts and not let pride get in the way. Society places such a high standard on positions that make us look important, that most of us feel we are being looked down upon if we aren't bringing home a big paycheck. The people I admire most are those that have menial jobs; custodians, trash collectors, fast food employees, and yet continue to do their job with joy and pride. The most admired people should be parents that stay home with their children. This is such an important, but seemingly unrewarding job at the time. We don't see the results of our efforts (the big picture) until much later in life, but what can be more important than to "train your child in the way that they should go?"

I love movies that portray God as a common man doing common jobs such as in *Oh God* and *Bruce Almighty*. The black God as a janitor in *Bruce Almighty* was especially impressive. Jesus teaches us that we need to take on a servant attitude in doing any daily, menial task with an attitude of love. In doing this, even the smallest task takes on great importance. For me, I think the answer was to continue doing the mission work I was presently doing at my church.

Did you clean that bathroom today with a good attitude? Were you full of joy when you took the trash out? Did you pout when things didn't go as you wanted them to recently? Put on an attitude of righteousness in everything you do. You never know when you'll meet God when you're doing even small things and the change of plans may have been a part of His bigger picture for you.

Prayer: *Lord, through faith we know You have laid a path for us. Let us recognize the path You have chosen and trust that "Father knows best" when it comes to the big picture You have painted for our lives. Help us let go of our human pride and continue to lead us where You want us to go. Help us to be content even with the most menial jobs and not feel the need for society's acceptance, but only Yours.*

Chapter 26
Handicapped

"Hear, you deaf; look, you blind and see! Who is blind but my servant, and deaf like the messenger I send? Who is blind like the one committed to me, blind like the servant of the Lord? You have seen many things, but pay no attention; your ears are opened but you hear nothing."

Isaiah 42: 18-20

"As he went along, he saw a man blind from birth. His disciples asked him, 'Rabbi, who sinned, this man or his parents, that he was born blind?'

'Neither this man nor his parents sinned,' said Jesus, 'but this happened so that the work of God might be displayed in his life. As long as it is day, we must do the work of him who sent me. Night is coming, when no one can work. While I am in the world, I am the light of the world.'"

John 9: 1-5

"To keep me from becoming conceited because of these surpassingly great revelations, there was given me a thorn in my flesh, a messenger of Satan, to torment me. Three times I pleaded with the Lord to take it away from me. But he said to me, 'My grace is sufficient for you, for my power is made perfect in weakness.' Therefore I will boast all the more gladly about my weaknesses, so that Christ's power may rest on me. That is why for Christ's sake, I delight in weaknesses, in insults, in hardships, in persecutions, in difficulties. For when I am weak, then I am strong."

2 Corinthians 12: 7-10

I know three young men who have one thing in common; they are all handicapped. The first has been a close friend of the family for many years. At a young age he was able to walk next door to our house, with the help of braces, and catch lightning bugs with my children. Another favorite pastime they enjoyed together was to ride Big Wheels very fast on the carport until they came to a screeching halt, skidding the whole way. We knew he had muscular dystrophy, but didn't think of him any differently.

That was twenty-two years ago. The disease has now restricted much of his livelihood and he hasn't left his house for five years now.

The second is a young man who is also close to our family. He was only eighteen months old when his mother left him and his two sisters with their father. The father and grandmother ended up raising them together at the grandmother's house. Later in life this young man made many bad choices. He is ended up being incarcerated in a state prison where he served a year and half.

The third has had a fairly good upbringing and normal childhood with maybe a few problems. As a young adult, he is beginning to party more and more. He's attending college and is doing okay, but his life mainly revolves around partying with his friends and having a good time. To him, it's important to have the right clothes and to say and do the right things to fit in with the crowd. Hard work is a bad word and there's not much concern for other people's feelings. Which one of these is handicapped?

The first one, with the physical handicap, has been an inspiration to many people by his perseverance at maintaining a normal life and good attitude when he actually has more to be grouchy about or more reason to feel sorry for himself than most of us do.

The second is being physically restrained for leading a lifestyle of bad choices of breaking the law and not being honest. Since he's been in prison, he has now earned his GED, is learning the plumbing trade and is attending a Bible Study class. He will be making a second attempt at life when he gets out. Once again, he will be free to make choices. His new life will depend on if he comes out of prison with a better or worse attitude and a relationship with Christ. His handicap has been his attitude and a feeling of a void in his life with the separation of his parents and little contact with his mother.

The third is still trying to find his way in life, and like the prodigal son is looking in the wrong places. This one has some hard life lessons to learn before he can become a complete person that can support himself, care for other people, and make a difference in society.

Yes, they are all handicapped in their own way. Aren't we all? Which one are you most like? What is your handicap? Maybe you are emotionally immature and fly off the handle at the least difficulty that you come across; maybe you're the one that gossips about your friends and really aren't as nice as you pretend to be; maybe you return friendliness with a cold shoulder and are suspicious of everyone's intentions.

Most people have dealt with some hardship or another during their lifetime. What's the difference between those who are able to go on with their life and be happy and productive even when faced with hardships and those that can't?—forgiveness and finding God. Without forgiveness we carry a big weight that only gets heavier and heavier the longer we carry it. Once that weight is gone, you are more open to receive and give love again.

Secondly, many people spend their lives trying to find happiness in other people or things; fancy cars, houses, drinking, sex, etc. What they find is that once they've reached or obtained what they thought they wanted so badly, there's still a void. This void can only be filled with God's love and mercy.

These are the ones I worry about the most. God desperately wants a relationship with all of us, but he gives us a free will to make that choice. For some reason, many of us have to hit rock bottom or be completely broken to choose Him.

Don't let a hard heart be your handicap. Choose God today! He is waiting for you with open arms. If you don't believe me, look at how he died on the cross. His arms are still open wide.

Prayer: *God, You know we don't need to have a physical handicap to be handicapped. Anything that separates us from You is a handicap. Help those that have eyes, but can't see, to have vision. Help those that hear, but choose not to hear, be able to hear Your voice. Help those who are offered love and forgiveness, to be able to feel it and give it in return. Heal my handicaps Lord. Only You can make me complete Lord!*

Chapter 27
Angels Among Us

"If you make the Most High your dwelling—even the Lord, who is my refuge—then no harm will befall you, no disaster will come near your tent. For he will command his angels concerning you to guard you in all your ways: they will lift you up in their hand, so that you will not strike your foot against a stone."

Psalm 91:9-12

"My God sent his angel, and he shut the mouths of the lions. They have not hurt me, because I was found innocent in his sight."

Daniel 6:22

End Times - *"At that time, Michael, the great prince who protects your people, will arise. There will be a time of distress such as has not happened from the beginning of nations until then. But at that time your people—everyone whose name is found written in the book—will be delivered."*

Daniel 12:1

"In the sixth month, God sent the angel Gabriel to Nazareth, a town in Galilee, to a virgin pledged to be married to a man named Joseph, a descendant of David. The virgin's name was Mary. The angel went to her and said, 'Greetings, you who are highly favored! The Lord is with you.'"

Luke 1:26-28

Many people, including myself, find angels fascinating. I have started a collection of angels, and often give one to people who are sick or hurting. Just the image of an angel can bring comfort in times of need.

There are only two angels that I could find that are actually given names in the Bible: Michael, the angel of protection in times of war, and Gabriel who announces to both Elizabeth and Mary the coming birth of John the Baptist and Jesus.

Other types of angels include; strengthening angels, encouraging angels, children's angels, angels of protection, rejoicing angels, guiding angels, ministering angels, messenger angels, destroying angels, and even angels of death.

Angels are portrayed in movies and songs in many ways: Trying to earn their wings as Clarence does in *It's a Wonderful Life*; The character in *Touched by an Angel* suddenly appears in many people's lives to help them make a change in the type of life they're leading; Children deal with the death of a loved one by thinking of them as becoming an angel when they die. Songs refer to what jobs angels do to help God, such as in "Help Pour Out the Rain" by Buddy Jewel or helping people in their time of need such as in "Angels Among Us" by Alabama. I never get tired of hearing these songs and I truly do believe that angels do help us in times of need or help lead us where we need to go.

There are books written even today about how angels have ministered to people in times of desperation. I would like to think that we all do have a guardian angel. According to Psalms vs. 91:11(above) we do.

The pastor at our church just gave a sermon about angels and reminded us that angels are special beings that God has created for His purpose. So, in actuality, people cannot become angels when they die. We do have a tendency to classify people that do good things as angels by earthly standards. By these standards it can be someone who happens to be where you need them to be at the right time. It could be someone who's there when you are really down to show they understand or to give encouragement and hope. Angels could be a neighbor, or friend, or—you could be an angel to someone else.

Do you have angels in your life? I think the best angels are those who care for those who are sick. It could be a mother caring for her own child or someone caring for his or her elderly parent; it could be a nurse or aid in a nursing home caring for someone that has no one to visit them; or a grandmother that helps raise her grandchildren because of a divorce.

Have you ever been an angel to someone else? Possibly stopping to help fix a flat tire; being aware of needs of people in your community; showing support to someone who has lost a loved one; visiting a homebound person who has no family members that show they care. It doesn't take a dramatic action to make a difference in someone's life. It could simply be a small gesture, such as smiling at a stranger or holding a door open for somebody. Many stories have been written about a time when a kindness shown at the right time has prevented someone from committing suicide.

Yes, I think angels are real, both the heavenly kind and the earthly kind. Several of my friends are angels. I'm an angel wannabe. Maybe one day I will earn my wings or help pour out the rain.

Prayer: *God, thank You for sending the angels I have had in my life in times of need. In return, open my eyes to see needs around me so I can be an angel to someone else. Work through me to make a difference, even if it's in just one person's life. Continue to send out Your army of angels every day to protect, guide, and show us the way.*

Chapter 28
Wrestling with God

"Jacob was left alone, and a man wrestled with him till daybreak. When the man saw that he could not overpower him, he touched the socket of Jacob's hip so that his hip was wrenched as he wrestled with the man. Then the man said, 'Let me go, for it is daybreak.'

But Jacob replied, 'I will not let you go unless you bless me.'

The man asked him, 'What is your name?'

'Jacob,' he answered.

Then the man said, 'Your name will no longer be Jacob, but Israel, because you have struggled with God and men and have overcome.'

Jacob called the place Peniel, saying because I saw God face to face, and yet my life was spared."

Genesis 32:24-29

"Lord, when I bring my case to you, you are always right. But I want to ask you about the justice you give. Why are evil people successful? Why do dishonest people have such easy lives?"

Jeremiah 12:1

"Praise be to the God and Father of our Lord Jesus Christ, who has blessed us in the heavenly realms with every spiritual blessing in Christ. For he chose us in him before the creation of the world to be holy and blameless in his sight. In love he predestined us to be adopted as his sons through Jesus Christ."

Ephesians 1:3-5

This story from Genesis about Jacob wrestling with God has special meaning for me since my son's name is Jacob, we call him Jake, and he was a wrestler.

I find it intriguing that God would even wrestle with someone, let alone let him win and then bless him. In Rick Warren's *A Purpose Driven Life*, a chapter about a friendship or relationship with God states that:

God isn't offended when we "wrestle" with him, because wrestling requires personal contact and brings us closer to Him! It is also a passionate activity and God loves it when we are passionate with Him." (pg. 95)[8]

After experiencing my son's wrestling matches I can easily relate to this. Wrestling is hard to watch when you are the mother of one of the wrestlers involved. Rather than being a team sport, each match is between one person and the other guy. Then, in the end, all the matches are totaled for a score to see which team wins.

The first time my son wrestled in junior high, it was all I could do to not go out and get the boy he was wrestling and spank him for hurting my son so badly. He pulled back on his hand so hard I thought he had surely broken his wrist. He pushed my baby's head down to his chest so hard I thought for sure his neck was going to break. Then, to top it all off, he even BIT him. I was such an emotional wreck I went to the bathroom and cried, not able to watch anymore. After watching several matches after this one, I was finally able to get to the point of watching without crying. However, if anyone else got hurt I would cry for them too. I don't like to see anyone get hurt, physically or emotionally.

I love the fact that in the story, God is willing to let Jacob win and then blesses him. According to Warren's book, God wants us to have an intimate relationship with Him so badly that He urges us to wrestle with Him. Think about it! In order to wrestle with someone you have to get VERY close. God desires us to be that close to Him even if it requires questions and doubts.

I have told my senior high Sunday School class that it's okay to question God. When you question something and try to understand it by thinking it through and testing, you come to have a better understanding of it. It is better to question something than to mindlessly accepting everything you hear and read without putting any thought into it. When you learn this way, you don't really internalize it. You also set yourself up for following false information to making bad choices and decisions. If anyone tells you they have a great deal, it's always wise to check it out to see if there are any strings attached or any gimmicks. As they say, be sure to read the fine print. If you don't understand something that God tells you or something someone else claims God said, don't be afraid to question the information and check it out.

Notice also in this story of Jacob wrestling with God, Jacob insists that God bless him. Do you remember a similar story about him when he was younger? He tricks his nearly blind, very old father Isaac into believing he is the elder brother Esau by putting animal skin on his arms to make him feel hairy in order to get the blessing of the first born son. Now, here he is again, years later, wrestling with God in order to get a blessing. Apparently Jacob understood the importance of blessings and would do anything to get them.

Is it wrong to want to be blessed? It seems self-centered, but according to scripture we are to ask for it. Yes, I want to be blessed and I want all the people in my life to be blessed also. I will continue to pray for blessings in my life and for others.

What are blessings and what kind of blessings should we ask for? The best blessings are spiritual blessings. The fact that Jesus died for us so that we can all be with Him one day as brothers and sisters in Christ is the best blessing of all. If you have spiritual blessings, the rest of your life will be good and you will be at peace.

Can you handle being close enough to God to wrestle with Him? When you are very intimate with someone you begin to know every aspect of his or her life. You understand how they tick and know how they feel about any particular subject. Close relationships aren't always "lovey dovey." You may yell and shout at each other until you reach closure on a situation that you don't agree on. Don't be afraid to yell and shout, Why! to God. Job and David did this and He continued to bless them even more. God doesn't want a mindless relationship with you. He wants you to really get to know Him. Wrestle with Him when you don't know why; wrestle with His word when you don't understand it; wrestle with your feelings of guilt when you know you have sinned. In the end you will be a different person—fully blessed.

Prayer: *God, You've been by my side all those times when I've been angry or didn't understand why things have happened to others or myself. I've questioned You, doubted You and, yes, I'm sure You heard me yelling too. Satan probably thought, Oh boy, I've got them now. But thank goodness*

You want to be a part of my life so much that you're willing to let me bear my soul to You and yet You still give me a shoulder to cry on. What big shoulders You have to put up with all our complaining and questioning. Please continue to bless us as we find our way to You. I love You, Lord!

Chapter 29
Let Go, Let God

"Commit your way to the Lord; trust in him and do this: He will make your righteousness shine like the dawn, the justice of your cause like the noonday sun.

Be still before the Lord and wait patiently before him; do not fret when men succeed in their ways, when men succeed in their ways, when they carry out their wicked schemes."

Psalm 37:5-7

"If anyone chooses to do God's will, he will find out whether my teachings comes from God or whether I speak on my own. He who speaks on his own does so to gain honor for himself, but he who works for the honor of the one who sent him is a man of truth; there is nothing false about him."

John 7: 17-18

"I thank Christ Jesus our Lord, who has given me strength, that he considered me faithful, appointing me to his service. Even though I was once a blasphemer and a persecutor and a violent man, I was shown mercy because I acted in ignorance and unbelief."

1 Timothy 1: 12-13

"Therefore, my brothers, be all the more eager to make your calling and election sure. For if you do these things, you will never fall, and you will receive a rich welcome into the eternal kingdom of our Lord and Savior Jesus Christ."

2 Peter 1: 10-11

It took twenty-five years of marriage, but now my husband and I have finally set aside a "date" night. When the children were young we made the mistake of not nurturing our marriage by not doing things together as a couple. Now we make it an effort to go to the movies or out to dinner at least every other week. One of the recent movies we went to was *Under the Tuscan Sun*. Since it was more of a chick flick—I liked it, but he didn't.

It was about a woman whose husband left her and she goes to Tuscany, Italy, to live and start a new life. She buys a dilapidated house and hires a strange mix of fellows to fix it up. During the entire time she is looking for love and romance, but finds only rejection and disappointment.

She also befriends a lady who is rather unusual, but passionate and interesting at the same time. She tells the main character a story that goes something like this:

> *Once there was a woman who had never seen a ladybug. She went in to a field and searched tirelessly to find one. After many hours of searching, she lay down in the field—exhausted from her search and fell asleep. When she woke, to her amazement—she was covered with ladybugs.*

This reminds me so much of how we go about life, trying to do things our own way—in frustration, but if we would go to God for guidance and seek His will, the good things in life would come to us.

It is very difficult to let go of trying to have control of our life and let God lead us where He wants us to go. We need to understand that God has a plan for each of us and if we can just let go of that control and trust Him, He will not steer us in a wrong direction.

As children, we have hopes and dreams of what we want to do with our lives. Most of us pursue those dreams and may end up leading the happy life we had imagined. God may have planted those dreams so that you would find His purpose. At the same time, His purpose for you may be completely different than what you may have thought it should be. Some that pursue what they thought was their dream, may end up feeling empty and wander aimlessly in search of what their true meaning is in life. This is a good indication that you need to let go and let Him show you the direction you should be taking. This may mean a career change at mid life or possibly not even following a career; but a service to people in need or maybe even called to be ordained into service.

Since society tells us success is seen in material things, this may be a hard path to follow. It may mean caring for a sick family member for many years; taking in foster children; helping to raise grandchildren that have been caught in the middle of a divorce; serving a need in your community, or, as in Mother Teresa's case, in the world. God can accomplish great things through you when He calls you and you respond to His call.

In the movie, the woman is finally willing to let go of finding love and be satisfied with the way her life has turned out—and then. . .you'll have to watch the movie to find out what happens.

Do you feel like you're not where you are supposed to be in life? Are you satisfied with where your life has led you? If not, open your heart. God is probably calling you for a special service.

Prayer: *Father, I can hear You calling me. Help me to let go of controlling my not so perfect life and just let You lead me. I know You won't fail me and will be with me every step of the way. Continue to be my Shepherd and I will follow.*

Chapter 30
Help! I've Got a Plank in My Eye and a Foot in My Mouth

"Do not judge, or you too will be judged. For in the same way you judge others, you will be judged, and with the measure you use, it will be measured to you.

Why do you look at the speck of sawdust in your brother's eye and pay no attention to the plank in your own eye?"

Matthew 7: 1-3

"You, therefore, have no excuse, you who pass judgment on someone else, for at whatever point you judge the other, you are condemning yourself, because you who pass judgment do the same things. Now we know that God's judgment against those who do such things is based on truth. So, when you, a mere man, pass judgment on them and yet do the same things, do you think you will escape God's judgment?"

Romans 2: 1-3

"He whose walk is blameless and does what is righteous, who speaks the truth from his heart and has no slander on his tongue, who does his neighbor no wrong and casts no slur on his fellow man."

Psalm 15: 2-3

"A malicious man disguises himself with his lips, but in his heart he harbors deceit. Though his speech is charming, do not believe him, for seven abominations fill his heart."

Proverbs 26: 24-25

Oh, what a sinful people we are! There are very few of us that aren't guilty of judging others without knowing all the facts. Even if we know the facts, we still aren't supposed to judge.

I have heard many stories that tell of someone who appears to be lazy or uncaring, then to find out later that they were ill with cancer or have had some tragic experience in their life. That certainly makes you feel like a schmuck when you've judged someone such as this.

Especially irritating are those who constantly criticize others and act as if they are self-declared saints. In their eyes they have never done anything wrong because they aren't breaking the Ten Commandments. Besides, they go to church every week AND give large amounts of money to the church. Surely they will be rewarded with a seat next to Christ in paradise. I say no, God has many lessons for these "saints." There's a little matter of helping them to look at themselves first; learning to love unconditionally; accepting people where they are and allowing for mistakes rather than judging others. In fact, we aren't worthy of judging anyone. Only God can do that. Yes, we need to get that plank out of our eye, be more concerned with how OUR relationship with Christ is before criticizing others for how they're living their life.

There is a difference between judging someone and dealing with difficult people. For instance, what about someone who has slandered you? Or what about someone who makes you look stupid in front of others? You may have reason to be angry, but look back in your life. Have you ever said a half-truth about someone trying to get others on your side? Or have you ever inadvertently said something about someone, which has caused them great embarrassment? Or possibly mentioned a situation involving someone, even telling the truth, but bringing it up again just added salt to the wound. Some things are better left unsaid. What is it that makes us want to make others look bad so that we can look good? Don't we realize we can just skip the making other people look bad step and just work toward making ourselves a better person.

There have been many occasions when I have had a conversation with someone and then—I do it—I say something negative about another person knowing the person I'm talking to probably feels the same way. After I hang up the phone I immediately begin to feel guilty. So much so that I sometimes call them back and retract what I said. This doesn't always work, sometimes the damage has already been done. That foot is hard to get out of my mouth.

No, I'm no better than anyone else who has judged or talked about someone else. I am a sinner at heart and the only way to remedy it is to ask God for help. Paul tells us in Romans 7:18-19 *"I know that nothing good lives in me, that is, in my sinful nature. For I have the desire to do what is good, but I cannot carry it out. For what I do is not the good I want to do; no, the evil I do not want to do—this I keep on doing. What a wretched man I am! Who will rescue me from this body of death? Thanks be to God—through Jesus Christ our Lord!"* (Vs. 24-25)

Even a man as dedicated as Paul wasn't free from sin. Is there any hope for us regular believers? It gives me comfort knowing that Paul, a major influence in spreading Christianity, had a hard time not sinning himself. Possibly, if I locked myself in a room—maybe then I wouldn't sin. No, I'd probably start having bad thoughts that would be sinful. Woe is me!

All this goes to prove how much we need God. Satan is such a powerful force we're hopeless on our own. Satan is so good at being bad that he can make something bad look good and something good look bad so that you don't even know you're sinning. How many times have you made a decision without going to God first and what you thought was a good decision turned out to be a bad one?

Do you intend to do good, but keep messing up? Know that you are in good company since most of the people in the world are in the same boat. Remember that through God all things are possible. Just be sure to include Him in your decision-making and pray for strength to be able to discern right from wrong and to make good choices.

Prayer: *God, I'm sorry for all those promises I've made and then have broken over and over again. Let me turn to You for my strength rather than relying on my own weaknesses. This plank in my eye and foot in my mouth make it hard to see clearly and speak good things. Help me to lead a non-judgmental life, Lord.*

Chapter 31
Amazing Grace, How Sweet the Sound

After Moses chiseled out two new stone tablets with the Ten Commandments:

"Then the Lord came down in a cloud and stood there with him and proclaimed his name, the Lord. And he passed in front of Moses, proclaiming, 'The Lord, the Lord, the compassionate and gracious God, slow to anger, abounding in love and faithfulness, maintaining love to thousands, and forgiving wickedness, rebellion and sin. Yet he does not leave the guilty unpunished.'"

Exodus 34: 5-7

"From the fullness of his grace we have all received one blessing after another. For the law was given through Moses; grace and truth came through Jesus Christ."

John 1: 16-17

"In Christ we are set free by the blood of his death, and so we have forgiveness of sins. How rich is God's grace, which he has given to us so fully and freely."

Ephesians 1: 7-8

"Consequently, just as the result of one trespass was condemnation for all men, so also the result of one act of righteousness was justification that brings life to all men. For just as through disobedience of one man the many were made sinners, so also through the obedience of one man the many will be made righteous."

Romans 5: 18-19

Wow! Do you realize that this last verse in Romans 5 spans 10,000 years in one sentence? I did some research and added up the years of the fathers from Adam to Noah, and then from the flood to the patriarchs, and then from the patriarchs to Jesus, and get about 10,000 years. Feel free to correct me if I'm wrong. But isn't that mind-boggling that from Adam and Eve's original sin, to Noah (6000 yrs.) the world continued to decline in moral decay—thus comes the flood. *Surely that will straighten out these sinful people!* God must have been thinking. *I'll let the good ones start over again.* But sure enough, sin starts to pop up again. Another 5,000 years pass between the flood and Moses. During this time, God's chosen people sin again, and as a result, are defeated and taken into exile to neighboring countries (mostly Egypt) until Moses comes along and pleads for their release. Of course, Pharaoh has a hardened heart, so it takes several plagues before he finally relinquishes. And then what do they do during the exodus? Sin again. That's a lot of years of sinning!

God puts His mind to work again and thinks, *There must be a way I can get through to these people.* After much sweat and tears, He thinks of one final solution. It's a very painful one, but it has to work. Although these people keep sinning, He still loves them very much. Maybe...if He sends His only Son to be a perfect example of how they should live that will surely work. This Son will heal people and show them how they should love and forgive each other. He can also teach those hardhearted Pharisees a few lessons while He's there too. And then comes the hard part—let Him die a very painful death for everyone's sins.

This way, when Jesus returns to Heaven He can start preparing a place for those who love Him. "Yes, I know they'll keep sinning," God says, "but since Jesus is willing to die for their sins, they will be given many chances—as many as they need. They can even accept Me at the last minute. I'll do whatever it takes to bring my people to me. I love them with their failures, sins, shortcomings and all."

Does this sound familiar? Has one of your children ever disobeyed you? If so, do you stop loving them? I hope not! Most of us will try any means we can to bring them around to the good people that we know they can be. We may try a different means of punishment, and then love them; take away privileges, then love them some more; give them second chances, then love them some more. No matter what they do, we might hurt deeply, but we will always love them. Guess what! God feels the same way about you. And what a joy we both feel when that child finally realizes their sin and comes back home to start a new life.

This is called grace. That is why God keeps giving it to us freely. We don't do anything to earn it—we are just loved dearly. Just as in the story of the prodigal son, to some it doesn't seem fair that those that sin have just as much of a chance of receiving grace as those who don't sin (much). None of us are capable of not sinning at all. With God's help we can try to reject sin; ask for strength to withstand it; use every ounce of willpower we have to avoid it, but we can't quite do it. We are all sinners! If you don't think you are—you better start reading the Bible more and reexamine your life more closely. If Adam and Eve hadn't committed the first sin, it wouldn't have been long before another one of us would have. Satan is too strong.

What exactly is grace you might ask? One year while on vacation I went to a small Baptist church in Nags Head, N.C. that gave some good definitions of grace. They are as follows:

The act of kindness to someone undeserving or helpless
The opposite of justice
To be gracious means to be forgiving
To be gracious means to take the initiative, to help people
To be gracious means to raise somebody up
To be gracious means to be loyal

Since I was struggling with giving someone else grace at the time, this was a good lesson for me. Receiving grace is one thing, giving it is another. Can you be kind to someone who doesn't deserve it? Can you let an unfairness drop rather than to lash out in retaliation? Can you forgive the unforgivable? Have you ever helped someone that didn't even ask for your help? Can you make a special effort to make someone feel good about themselves? Can you remain loyal, even if it may hurt you? Since God gives us these things, we should strive to give them to others also.

Have you made a lot of bad choices? Do you feel God couldn't love someone like you? You're wrong! He loves you dearly and will celebrate with the angels when you come to Him. You don't have to be perfect. You don't have to be a saint. You don't have to have a perfect family. You don't have to do anything except believe in Him. He loves you that much!

Those words from that beautiful old hymn we are all familiar with are so true: "Amazing grace, how sweet the sound, that saved a wretch like me. I once was lost, but now I'm found, was blind, but now I see." Pray them when you feel there is no hope left for you or someone you love.

Prayer: *God, what a gracious God You are; Loving and accepting us as we are; forgiving us time and time again; picking us up when we fall down; letting Your Son die for us as a perfect example. Help us to give grace to others as freely as You give it to us. Thank you, Lord, for Your AMAZING grace!*

Chapter 32
Pride

"He chose the lowly things of this world and the despised things—and the things that are not—to nullify the things that are, so that no one may boast before him. It is because of him that you are in Christ Jesus, who has become for us wisdom from God-that is, our righteousness, holiness and redemption. Therefore it is written: "Let him who boasts, boast in the Lord."

I Corinthians 1:28-31

"We know that we all possess knowledge. Knowledge puffs up, but love builds up. The man who thinks he knows something does not yet know as he ought to know. But the man that loves God is known by God."

1 Corinthians 8: 1-3

"The brother in humble circumstances ought to take pride in his high position. But the one who is rich should take pride in his low position, because he will pass away like a wildflower."

1 James 1:9-10

"If you respect the Lord you will also hate evil. I hate pride and bragging, evil ways and lies."

Proverbs 8:13

Pride: *Inordinate self-esteem; glory or delight; splendid show; to value oneself.* (Webster's Dictionary & Thesaurus)

In my mind there are two different types of pride: One is the type where someone thinks that they are better than others, placing great value in themselves and their works. The other is a sense of pride in accomplishment. It could be about something you worked very hard to accomplish and the results were pleasing. It could also be pride in the accomplishments of those close to you.

Dogs have a sense of pride that is far different than that of people. They take pride in rolling in stinky things and killing animals and bringing them to you. Although these animal behaviors sound bazaar—don't we do similar things. As I look back on my life, I recognize strange behaviors I have done in search of recognition.

At one point in my life I would often leave several large loads of clothes lying on the bed for quite awhile after I folded them. When my husband would go to bed he'd have to call me to put them away. One day when he was asking me, again, to put the clothes away so he could go to bed, I jokingly replied, "I just wanted you to see how much work I did today." Although I said it jokingly, I surprised myself when I realized this was true. Washed and folded clothes that are put away aren't noticed; as well as washed and dried dishes, a vacuumed house, a dust free house, and the 100 toys that are picked up during the day. This way he could actually see something I had done before it was put away. I didn't do this consciously, but now I realize why I did it. Being a housewife and stay at home mom can be very unrewarding, and at times you need a little pat on the back and need to feel you are contributing to the world in some way. It isn't until your children are older that you start to reap the rewards of the labor from the years spent at home raising them.

As parents we have a sense of pride when our children achieve many goals throughout their lives. Just as parents take pride in their children's accomplishments, God must also take pride in things we do to show our love for Him. I can imagine Him saying, "Look at Joe down there helping his neighbor. That's my boy!" Or "Good job, Lisa, through your words and encouragement another person has come to know Me today."

One danger of receiving compliments or praise is to not let it "puff" you up. It becomes very easy to start thinking highly of yourself if you are talented in an area or have learned a skill well over time. You should remind yourself daily that anything you do is only possible with gifts that God has given you. (Good health, social status, education opportunities, and the country you're born in)

Its also easy to think that the accomplishments you have made in life should be easy for others to accomplish also. You never know what circumstances are involved in other people's lives and you should never judge them or look down on them because of their lack of success. Pride and bragging is a very dangerous thing and something that God despises. (Proverbs 8:13)

Pride has also been the ruination of many relationships and marriages: A pride that is so strong that you can't say you're sorry, admit you're wrong or let your significant other feel good about themself, a pride that won't let you change your ways even if you know they're wrong, a pride that won't let you show someone your feelings because it might make you look weak.

Oh, how pride is a subtle yet strong influence on our lives! This isn't to say that you shouldn't be proud of anything in your life. Just be careful with what it is that you are proud of. Don't revel in how your child has excelled to great heights to a neighbor who's having problems with their child. Don't think that your talent is so invaluable that you are indispensable. God and life have a way of teaching you lessons when you're too "puffed" up. As the saying goes, "The bigger they are, the harder they fall." The bigger you think you are, the harder the lesson you will learn. Just be sure to give credit to God and hope that anything you achieve during this life will bring Him the glory, not you.

What are you proud of? A large load of laundry neatly folded and put away; a large event you may have planned that went well; a trophy or plaque you may have received for outstanding service; or could it be the way you show your love for Christ to others? You may work all your life to have cars and a house you're proud of—but have you left a mark on the world? Do something that makes God proud of you today: Love, care, and share. Make the world a better place because you were here. Make the world proud that they knew you!

Prayer: *God, we go through life trying to find our way, trying to make people notice our accomplishments. Help us to seek only Your approval. Let what we do be to Your glory. When we succeed, Lord, help us to not be puffed up. Let what we do be done to make You and You only proud. (Did you notice that big load of clothes I folded today?)*

Chapter 33
Music

"These are the men David put in charge of the music in the house of the Lord after the ark came to rest there. They ministered with music before the tabernacle, the Tent of Meeting, until Solomon built the temple of the Lord in Jerusalem."

1 Chronicles 6:31-32

"Clap your hands, all you people. Shout to God with joy. The Lord Most High is wonderful. He is the great King over all the earth!"

Psalm 47:1

"Sing to the Lord a new song; sing to the Lord all the earth."

Psalm 96:1

"Shout for joy to the Lord, all the earth, burst into jubilant song with music."

Psalm 98:4

"Let the word of Christ dwell in you richly as you teach and admonish one another with all wisdom, and as you sing psalms, hymns and spiritual songs with gratitude in your hearts to God."

Colossians 3: 16

*****

I finally did it! I got to go to the Grand Ole Opry. It was every bit as exciting as I had hoped it would be. The building (The Ryman) was old, but you could feel the history that had taken place there by just standing in the room. Many great artists that made their debuts in the country music world sang their first songs here. Young and old singers offered songs that were both old time favorites and new ones never heard before.

How blessed these people are to have been born with such musical talent. There are some of us, that no matter how hard we try, cannot make a pleasing sound with either our voices or an instrument.

I love music and love to sing along to songs. However, I've never had talent in this area. I've tried very hard to learn to play the guitar, but as they say, "You can't teach an old dog new tricks." I wish so badly I had started when I was younger, then maybe it would have come more naturally. (Kids, if your parents tell you to practice, do it!)

How much lovelier this world is because of music. God must of thought it was important also since He created birds and crickets to sing tunes and all through the Bible, especially in Psalms, you see the importance of music for all types of occasions. Songs of joy, sorrow, love and pain are expressed throughout. Even the angels sing at Christ's birth. (Actually my Bible explains that the angels "said" rather than sang. It is believed that the angels won't sing again until the redemption.)

The most popular songs are often those sung about life experiences that are shared by everyone. Lyrics that we can relate to and helps us realize that others have faced circumstances similar to ours. We are drawn to particular types of music for different reasons. It may be the type of instrument or the rhythm that makes a song pleasing or the words.

Crazy words put to a good tune can even produce a number one hit. Songs about "sexy tractors" or "letting the dogs out" or "achy breaky hearts" can get stuck in your head and you may catch yourself singing them all day long.

There is something magical about a room full of people singing a song. It seems to bring everyone together spiritually as one. In a church service, what may have been words spoken rotely with little meaning, come to life when put to a melody. On this "note" there are many times a song will bring a tear to my eye because the meaning of the words are so touching they make me feel close to God.

Music is more likely to be sung when we are happy. You hear people whistling and humming when they are happy. Music played at important occasions, such as weddings, is picked carefully to create a mood. My daughter and her husband chose Louis Armstrong's "It's a Wonderful World" for the end of their ceremony. It brought mixed tears of joy and remembrance to many people's eyes.

Funeral songs are often solemn to reflect the mood of those attending the funeral. Most worship services are a joyful time in most churches with the exception of Ash Wednesday, Maundy Thursday, and Good Friday. Music for all these types of events is picked to project the mood. Churches that want to attract young people use contemporary, upbeat guitar music while there are others who prefer traditional music singing the old hymns using the piano or organ.

Music is a very important part of a church service. Otherwise, we would have nothing but a sermon. (Yikes!) Many parts of God's Word are put into song to make or express a point and to take us to a higher level of worship.

When I was a teenager I was especially drawn to the Folk services offered at Catholic mass. During this they simply played a guitar and sang meaningful songs. This was so important to me that I pushed for a contemporary service at our Methodist church a few years after I changed my membership. There were some old-fashioned people who didn't think that type of music was proper for a church service. Thank goodness we were able to get one started after many years of trying. Now I feel I can express my love for God in a more vibrant and happy way. I especially love many of the psalms and different verses put to song; "Create in Me a Clean Heart," "Rejoice in the Lord Always," "Thy Word," "On Eagle's Wings," are some of my personal favorites. "Amazing Grace" is an all-time favorite that will bring me to tears no matter how many times I sing it.

Sounds in nature can represent or make just as pleasing a sound as music; a waterfall, a rushing stream, frogs, crickets, whippoorwills, and rain on a tin roof can actually make music of their own. God surely has blessed us with many good things.

Don't have a good voice? Sing anyway! A heartfelt song sung to God is pleasing to Him regardless of how it sounds to human ears. Love that song on the radio? Turn it up and sing along. (It makes you sound better) Are you in love? There is nothing more romantic than for a man to look into a woman's eyes and sing her a love song.

Did you get some joyful news today? Go ahead, get crazy and sing and dance around the house. Make a joyful noise—sing a new song!

Prayer: *God thank You for the many talents You have given people, especially a pleasing voice and the ability to make beautiful music. Although all of us are not so blessed, let the songs we sing be pleasing to Your ears. Thank You for making the world a better place because of music. "I love You Lord, and I lift my voice, to worship You—my soul—rejoice."*

Chapter 34
Is There Hope?

"Even if God kills me, I have hope in him; I will still defend my ways to his face."

Job 13:15

"But those who have troubles will not be forgotten. The hopes of the poor will never die."

Psalms 9:18

"But I have hope when I think of this: The Lord's love never ends; his mercies never stop."

Lamentations 3:21-22

"There was no hope that Abraham would have children. But Abraham believed God and continued hoping, and so he became the father of many nations. As God told him, 'Your descendants also will be too many to count.'"

Romans 4: 18

"Praise be to the God and Father of our Lord Jesus Christ. In God's great mercy he has caused us to be born again into a living hope, because Jesus Christ rose from the dead."

1 Peter 1:3

*****

Sometimes you hear stories of atrocities that people have suffered and you wonder "Is there hope for that person?" One of Satan's favorite lies is to convince you that there is no hope. Without hope there is no desire for life.

I know of a woman whose husband raped their daughter as a teenager. As a result she became pregnant at fifteen. The same man was abusing another daughter's two-year-old handicapped son. In desperation, the daughter shot and killed her father to make him stop.

I also know some young adults who were sexually abused by their mother when they were very young. They still struggle with this today. How could a mother do such a thing to her own child? Can they recover from this type of act by someone they thought they could trust and love?

For people such as these, you may wonder, "Will they ever find peace and be able to lead a normal life?" or "Why did God allow this to happen?" In most cases the person that is doing this terrible thing has been abused themselves as a child and the cycle continues.

Have you seen the movie *Dead Man Walking* with Susan Sarandan? The man in this story and some friends brutally murdered a young couple. The main character is on death row and denies his guilt until the very end. Susan Sarandan, who plays a nun, keeps telling him about Christ and His love and forgiveness. When he finally confesses, the pain is almost unbearable. He doesn't know how someone such as him could possibly find forgiveness. He comments, "It's ironic that I have to die to find love."

Do you think this could possibly be the reason why God sent Jesus to die the terrible death He died for us? Since He suffered so badly, we can find comfort in knowing He truly understands our suffering. Instead of thinking this way though, we usually ask, "Why did He let it happen to me or someone I love?"

Can you imagine how it would feel to see your son die as God allowed Jesus to die the terrible death He did? Surely God has feelings and it had to have hurt Him deeply. But He was willing to go through the pain so that we would know that He loves us so much—that He was willing to suffer Himself by letting His son suffer.

He still hurts deeply when He sees one of His own suffering today. Unfortunately, Satan does have some power in this world and bad things do happen.

It's important to know that His death as well as the bad things that may happen to us, is not the end of the story. If we prevail, a better place awaits us with no more pain and suffering. Yes, He knows your pain and He hurts with you. Let Him help you carry the load. Give Him all of your troubles. He can't prevent all pain, but He will walk with you to help you get through and will then make other beautiful things happen in your life.

Prayer: *God, sometimes the pain of this world is too much to bear. I can't do it alone. I need You! When Satan tells me lies, keep me strong to not believe him. Please give me peace and let me feel hope again. Hope for a better future and no pain. Hope for eternity spent with You in paradise.*

Chapter 35
Changed Hearts

"There was a man who had two sons. The younger one said to his father, 'Father, give me my share of the estate.' So he divided his property between them.

Not long after that, the younger son got together all he had, set off for a distant country and there squandered his wealth in wild living. After he had spent everything, there was a severe famine in that whole country and he began to be in need. So he went and hired himself out to a citizen of that country, who sent him to his fields to feed pigs. He longed to fill his stomach with the pods that the pigs were eating, but no one gave him anything.

When he came to his senses, he said, 'How many of my fathers hired men have food to spare, and here I am starving to death! I will set out and go back to my father and say to him: Father, I have sinned against Heaven and against you. I am no longer worthy to be called your son; make me like one of your hired men.' So he got up and went to his father.

But while he was still a long way off, his father saw him and was filled with compassion for him; he ran to his son, threw his arms around him and kissed him.

The son said to him, 'Father, I have sinned against Heaven and against you. I am no longer worthy to be called your son.'

But the father said to the servants, 'Quick! Bring the best robe and put it on him. Put a ring on his finger and sandals on his feet. Bring a fattened calf and kill it. Let's have a feast and celebrate. For this son of mine was dead and is alive again; he was lost and is found.'"

Luke 15:11-24

On the trip my husband and I took to Nashville, we not only heard great music, but we learned some history too. The most memorable part of the trip was a tour of the Ryman Auditorium where the Grand Ole Opry was held from 1943-1974. The amazing part of the history there is the fact that it was built in 1892 as a tabernacle by Captain Thomas Ryman. Ryman was a successful steamboat captain and Nashville businessman. Part of his businesses included many local bars and a shipping company.

"During this time a preacher by the name of Samuel P. Jones was preaching against drinking and the wayward life many were leading in this area. On March 10, 1885 he held a tent revival where he planned to preach about these sinful acts.

"Hoping to challenge the preacher and to cause trouble, Thomas Ryman attended the revival. As a result, his life was changed forever. Something he heard during the revival moved him and as a result he came forward and was saved. Eventually he went as far as building a tabernacle for Samuel Jones so he wouldn't have to preach in a tent there again. After fifty years the upkeep of the church became too expensive for a regular congregation and it was eventually sold to a company that turned it into a performance hall. The acoustics in the hall are said to be second only to the Mormon Tabernacle."[9]

It's exciting to hear how people can change their hearts after experiences such as this. These are the people that God can use the best. They are usually very passionate about their mission and do it with a sense of urgency.

There are many people who have started their adult life on a wrong path, but were able to turn their lives around: Johnny Cash, Charlie Daniels, Randy Travis and many more. Just as in the story of the prodigal son, there is much celebration when these and many more make a positive change their life. As the verse says, "These were lost but now are found." (Luke 15:24)

The story of Saul, who later becomes Paul, truly shows how God chooses unlikely people to do His work and causes them to change. (Acts 9: 1-19) Those of us who have been forgiven the most are also the most grateful for forgiveness when it is given and will go to great lengths to prove it. Knowing that you have caused so much pain and yet are stilled loved is an overwhelming feeling.

Many of us have committed smaller infractions that may torment us. Can you imagine the torment you would feel if you killed someone? Can you imagine the weight that would be lifted when you were forgiven?

I have heard of families of murder victims being able to go to the murderer in prison and tell them that they forgive them. In doing so, a great weight has been lifted for them also. Others are never able to get to this point. I honestly don't know if I could either.

Does your heart need to be changed? Do you have a calloused heart due to past hurts done to you? The only remedy is to open your heart to feel God's love. In so doing, you too will be able to forgive even the worst offenses that have been done to you. Likewise, God can forgive you of any offense you have committed. Let God have your heart and see what great things He can accomplish through a forgiven soul.

Prayer: *God, sometimes I have a heart of stone. Soften my heart so that I can feel, see, and accept the many gifts You have freely given me: Love, life and forgiveness. Forgive me for all those I may have hurt along the way. Heal their wounds and let them see the new person I have become through You. Keep me from sin and help me not to hurt others again. Amen*

Chapter 36
Nakedness/Wisdom

"When the woman saw that the fruit of the tree was good for food and pleasing to the eye, and also desirable for gaining wisdom, she took some and ate it. She also gave some to her husband, who was with her, and he ate it. Then the eyes of both of them were opened and they realized they were naked; so they sewed fig leaves together and made coverings for themselves."

Genesis 3: 6-7

"The Lord God made garments of skin for Adam and his wife and clothed them. And the Lord God said, "The man has now become like one of us, knowing good and evil."

Genesis 3: 21-22

"One evening David got up from his bed and walked around on the roof of the palace. From the roof he saw a woman bathing. The woman was very beautiful, and David sent someone to find out about her. The man said, 'Isn't this Bathsheba, the daughter of Eliam and the wife of Uriah the Hittite?' Then David sent a messenger to get her. She came to him, and he slept with her."

2 Samuel 11: 2-4

"Behold, I come like a thief! Blessed is he who stays awake and keeps his clothes with him, so that he may not go naked and be shamefully exposed."

Revelation 15: 15

When you think about it, nakedness is a weird thought. When you see naked babies you don't think of it as bad, you see innocence and beauty of God's creation. Then as a child gets older, it becomes more important to cover all of the "private" parts. It becomes very embarrassing for anyone to see you, especially after adolescence.

I went through a period in my life where I felt God just didn't want me to wear clothes. They were all bathing suit incidents.

When I was a teenager we would go boating on the Shenandoah River regularly. I was a fairly accomplished water skier and was able to ski off the dock. It was a big surprise when my bathing suit got stuck on a nail on one occasion. When the boat pulled me up, the whole back of my bathing suit bottom ripped, leaving me exposed to the whole world. I fell into the water quickly when I realized what had happened.

Another time we stopped the boat in the middle of the river to swim. As I was sliding off the front of the boat to get into the water, my bathing suit bottom got caught on a tie off hook. My whole bathing suit ripped except for the elastic. People on shore could see me dangling with my bottom exposed. I had to bounce up and down until the elastic broke as I laughed hysterically and almost drowned when I finally fell into the water.

As I read the Bible verses about Adam and Eve discovering their nakedness after eating the fruit, I find it interesting that awareness of nakedness was a sign of "knowledge of good and evil." Does this mean that if no one would have eaten from *The Tree of Knowledge of Good and Evil* we would all be going naked and not be aware that this was a "bad" thing? What is it about nakedness that is so bad? There are nudist camps all over the world and in some European countries people sunbath naked regularly. I must admit nakedness makes me feel uncomfortable. I definitely have acquired the "knowledge of good and evil."

One summer when my family was riding a ferry to Ocracoke Island in North Carolina, a woman was wearing a thong bathing suit. Several small children that were there and her bare bottom was right at their eye level. I kept watching the children to see what their reaction would be. They didn't even seem to notice, but the men sure did! Maybe this is what Jesus meant when He said we should have the mind of a child.

Can you imagine a world of nakedness where people don't think anything of being completely exposed? We wouldn't have to decide what to wear every day, and we wouldn't have to spend thousands of dollars trying to look good and buying the latest fashions. However, I wonder what God's plans would be for cold weather or would there be cold weather? Now we're getting into a whole different weather pattern on earth as we know it. Since Adam and Eve did eat the fruit of *The Tree of Knowledge of Good and Evil*, and now we do know that nakedness is bad, I guess we'll be keeping our clothes on for a while.

Nakedness can be compared to complete exposure. When you are completely exposed, you can't hide anything; that scar or birthmark that you didn't want anyone to see, that big belly that you can somewhat hide under clothing, and other parts of your body that are beginning to sag. This humiliation we feel from complete exposure is similar to what we will feel when we meet Christ. He knows everything we have done and we can't hide behind the "garments" of our shame any longer. Deception and lies will not work with Him.

Do you have parts of your body (past) that you are ashamed of? Confess your sins to Christ and stand in shame no longer. He has made your body beautiful for all to see. Seek redemption so that you can stand "naked" in His presence without a sense of shame, proud of the "temple" He has given you—not ashamed to show the world its beauty.

Prayer: *God, You have created us in Your image—every part of us. (Well, if You are a man, women are a little different) Each part has it's own purpose. Help us to remember that our body is a gift and a temple. So being, we should take good care of it by keeping it clean, strong, and healthy so others can see what a good job You have done in creating us. Also help to keep our thoughts and acts pure so that we can one day stand in your presence, unashamed because we have asked for forgiveness and strive to lead an unblemished life with You.*

Chapter 37
Birth

"To the woman he said, 'I will greatly increase your pain in childbearing; with pain you will give birth to children."

Genesis 3: 16

"The King of Egypt said to the Hebrew midwives, whose names were Shiphrah and Puah, 'When you help the Hebrew women in childbirth and observe them on the delivery stool, if it is a boy, kill him; but if it is a girl, let her live.' The midwives, however, feared God and did not do what the King of Egypt had told them to do; they let the boys live. The King of Egypt summoned the midwives and asked them, 'Why have you done this? Why have you let the boys live?' The midwives answered Pharaoh, 'Hebrew women are not like Egyptian women; they are vigorous and give birth before the midwives arrive.'"

Exodus 1: 15-19

"At this my body is racked with pain, pangs seize me, like those of a woman in labor."

Isaiah 21:3

"I tell you the truth, you will weep and mourn while the world rejoices. You will grieve, but your grief will turn to joy. A woman giving birth to a child has pain because her time has come; but when her baby is born she forgets the anguish because of her joy that a child is born into the world."

John 16: 20-21

I find it interesting that in many instances in the Bible, when they refer to an incident that is very painful, they often will compare it to childbirth. Since I am a small person, people thought I might have a hard time having babies. In my case size had no effect on the matter whatsoever.

When we had our first child, I was twenty-three. She was ten days late, but once I went into labor it went fairly smoothly, with the total labor only lasting about four hours. This was our daughter Cassie, who changed the focus of our lives, which now shifted from a relationship between my husband and I to now include this bundle of joy.

When our second child was ready to make her entrance into the world, Tim had worked a night shift. When he came home that morning I knew I was in labor. "Knowing" I wasn't ready to go to the hospital yet, since the pains weren't close together, I told him to go lay down for a while and I'd wake him up when it was time. The contractions seemed to get stronger, but never got regular, so I kept waiting. With so much time to think, I kept trying to plan every detail in hopes of making the delivery go smoother. I was concerned about Tim being hungry when he woke, so I made him some hot dogs.

The contractions were still not regular, but were getting very strong, so I thought I better wake him up to get ready to go. He could see I was in a lot of pain and wanted to leave right away, but I insisted that he eat the hot dogs. He ate them quickly to appease me since I was already starting to do the breathing routine. On the way to the hospital the contractions finally did get regular—at two minutes apart—and the pain was very intense. This scared Tim to the point that he feared I might have the baby in the car. He drove very fast and was very perturbed with me for making him eat those "damn" hot dogs. When we finally arrived at the hospital, the contractions slowed enough for me to be able to walk to the maternity ward. While in the bathroom getting a urine sample as required, I began having severe contractions and knew I was ready to push. I was in so much pain I couldn't yell, but only breathe rapid breaths. I held on to the wall to make my way out into the hall. As soon as the nurses saw me, they knew they needed to prep me right away. They put me on a gurney in the hall and examined me, realizing I was fully dilated. Within minutes I had my daughter before the doctor could even get there. Tim arrived (sprinting) from trying to check me in as I was having her. (Twenty minutes after we got to the hospital.) This was our daughter Robyn, who has also become a highlight of our life and gave us a good story to talk about.

Fearing the same thing would happen with our third child (fifteen months later), I went to the hospital as soon as the contractions started. When we got there, the contractions were twenty minutes apart. After walking the halls for an hour my doctor decided to break my water to bring the contractions on faster. A half-hour later he checked me and I was three centimeters dilated. As he was getting ready to walk out of the room I wanted to tell him not to go, but couldn't talk since I was having a terrible contraction. I was in a birthing chair with no bottom to it and a nurse had to literally run over to catch my son as he was born. My husband was so excited about having a boy that he began hitting me in the arm excitingly yelling, "It's a boy! It's a boy!"

Thus came our delightful son Jake, the last child for this weary young mother.

After the baby and I were taken care of and were finally put into a room, a nurse came in holding a tape that was a printout of my contractions. It showed that I had broken the hospital record by going from three centimeters to delivering in forty-five seconds. (Thank goodness I didn't make Tim eat a hot dog this time!)

Although childbirth is painful, I was very fortunate that my labors went very quickly. It's ironic how you quickly forget about the pain of childbirth as these new members of your family begin to grow and become so important in your life. These same feelings are reflected in John 16: 20-21. *"When her baby is born, she forgets the anguish because of her joy that a child is born into the world."*

According to Genesis 3:16, childbearing became painful only after Adam and Eve ate the fruit from *The Tree of Knowledge of Good and Evil* as a punishment for the woman since she sinned. I wonder what His plan was for how we would have had children before this? Would it not have hurt? Thanks a lot, Eve!

What other pain do we experience that results in something so wonderful? After giving birth and witnessing this miracle, you can have no doubt that there is a God. You can't help but stare at those tiny fingers and toes and feel a deeper respect for a God that can create such a beautiful thing. (I guess we can take a little credit for it too.)

The Bible tells us that even at the minute of conception, God already had a plan for us: If we would be a boy or girl, tall or short, blonde hair or brown, blue eyes or green.

What a perfect plan, for chromosomes to be released by each parent to make a new and unique individual with no match quite exactly the same. (Unless you're a twin, another miracle in itself.)

I find it clever that the midwives in Exodus 1:15-19 refuse to kill the sons born to the Hebrew women and are able to save their hides by saying they couldn't get there fast enough because "the Hebrew women were so vigorous they had them too quickly." (I can relate to that.) And to think Pharaoh even believed it.

Let's never forget these miracles we take for granted every day. Whether it be your child, a grandchild, a neighbor or friend's child, enjoy their uniqueness and wonder as they begin to explore this new world out of the safety of their mother's womb. Take it even a step farther—look at each person you meet and realize that each and every one of them is a walking miracle. Appreciate the multitude of life around you as God continues to bless us in so many ways.

Prayer: *God, thank You for the gift of conception and the ability to grow and development a living "being" inside our bodies. Not everyone is so blessed God. Be with those who are unable to conceive. Possibly Your plan for these is adoption of another child that needs to feel loved and cared for. Either way, Lord, give them a child to love. Let us all realize that a child is a precious gift. None more precious than the gift of a baby named Jesus born to Mary and Joseph in a stable two thousand years ago.*

Chapter 38
Weeds/Farming

"Now the Lord God had planted a garden in the east, in Eden; and the Lord God made all kinds of trees grow out of the ground-trees that were pleasing to the eye and good for food."

Genesis 2:8-9

"The Lord God took the man and put him in the Garden of Eden to work it and take care of it. And the Lord God commanded the man, 'You are free to eat from any tree in the garden; but you must not eat from the tree of knowledge of good and evil, for when you eat, you will surely die.'"

Genesis 2: 15-17

After Adam and Eve ate the fruit:

"Cursed is the ground because of you; through painful toil you will eat of it all the days of your life. It will produce thorns and thistles for you, and you will eat the plants of the field. By the sweat of your brow you will eat your food until you return to the ground, since from it you were taken; for dust you are and to dust you will return."

Genesis 3: 17-19

"I planted the seed, Apollos watered it, but God made it grow. So neither he who plants nor he who waters is anything, but only God, who makes things grow. The man who plants and the man who waters have one purpose, and each will be rewarded according to his own labor. For we are God's fellow worker; you are God's field, God's building."

1 Corinthians 3: 6-9

When I graduated from high school, my family moved to a forty-acre farm in the country. I had never thought about farming or living in the country before because I was very content to grow up in a neighborhood with friends to ride bikes, play army, and build forts with.

When you own a farm, the first thing you're required to do is to buy the animals that go along with it. We immediately bought ten Black Angus cows and six large pigs. My husband, who was my boyfriend at the time, even bought me my very own horse. In addition, we had the other usual animals that come along with a farm, barn cats and dogs. It didn't take long for us to realize that living on a farm and raising animals requires a lot of hard work.

After this experience, I have become very respectful of farmers and admire them for the hard work they do. I fear that farming, as we know it, will one day become a thing of the past with all the new higher technology methods they have developed. No matter what new technique they may come up with, there is nothing like homegrown natural tomatoes, corn on the cob, cucumbers or cantaloupe.

After years of living in neighborhoods as my own family grew, we have recently had a dream come true. We have moved to the country, surrounded by farmland consisting of acres and acres of cornfields, hayfields, orchards, and hundreds of beef and dairy cattle. We see deer almost daily and our dogs can roam without fear of a neighbor complaining that they have come into their yard. I watch the local farmer with awe as he starts early in the morning with his daily routine of feeding cows, plowing fields, and spraying crops. The fulfillment of working the ground must bring great satisfaction to farmers, as well as the thrill of operating those big tractors and other various pieces of farm equipment. (Being the farmer wannabes that we are, we have purchased our own Kubota tractor, but don't do the hard work they do)

In addition to loving country life, I have a love for barns—the older the better. I am fascinated with the craftsmanship that goes into building a barn. The older ones in particular that have hand-honed logs are a work of art in themselves. Since newer ones are not even near this caliber of craftsmanship, I fear that they will also one day become a thing of the past.

Farming requires a lot of diligence with having to deal with all the obstacles they face: drought, insects, flooding, high winds, and early freezes. Unless many turn toward higher technology techniques or sell portions of their property, it is very difficult for them to survive. It amazes me to think about how much food they must produce to feed a nation that consumes as much food as the United States.

It's interesting to read the verses in Genesis 3:17-19 about when God created Eden and put man there to "work it and care for it." But then after they ate the fruit from the "Tree of Knowledge of Good and Evil," now there would be weeds and thistles and man would do it "by the sweat of his brow." (Here we go again, more pain from that same sin) Can you imagine a world with no weeds? Although it says he would have had to work the land and care for it before, the work became much more difficult after they sinned.

Try to imagine what life would have been like if no one had sinned. (This is very unlikely because I'm sure someone else would have sinned along the way—probably me.) Would we have had to work for our food? Even if you are not a farmer you have to work hard to make enough money to buy your food. Would it have been a life of ease as the paradise of Eden portrays?

There are some who are less fortunate and are unable to make enough money to buy all the food they need for their family. Some may argue that if they worked harder they would have all they need. But, just the way the weather can affect a farmer, people's life situations can affect their prosperity. Bad choices, dysfunctional families, health problems, unaffordable education and mental health issues are all factors that contribute to a persons success or failure.

However, there are those that are too lazy to work and rely heavily on government assistance. In contrast, there are those who come here from other countries, starting with nothing, but through hard work and determination are able to become successful. They have a dream for a better life and are willing to do what they can to make it come true.

Again, like the farmer who gets satisfaction from working the land, they get satisfaction from being able to support themselves through the work of their hands.

It's easy to take the food we buy from the store for granted, not thinking about what was required to get it there. Try to remember the farmers in your prayers. Thank God for them and the hard work they do to provide food for the world and for us.

Prayer: *God, here we go back to that original sin in the Garden of Eden again. Now we have to work for our food by the "sweat of our brow."*

With that being so, thank You for the farmers and all the people that it requires to make food available for us daily. Even if You gave us weeds, farmers are still able to produce fruits of the earth from the many other gifts You have given us: soil, seeds, rain, sunshine, processors and the loving hands that prepare the food. Thank You, God. All of this just to nourish our bodies and yet we still continue to sin and take what You've given us for granted. Thank You for continuing to care for us, even in our sinfulness.

Chapter 39
If You're Happy (or Sad) and You Know It, Clasp Your Hands

"In the morning, O Lord, you hear my voice; in the morning I lay my request before you and wait in expectation."

Psalm 5:3

"He will answer the prayers of the needy; he will not reject their prayers."

Psalm 102:17

"Ask and it will be given to you; seek and you will find; knock and the door will be opened to you. For everyone who asks receives; he who seeks finds; and to him who knocks, the door will be opened."

Matthew 7: 7-8

"Until now you have not asked for anything in my name. Ask and you will receive, so that your joy will be the fullest possible joy."

John 16: 24

"Cast all your anxiety on him because he cares for you."

1 Peter 5: 7

"Now to Him who is able to do immeasurably more than all we ask or imagine, according to his power that is at work in us, to him be glory in the church and in Christ Jesus throughout all generations, forever and ever, Amen."

Ephesians 3: 20-21

As a child, I would pray at night when I went to bed. A child's prayer often begins by thanking God for many people and things and then requesting help for those we know and love. As I've grown in my faith I've learned that there is a good formula for prayer:

> First, thank and praise Him for all the good things He's done in your life.
>
> Second, ask for forgiveness for your sins.
>
> Third, make a plea for others you have concerns for.
>
> Fourth, make a plea for concerns in your own life including guidance and blessings.

When you first come to God in prayer, it's important to thank Him for the many blessings He's bestowed upon you. Can't think of any today? Look around you at this big beautiful world. Look at your body, how it works, grows and heals itself. Look at the cross and how He allowed His Son to die for you; look at the food you have in your refrigerator. Notice the warmth in your home in the winter and coolness during summer. Look at the great country that we live in. The list can go on and on and if you really get into it, this could take some time.

Next you need to ask for forgiveness. You haven't killed anybody lately or stolen anything or committed adultery? You're in pretty good shape with those Ten Commandments? Well, how about the "Love your neighbor as yourself" one, or maybe the coveting your neighbor's wife or belongings? Maybe it wasn't his wife/husband, but you have an unending desire for bigger and better things for yourself rather than spending more time and money helping others. How about gossiping or judging others? Humble yourself and you will surely find areas that can use improving.

Next, we need to show our love for others by praying for them. Just like in many things in life, there is strength in numbers. The more prayers God receives, the louder they are. In the same way a fervent, desperate prayer will be heard very loudly too. It is important to pray for others in need. You may be the only person that has ever prayed for that particular person and it can lead to a life changing experience in their life.

Lastly, pray for yourself. Ask for relief from what is ailing you. Ask for guidance in your life. Ask for continued blessings. Ask for strength when you are weak in facing a temptation. God WANTS you to go to Him for help. Don't feel you are overburdening Him.

Have you heard the Prayer of Jabez? It's very short and simple, but very meaningful: *"Oh, that you would bless me indeed, and enlarge my territory. That your hand would be with me, and that you would keep me from evil, that I may not cause pain."* 1 Chronicles 4:9-10

When I first started saying this prayer I felt selfish asking for blessings for myself. I had no problem asking blessings for others, but felt uncomfortable for myself. I did it anyway and the blessings have abounded.

Enlarge my territory, what does that mean? To me it means helping to bring others to Christ. We can't do this alone, but only with God's help. What can you do to bring others to Christ? Sermons and preaching probably isn't your thing. Your example is the best message you can give. I kept having thoughts of what I would preach about if I were a pastor. Knowing that my knees knock too much when I get in front of people, it came to me, "Write a book!" What a better way to reach people and tell them of His love! (Especially if the words don't flow smoothly from your mouth.) But you don't have to write a book. Just do things that show God's love.

"Keep me from evil and may I not cause pain." This is important because we are faced with evil or temptations every day. Even little things that are done unconsciously can have a big effect on other people's lives. There are times where we may hurt others without even being aware of it. We need to pray to be more conscious of what others have been through and experienced so that we don't do or say something to hurt their feelings. I have been hurt by other people's words. Knowing this pain helps me to be more sensitive to others feelings and I feel horrible if I inadvertently say something that may hurt someone. (There is a difference between hurting someone and disagreeing with them.)

When my children were young, my favorite time of day was when I put them to bed. Not just because that I would now get some well-deserved rest, but also because I enjoyed saying their bedtime prayers with them. My daughter Robyn even made up one of her own when she was about six years old that I will always treasure:

My Lord is special because He does everything for me.
I'm sorry for all the bad things I've done.
I love God and I love Jesus.
Thank you for leading me everywhere I go.

Needless to say, I was very proud of her!

I find that if I try to pray at night when I go to bed, my mind wanders and I can't finish a prayer. Now I do my devotions in the morning to open my mind to God first, then go to Him in prayer. Being more focused in this way, my prayers may last 20-30 minutes. Now, this is my favorite time of day.

In *A Purpose Driven Life* by Rick Warren, he tells us that prayer doesn't have to be at a particular time, that we should be in constant conversation with God throughout the day. He wants to be your best friend and be included in all aspects of your life.[10]

When do you go to God in prayer? When you are happy, sad, desperate, making decisions, concerned, or all of the above? He wants you to come to Him for all of these. Just remember—when you're happy (or sad) and you know it, clasp your hands.

Prayer: *Hi, Friend! Thanks for being with me today and all the times I needed You. Thank You for the delicious food I had to eat today; for the car I had to go to work in; for my job; for the beautiful day; for my healthy family; for this beautiful world; for love; for friends; and especially for sending us Your Son. You're the "Bestest" Friend that anybody could have!*

Chapter 40
Who Needs God?

"After the whole generation had been gathered to their fathers, another generation grew up, who knew neither the Lord nor what he had done for Israel."

Judges 2:10

"There are those who rebel against the light, who do not know its ways or stay in its paths."

Job 24:13

"In spite of all this, they kept on sinning; in spite of his wonders, they did not believe. So he ended their days in futility and their years in terror."

Psalm 78:32

"All those who stand before others and say they believe in me, I will say before my Father in Heaven that they belong to me. But all who stand before others and say they do not believe in me, I will say before my Father in Heaven that they do not belong to me."

Matthew 10:32-33

"As newborn babies want milk, you should want the pure and simple teaching. By it you can grow up and be saved, because you have already examined and seen how good the Lord is."

1 Peter 2:2

My guess is that you probably know many people in your life who don't believe in God? Do you try to convince them that there is a God? If so, what do you say?

Reasons for not believing may vary from: "If there is a God, why does He allow so many bad things to happen?" "Yeah, look at all those who do believe and how they fight and kill in his name." "So many Christians are hypocrites." "If that's what it's about I don't want any part of it."

The book *The Shepherd* by Joseph Girzone has a good explanation for a non-believer. Joseph Girzone has some good explanations for those who are non-believers. He gives examples that may help some unbelievers to believe. The example of how we may not see heat but may feel it doesn't mean the source of the heat isn't there. Just as when you smell a delicious odor, but don't know where it coming from doesn't mean the source of the good smell doesn't exist. In the same way, why do so many have a difficult time believing in God after they have seen the beautiful things He has created in this world. A good scenario for me would be when a waitress brings you a delicious plate of food. You didn't see the chef prepare it, but there's no doubt in your mind that a chef prepared it for you. God, the Chef, has also prepared many things in this world for you.

Girzone also places emphasis on the over abundance of natural resources in the world. Rather than blaming God for the misfortunes of those that have so little, he stresses the responsibility each one of us has for taking care of those in need. We are to be "the hands of lips and heart of Christ." Girzone states that by doing this "we become the strongest proof that God exists."[11]

What do you think? Could these ideas convince someone or at least make them think seriously that there may be a God? Not only does it give an example on how to experience God, but also makes us responsible for doing God's work.

There are so many problems in the world that it often feels overwhelming to try to do anything about them. Making a difference doesn't require making a drastic change, just start with one person at a time and pray for God's guidance.

If someone is truly against God, all the talking in the world won't change his or her mind. However, there is a possibility that they can see Christ's love and peace in you. In so doing, they may come to think, *I wish I could be like that.*

Some have turned away from God because a terrible tragedy has happened in their life. A beautiful story that portrays this is *Gideon"s Gift* written by

Karen Kingsberry. The story revolves around a homeless man that has lost hope and no longer believed in God after the tragic loss of his wife and daughter. Through the friendship of a little girl and a lot of prayers, he has a dramatic awakening and finally believes again.[12]

In most cases, those who have developed the hardest hearts are the ones that have the most dramatic change when they come to God. These are the ones that need to hit rock bottom before they believe. And when they finally do, they are hit hard—nearly to the point of unbearable pain at the realization of their sinfulness. Yet these are the ones that become the most passionate about God's love. The ones that can share Christ's love best with other non-believers. They can sympathize with an understanding and patience that only one who has shared the same experiences can do.

As a child, believing was easy. Don't let your adult "reasoning" get in the way. Enter into the faith ready to believe and explore the many possibilities Christ has prepared for you. A wonderful journey lies ahead in a new life with Christ. The closer you get to Him, the easier it is to admit that yes, I do need God/Jesus/The Holy Spirit all in one.

Prayer: *Lord, as You know, Satan revels when people turn against You. But when we do realize that we do need You, it causes him anguish. Help to soften our hard hearts and open our closed minds when it comes to knowing You. Through Your grace and mercy You continue to give us many chances and opportunities to help us believe. Let the whole world know and "Let every knee bow and tongue confess that you are Lord."*

Chapter 41
This Is Love?

"Place me like a seal over your heart, like a seal on your arm; for love is as strong as death, its jealousy unyielding as the grave. It burns like blazing fire, like a mighty flame. Many waters cannot quench love; rivers cannot wash it away. If one were to give all the wealth of his house for love, it would be utterly scorned."

Song of Songs 8: 6-7

"Later I passed by, and when I looked at you and saw that you were old enough for love, I spread the corner of my garment over you and covered your nakedness. I gave you my solemn oath and entered into a covenant with you, declares the Sovereign Lord, and you became mine."

Ezekiel 16: 8

"May your fountain be blessed, and may you rejoice in the wife of your youth. A loving doe, a graceful deer—may her breasts satisfy you always, may you ever be captivated by her love."

Proverbs 5: 18-19

"Love is patient, love is kind. It does not envy, it does not boast, it is not proud. It is not rude, it is not self-seeking, it is not easily angered, it keeps records of no wrongs. Love does not delight in evil but rejoices with the truth. It always protects, always trusts, always hopes, and always perseveres."

1 Corinthians 13: 4-7

As a young girl I always imagined what my dream man would be like. He would be handsome, gentle, kind, but tough, and most of all—madly in love with me.

The attraction to the "man" I ended up marrying began in 7th grade. We found out through mutual friends that we liked each other, that was until…*the haircut*.

I was dumb enough to let a friend convince me to let her cut my longer than shoulder length hair up to my ears. "You would look so cute with your hair short." she told me over and over. I finally conceded, totally convinced I would surely be beautiful when she was done.

To make a long story short, it was plain ugly and so was I. If you think I'm exaggerating, ask my friends that went to school with me. When I walked down the hall, everyone stared. I'll never forget one boy saying in the most sympathetic voice I've ever heard, "Oh, Cathy!" It was so bad that my P.E. teacher got someone to take over her class while she tried to style it for me. Well, to say the least, Tim (my husband to be) lost his attraction to me.

Four years later my hair had grown back to an acceptable length and we ended up in a short study hall class together in high school. It was a class of about ten boys, myself and one other girl. Being the only girls, the other girl and myself (mostly me) became the target of much teasing and harassment. (I'm not complaining)

The teacher would often take the opportunity to take short breaks during this time, leaving us two girls alone with these wild boys. By now, Tim was beginning to be attracted to me again and he was the "ringleader" of this group. Some boys show their attraction by picking on a girl—this was his style. If picking on someone is an indication of love, he must have been madly in love with me. He would lift my dress in front of the class; take personal items out of my pocketbook and throw them around the room to the other boys; push me down the hall in my desk into the boy's bathroom and hold the door shut. For some strange reason, I still liked him.

We began dating at the end of that year after I (believe it or not) asked him out. We dated for four years and then got married during spring break of my junior year in college. His original proposal went something like; "I joined the Air Force, so we need to get married sometime in the next two months." (I did get a better one later.)

We have now been married for thirty-some years and have three grown children. I will not say they have all been years of "wine and roses." Like most marriages, we have had our ups and downs. He hasn't exactly been the "Prince Charming" I dreamed of. Forget flowers and romance, but he has shown his love in many other ways. He is one of the hardest workers and providers you'll ever meet. Friends were always jealous about how great of a father he was with the kids. Dirty diapers didn't bother him a bit and he always enjoyed taking the kids with him on special excursions. Going to the dump and to get his paycheck were days the kids looked forward to with excitement since they were always treated to chocolate milk and Slim Jims.

The sweetest thing he ever did was when I left the carpet cleaner on our wood floor overnight. It leaked, leaving a huge black mark on the floor. I was scared to death to tell him—thinking the entire floor now needed to be sanded to fix it. Thinking my life was over; I left a very sweet "Hi Honey Bunny" note on the table explaining what happened. My plan was to come home an hour later, giving him time to calm down.

I finally got the courage to go home and to my surprise he came out to meet me and he didn't seem mad. Matter of fact, he didn't even bring it up. I came into the house, went directly into the kitchen to make sure he got my note only to find that he left me a note saying, "What are you talking about?" I went to look at the spot and it was gone! How did he do that! It turns out he was able to sand it down and shellac it before I got home.

This one act made up for the dozens of roses he could have bought me. I then realized he must really love me after all these years. Maybe he is my Prince Charming after all.

It surprises me how some of the Bible verses mentioned earlier are so sensual. Speaking of "being old enough for love," "covering her nakedness," and "satisfying breast." The authors of these verses were definitely trying to get our attention on a subject that we all know well and are very interested in.

In my opinion the ultimate love verse of all is 1 Corinthians 13:4-7: *"Love is patient, love in kind. It does not envy, it does not boast, it is not proud. It is not rude, it is not self-seeking, it is not easily angered, it keeps records of no wrongs."* This is what Tim did when he fixed the spot. He was patient, kind, and he didn't take pleasure in reminding me of my mistake. In fact, he even covered it up for me. If we both could always be this forgiving and loving with each other every day our marriage would be so much better. Isn't this what Christ did when He died on the cross for us? He took our red stains of sin and covered them up for us. He loves us that much! How do you react when a loved one makes a mistake? Do you get angry and degrade them or do you chalk it up to experience and show them you love them mistakes and all?

Prayer: (for those with a spouse): *God, thank You for sending me a spouse that has been able to endure the hills and valleys of our life together. Help me to be a good husband/wife in return and to not sweat the small stuff. Some days aren't so easy Lord. But if love truly is patient and kind, it will persevere. Of all Your gifts Lord, thank You for giving us love. The love of spouses, friends, family and most importantly—Your unfailing, perfect, taking away our sins love. The best love of all!*

Prayer: (for those who are single or divorced): *God, love is a difficult thing. It takes a lot of giving and taking and finding the right person. God lead me to the person You have chosen for me. Let me be forgiving and understanding as You are with me during the difficult times. And Lord, if You think it is best I stay single, be with me and guide me on the path You have chosen and help me to be satisfied with Your love alone.*

Chapter 42
Chaos Happens

"One day when Job's sons and daughters were feasting and drinking wine at the oldest brother's house, a messenger came to Job and said, 'The oxen were plowing and the donkeys were grazing nearby, and the Sabeans attacked and carried them off. They put the servants to the sword, and I am the only one that has escaped to tell you!'

While he was still speaking, another messenger came and said, 'The Chaldeans formed three raiding parties and swept down on your camels and carried them off. They put the servants to the sword, and I am the only one who has escaped to tell you.'

While he was still speaking, yet another messenger came and said, 'Your sons and daughters were feasting and drinking wine at the oldest brother's house, when suddenly a mighty wind swept in from the desert and struck the four corners of the house. It collapsed on them and they are dead, and I am the only one who has escaped to tell you.'"

Job 1:13-19

"People on earth did what God said was evil, and violence was everywhere. When God saw that everyone on the earth did only evil, he said to Noah, 'Because people have made the earth full of violence, I will destroy all of them from the earth.'"

Genesis 6:11-13

"I tried to understand all that happens on earth. I saw how busy people are, working day and night and hardly ever sleeping. I also saw all that God has done. Nobody can understand what God does here on earth. No matter how hard people try to understand it, they cannot."

Ecclesiastes 8:16-17

You're probably familiar with that '70s saying similar to the title of this chapter. There's no doubt in my mind that whoever made up that saying had surely experienced chaos before. Although few of us will ever experience a day as bad as Job's described in the chapter of Job (God forbid), we have all had days where chaos has definitely happened. Stories told from these bad days are the stories that are passed down from generation to generation in families. And in almost all cases, this chaos has been a defining moment in the person's life—changing their course to new and different paths. As Paul Harvey's saying goes, "And now you know the rest of the story." If you do know the rest of the story, you know that Job does get through this horrible ordeal and goes on to lead an even better life than he had before.

Another Bible figure that goes through some pretty bad times, but ends up in unexpected prominence because of his ordeal, is Joseph. Genesis 37 tells the story of Joseph being the favored son of Jacob. Joseph's brothers become jealous of him since their father openly shows his favoritism by making Joseph a beautiful robe. On top of this, Joseph acts like he's better than everyone else by having dreams that portray him as a great person that everyone bows down to. This is too much for the jealous brothers to take so they plan to kill him and throw him into a cistern saying a wild animal killed him. Thank goodness Reuben encourages them to sell him to some Ishmaelites as a slave instead. Joseph then becomes Potiphar's (an officer of the King of Egypt) attendant and finds great favor with him—until his wife accuses him of sleeping with her (because he won't) and then he's sent to prison. Now what? More chaos happening! Well, in case you don't know the rest of the story—Joseph finds great favor (again) with the prison guard and soon earns great respect while in prison. So being, when Pharoah has a dream that greatly disturbs him the prison guard tells him about Joseph. Now Joseph (the dreamer) is able to interpret the dream telling him that it means a great famine is going to take place. Now Joseph is put in charge of Egypt, in effect being able to save his family. Another example of chaos with a happy ending.

A more modern day story that portrays bad things happening to a good end is the movie *Cold Mountain.* I love the character that Renee Zellwiger plays. Because of the abuse and neglect of a drunken father when she was a child, she becomes a very tough and independent person. During the Civil War this proves very beneficial, since few men are around and the women and older people need to learn to survive on their own. Although this is a fictitious character, there are many real life stories where bad experiences in life have helped people weather bigger storms later in life.

Is it possible that God uses the bad things that happen to us to prepare us for future trials that may prove to be even more difficult? Have you ever had something bad or tragic happen in your life and wondered, "Where was God?" "Why did He allow this to happen to me?" Just as Job and Joseph finally got their answer, you will get yours one day too. You may come to this realization before you die—or you may not find out until you meet God face to face.

This is why Paul tells us in many instances that we should be thankful for both the good and bad things in our life. God uses both to accomplish the plans He has for us.

Unfortunately, Satan does have power to make bad things happen, but then God has His wonderful way of turning these bad things around to make them result in something good.

Is chaos happening in your life? Try to go with the flow as Joseph did as he was used as a slave and imprisoned and yet was able to make the best of a bad situation—resulting in great things. Have faith that God will take even the worst situations in your life and turn them into something good and beautiful. In the meantime, continue to pray for others who may be experiencing similar situations. Pray for strength for them to get through tough times and remain faithful—receiving God's blessings in greater abundance than even before.

Prayer: *Yes God, chaos certainly happens. We may never know the reason why, but if we can remain faithful in good times and in bad we will prevail. As the saying goes, we need to learn to take the sweet along with the sour. Let us know that no matter how tough the tough gets going, in the end You will always carry us through and show us greater things than we could have ever imagined—things that are waiting to be revealed at the perfect moment in Your time.*

Chapter 43
Thirst/Desire

"As the deer pants for streams of water, so my soul pants for you, O God. My soul thirsts for God, for the loving God. When can I go and meet with God?"

Psalm 42: 1-2

"Like newborn babies, crave pure spiritual milk, so that by it you may grow up in your salvation, now that you have tasted that the Lord is good."

1 Peter 2:2

"When a Samaritan woman came to draw water, Jesus said to her, 'Will you give me a drink?' The Samaritan woman said to him, 'You are a Jew and I am a Samaritan woman. How can you ask me for a drink?' (For Jews do not associate with Samaritans.)

Jesus answered her, 'If you knew the gift of God and who it is that asks you for a drink, you would have asked him and he would have given you living water. Everyone who drinks this water will be thirsty again, but whoever drinks the water I give him will never thirst.'"

John 4: 7-10, 13

"My soul yearns for you in the night; in the morning my spirit longs for you. When your judgments come upon the earth, the people of the world learn righteousness. Though grace is shown to the wicked, they do not learn righteousness; even in a land of uprightness they go on doing evil and regard not the majesty of the Lord."

Isaiah 26: 9

I was raised, baptized, confirmed and married Catholic. As a Catholic, Sunday School classes were what we called CCD classes, which were held on Saturday mornings in preparation for confirmation. Since this was during my pre-teen years, it was a big deal to have to get up on Saturday mornings to do this.

The CCD class basically taught many Catholic doctrines and traditions, and occasionally you would get a Bible story in here and there. I remember having to memorize 100 questions that the Bishop or some important person could possibly ask you for confirmation. If you didn't know the answer when he asked you, as far as I remember you flunked confirmation. (Or were just the embarrassment of the whole church.) Catholic worship consisted of singing, standing, kneeling, reciting, and making the sign of the cross at the appropriate time. Through it all, one of my fondest memories of the Catholic Church was the sense of holiness. The painting of Jesus in the clouds with the cherubim on the ceiling, the profound statue of Him hanging from the cross, the beautiful stained glass windows, and the Stations of the Cross were constant reminders of what we were there for. But as far as the sermons, I rarely remembered or paid attention to what was being said.

As I got older and started to raise a family of my own, the desire for my children to have Bible learning became of great importance to me. Knowing that things had not changed since I was a child, I began to consider leaving the church. You have to understand—being raised a Catholic you are made to feel that if you leave the church you are committing a great sin. The decision to leave did not come without a lot of guilt feelings and soul searching.

I began my search for a church that had an active children's program and was led to the Methodist Church I am still attending—twenty-some years later. I no longer feel that I will go to Hell for making this decision (actually I feel God led me there) and my life has changed drastically since then.

I was so naive about other religions that I was surprised to learn that there was a Sunday School class for adults. If they had been coming all their lives, didn't they already know everything? Regardless, I was excited about going to one for my first time. There were also many programs for my children to get involved in and a lot of their friends attended the same church.

Since my knowledge of the Bible was very slim, it was very interesting for me to study the chapter of Job as my first. If you are familiar with Job, you know it is very perplexing, and yet interesting. In many cases it creates more questions than answers—as many Bible stories do. I read my lessons fervently and answered the questions from the study guide in detail and took lots of notes. When I looked at other people's books, I noticed they weren't answering the questions. I attributed this to the fact that most of them had been going to Sunday school most of their life and they probably already knew the answers. I just wished that one day I could know as much as they did. However, the teacher was impressed with my enthusiasm and even asked me to show everyone my book and how I was doing my lessons. It was a little embarrassing, but at the same time I felt a sense of pride—still wondering why the others weren't as excited.

When I became a member of the church, I immediately became involved in some leadership roles and it wasn't long before I was teaching a first grade Sunday school class; Bible School (another new concept to me); became Acolyte Coordinator (they're the ones that light the candles), and helped in any way I could with three young children tagging along.

Years later, I took an intensive adult Bible study called "Disciple." In this class you read the Bible daily and meet once a week for two and a half hours with your group of twelve to discuss the weeks readings. It required a lot of reading; which caused me to take my Bible and study book along on many trips to children's functions in order to finish the required readings for the week. When the class was over, I felt a void from not having to do the readings any longer. I then began reading the "Upper Room" devotional every day and added inspirational Christian books to fill my desire to know more. I went on to take two higher-level "Disciple" classes and read every Christian book I could get my hands on.

Since then, my relationship with Christ has gotten stronger and stronger. I still keep messing up, but He is always willing to forgive me and lift me up to start over again. It seems as if I've acquired an unquenchable thirst to know Him more.

A relationship with Christ is similar to that of a dear friend that you can't wait to see, talk to, share your experiences with, cry with, and empty all your hurts to—bearing your soul to them. In the same way, you want to know everything about the other person and share their experiences also. I have learned that this is the type of relationship that God desires to have with all of us.

Are you thirsty for Christ? Do you know Him intimately? You say you don't have time! Make time, read His word and talk to Him daily. You will understand what it means when Jesus told the woman at the well that He offers living water—"but whoever drinks the water I give him will never thirst." (John 4:14) But to receive the water, you have to thirst for it first. Seek Him and thirst no more.

Prayer: *God, most of us don't realize it, but what we thirst/yearn for is You. Thank You for offering us living water. Create a thirst in all people so that they will learn how to fulfill that insatiable desire with You alone. Will You meet me at the well today, Lord?*

Chapter 44
Prejudice/Human Rights

"When God created man, he made him in the likeness of God. He created them male and female and blessed them. And when they were created, he called them man."

Genesis 5:2

"Is he not the One that says to kings, 'You are worthless,' and to nobles, 'You are wicked,' who shows no partiality to princes and does not favor the rich over the poor, for they are all the work of his hands?"

Job 34:18-19

"In the Lord, however, woman is not independent of man, nor is man independent of woman. For as woman came from man, so also is man born of woman. But everything comes from God."

I Corinthians 11:11-12

"Then Peter began to speak: 'I now realize how true it is that God does not show favoritism but accepts men from every nation who fear him and does what is right.'"

Acts 10:34-35

*****

Why is it that since the beginning of time there has always been one group of people that has thought they were better or superior to another group of people? My answer is that this is just another one of those tricks Satan likes to entice us with. Think about it honestly, is there any group, race, gender or even an individual that you think you are better than?

An article I read in the newspaper recently showed Afghan women walking in the streets with their heads and bodies covered with a "burguas." The article was about how the country is ratifying its constitution after years of strict Taliban rule. Those rebuilding the country hope that a new constitution and the first democratic elections in decades will bring the country stability. Most importantly to me, are issues that will include women's rights. They will have rights equal to men in a society where they have been discriminated against for as long as most of them can remember. In a society where women cannot work, go to school, or even show their face in public; you have to wonder how they feel about that. In this case and many others, religion is what people/men have used as the reason for the prejudice. How this must hurt a loving God who has created us all equal!

After the fall of man in the Garden of Eden, God does tell Eve that women will now be under the control of man. I honestly don't think from that He meant they should be treated as if they are worthless and a less significant people.

Do men in that society have such little willpower that they have to make women cover their whole body so they won't be tempted? History has shown over and over again that certain groups of people have oppressed other groups of people in an attempt to makes themselves look more powerful and important. The dominance over the other group is almost always done in a violent way or may start out by sounding like they care about people but then end up turning bad with the more power they get.

Apparently in Bible days prejudice was prevalent: Jews against Greeks, Samaritans against Gentiles, Pharisees against Sadducees, men over women. It seems that man has had an inborn nature to feel superior over someone else since the beginning of time. Otherwise known as a self-esteem problem. If you feel good enough about yourself, you don't have to put others down or make yourself puffed up to show your value.

As seen in the verse from Genesis 5:2, God created male and female and called them "man." He states that everyone He has created are all the work of His hands. And then finally in Acts 10, Peter tells us that "God doesn't show favoritism but accepts everyone who fears Him and does what is right."

The body—whether it be male, female, black, white, Mexican, Asian, or from Timbuktu—isn't what's important. It's what's on the inside that counts. If you ever begin feeling like you're better than someone else or that someone else isn't good enough for you, then you're in trouble. This isn't the example that Christ gave us. He gave us the example of accepting all people: Examples such as of the Samaritan woman at the well, of helping beggars who were considered the lowest people in society, of letting children come to Him, eating with sinners, and dying for all of our sins. In God's perfect world, all are born with a clean slate and are of equal value. It's man that has created a much different picture.

In the past our church provided a Hispanic ministry to an especially poor area where many live in a trailer park. I also taught many children in my Head Start class of three and four year olds from the same neighborhood. Even from within this group there were prejudices amongst each other. The blacks consider the Mexicans of less value and even within the Mexican society, different groups are considered lower on the social ladder depending on what part of Mexico they are from.

Will the world ever move beyond this? Why can't we just look at each other's hearts and learn to love and respect each other for who we are? We are all people who laugh, cry, love, need love and respect, and want to provide for our families. Instead of looking at our differences—why can't we see the similarities?

I always found it interesting when I was teaching preschoolers, that when we did a project that involved making a picture of themselves, some wanted to be a different color than they were. To be politically correct we were required to provide construction paper of all colors for them to choose from, babies of all colors, posters with all nationalities, and stories with all types of children from around the world. (I do think this was important so that no one race was considered to be better than another.) It tickled me when the white children wanted to use black or yellow paper for their face, or the African-Americans wanted to use a white or red face. Unless the children's parents or others had tarnished them, they didn't even think of each other as being different in a bad way, or, in some cases, wanted to be a different color than they were liking that color better.

At a teacher meeting it was being stressed that we should make all children feel comfortable by talking about their differences. I protested saying that until we do that, most kids don't even notice the differences. Unfortunately, as they get older they become tarnished very quickly. I just wanted to protect that innocence a little longer. This must be what Jesus meant when he said, "Anyone who will not receive the Kingdom of God like a little child will never enter it." Matthew 10:15 (I know I've mentioned this several times. Apparently it is an important lesson since I keep coming back to it.)

I honestly try to look at each person I meet giving them a clean slate. No one race should think they should get special privileges over another because of their color. That goes for special working or education privileges. Everyone should start with from scratch proving himself or herself as the valuable person they are and accepting struggles they may encounter as challenges to conquer along the way.

Prayer: *God, You made us in Your image, but thank goodness we don't all look the same. Each of us has our own unique personality, color, nose, voice, and shape, with not one kind being any better than another. What an awesome God You are to use such creativity when You made us. Help us to see the likenesses in each other, but especially work on the hearts of those that put others down to make themselves feel better. Let them feel Your love and worthiness without hurting others to feel worthy.*

Chapter 45
A Dog's Life/Lessons Learned

"A righteous man cares for the needs of his animal, but the kindest acts of the wicked are cruel."

Proverbs 12:10

"Like one who seizes a dog by the ears is a passer-by who meddles in a quarrel not his own."

Proverbs 26:17

"But among the Israelites not a dog will bark at any man or animal. 'Then you will know the Lord makes a distinction between Egypt and Israel.'"

Exodus 11:7

"There was a rich man who was dressed in purple and fine linen and lived in luxury every day. At his gate was laid a beggar named Lazarus, covered with sores and longing to eat what fell from the rich man's table. Even the dogs came and licked his sores."

Luke 16:19-21

"The woman came and knelt before him. 'Lord help me!' She said. He replied, 'It is not right to take the children's bread and give it to the dogs.' 'Yes Lord,' she said, 'but even the dogs eat the crumbs that fall from the master's table.'"

Matthew 15:25-27

When God created the world, I wonder if He intended for animals to become pets? Animal lovers have pets ranging from anything as strange as lizards and snakes to pet pigs. Dogs have always been the preferred pet of many and are mentioned in the Bible as a pet, although they aren't given much respect and are usually only fed scraps and crumbs. (There were no references I could find as to cats.)

Our entire family loves dogs and even spoils them to a degree. We leave the radio on for them while we're gone so they won't feel lonely. We often buy chewies and treats for them at trips to the store. We make an extra effort to find a beach house that allows pets so they can come along for vacations.

Our oldest dog, Ginger, is fourteen years old and is part Cock-a-Poo. She has been an active part of our children's growing up years. When she dies, we will mourn as if she were another member of the family.

Bailey, our newest addition, is half Bulldog and half Blue Healer, which makes for quite an odd combination. He is very loyal and a good listener. Both of them will walk beside me when we go for walks—without a leash.

They are both very emotional and yet very smart. If you tell Ginger she's stinky, an hour later you'll find her waiting in the bathtub for a bath. Bailey gets very upset if anyone raises his or her voice and will go hide under the bed for a couple hours until he's sure it's safe to come out. He's also very selfish—and isn't shy about showing it. I'll give both of them a bone to chew on. He will sit and pout, staring at Ginger's the entire time until she's finished chewing hers, then he'll take it so he'll have two. If Ginger is getting pets and hugs, he comes and butts his way between us so he'll get them instead.

When you come home, even if you've only been gone for a little while, they are very excited to see you. Bailey wags his tail so hard you'd think he'd put a hole in the wall. It makes a person feel very loved. They have been good companions since our children are grown and have moved away from home. There is no better remedy for loneliness than a loyal dog or some may prefer cats.

When my daughter Robyn was at a low time in her life, she found an abandoned dog when she was running one day. She took her home and spent much money on vet bills getting her back to good health. The poor dog had mange and three types of worms, so it took some time to get her healthy. She has turned into a beautiful dog, being part Chow and part Samoyed. This is not a good mix for the Myrtle Beach area where she lives (thick white hair), but she is well loved. Since Robyn feels that God sent her to her, she named her Halo.

Dogs will even be loyal to an owner that doesn't treat them well. I met a lady at the vet who wouldn't let her dog get near Bailey when he was trying to make friends. I asked if hers was friendly. She said, "Yes, but she's not allowed to be around other dogs." I left it at that for a while, but couldn't help but wonder why, so I asked her why later. The lady explained that she's a kennel dog and is not allowed to have contact with other dogs or people so that the dog will think she (the owner) is wonderful when she spends time with her. She said when the dog sees her, "She stares at me as if to say, I love you so much and you're so wonderful." I sat there thinking, "Okay, that's pretty strange." Poor dog. Doesn't the woman realize that she doesn't have to treat it like that for the dog to love her?

Thank goodness God isn't like that with us. He could go to all kinds of similar extremes to make us loyal to Him, but He gives us a free will instead. If people could be near as loyal to God as dogs are to people, His job would be much easier.

I'd like to share guidelines about "Life Lessons Learned from Dogs" taken from some Sunday School material from Standard Publishing. I used this in my high school Sunday School class and thought it was refreshing and true:

Life Lessons Learned from Dogs

- When a loved one comes home, always run to greet them.
- Never pass up the opportunity to go for a ride.
- Allow the experience of fresh air and the wind in your face to be pure ecstasy.
- Let others know when they've invaded your territory.
- Take naps and stretch before rising.
- Run, romp, and play daily.
- Thrive on attention and let people touch you.
- Avoid biting, when a simple growl will do.
- On warm days, stop to lie on your back on the grass.
- On hot days, drink lots of water and lay under a shady tree.
- When you're happy, dance around and wag your entire body.
- No matter how often you're scolded, don't buy into the guilt thing and pout...run right back and make friends.

- Delight in the simple joy of a long walk.
- Eat with gusto and enthusiasm.
- Stop when you have had enough.
- Be loyal.
- Never pretend to be something you're not.
- If what you want lies buried, dig until you find it.
- Seek only your master and delight in his affection![13]

Prayer: *God, thank You for animals that have become pets that we love dearly and that they love us back even more. Be with animals that aren't loved, but are neglected and abused. Even creatures as these deserve love and caring. All creatures are part of the perfect plan You have made to make us happy. Let them be an example to us of the loyalty we should show to You every day. Master, lead me and I will follow. No leash required and I won't bite.*

Chapter 46
Real Religion?

"All the believers were one in heart and mind. No one claimed that any of his possessions was his own, but they shared everything they had. With great power the apostles continued to testify to the resurrection of the Lord Jesus, and much grace was upon them. There was no needy person among them."

Acts 4:32-34

"My command is this: Love each other as I have loved you. Greater love has no one than this; that he lay down his life for his friends. You are my friends if you do what I command. I no longer call you servants, because a servant doesn't know his master's business. Instead, I have called you friends, for everything I have learned from my Father I have made known to you. You did not choose me, but I chose you and appointed you to go and bear fruit-fruit that will last. Then the Father will give you whatever you ask in my name. This is my command; Love each other."

John 15: 12-17

"Do not merely listen to the word, and so deceive yourselves. Do what it says. Anyone who listens to the word but does not do what it says is like a man that looks at his face in the mirror, and after looking at himself, goes away and immediately forgets what he looks like."

James 1: 22-24

Our church had one of those rare blessings in that we received a large amount of money from an inheritance donation. This was especially exciting for me since I am on the Missions Committee and it was to be used for missions. While we were in search of some good projects where the money could be used best, we went to look at a house that belongs to a handicapped man that was in severe need of repair. Upon looking at what needed to be done, we noticed a sign in his kitchen that read, "I'm looking for a church that loves you the way you are." I shook my head to myself in understanding.

I know churches that are very judgmental and give you the feeling that you need to be "holy" to go there. Apparently this man has had contact with a church such as this—and now church or religion in general has a negative connotation to him. Hopefully, the work we do for him will convince him otherwise.

In looking for the word "religious" in a Bible reference book that I use to find needed verses, nearly all the references for "religious" were negative. The "religious" were almost always referred to as people who read the word and give all kinds of advice, yet do not live it. As it says in James 1:24: this is like "looking at yourself in the mirror and then immediately forgetting what you look like when you turn away." In other words, you read the word, but you're not internalizing what it means or doing what it says.

A story of a situation that reminds me of this happened on one of our mission trips to Appalachia. We shared a large room that had been used for band practice in an old school with a group from Florida. It was a very hot summer and the room we slept in had no windows or air conditioning, and there were about fifty women and teenagers sleeping together. (As you can see, the mood is set for trouble?) At first I was impressed with the group from Florida. They would get together with their leaders every evening to do a Bible study, in addition to the daily devotions and activities we did together as a group. This made me feel like I wasn't doing a very good job as a leader and I should be doing more.

However, it soon became clear that although this group did a lot of Bible study, they lacked love and unity. It started with them complaining to the center's leaders that our kids were playing with their flashlights making designs on the ceiling during lights out time. I thought, *That's odd, I didn't see anything.* And I'm a light sleeper. Then they would take the few fans we had and put them on themselves and yell if we opened the doors to let air in saying that bugs were coming in. It turned out to be a trying week to say the least.

When unbelievers experience these types of "religious" people, it's no wonder they are turned off by religion. Reading the Bible and knowing what it says is important, but it means nothing if we don't take it to heart and begin to live it by showing our love the way Christ calls us to. If we don't, we all become like the Pharisees of Jesus' day. This is like reading directions on how to do something and then throwing them aside and doing it your own way instead. Just as many families have at least one black sheep, so do churches. Some may have been going to church all their life, but have made no changes in their life or attitudes. Other than seeing them attending church on Sunday, there's no evidence that they are Christians.

I'll never forget an experience described in the book, *A Secret Place* by Dale A. Fife that describes how Christ must feel about how the church is used in negative ways in His name. The story reads like Revelations and is very thought provoking. The man was walking with Jesus along a long dirt road. Jesus is crying profusely as He passes several 3-D billboards that have torn off body parts on each one of them.[14] The body parts represent the churches of the world and how man has torn them apart with his own thinking. Isn't this so true!

God intended for us to love each other and help those in need as described in Acts 4:32. Oh how God would be so happy if His whole church would follow the plan to love, and not to act holy while doing unholy acts. If we truly loved each other that much—you couldn't sit back and watch a brother or sister in need. You would actively participate in His work. You would be able to experience more joy in your life, both in good times and bad. You would strive to make the world a better place for all rather than sitting back and enjoying the blessing you have.

Experience "Real Religion" today: The religion of love and compassion. If your church is lacking in this area, be a doer. Begin by spreading this message so that others will also begin to share it with others too. This type of religion is contagious and one that all will want to experience.

Prayer: *God, help those "religious" amongst Your believers to know that Your words are meaningless without love. Help to open our eyes to see the needs of those in our communities so that they will know true religion is one of love, forgiveness, and acceptance—a fun and joyful religion, where all are welcomed, not just the "holy."*

Chapter 47
Warm Fuzzies

"But it is you, a man like myself, my companion, my close friend, with whom I once enjoyed sweet fellowship as we walked with the throng at the house of God."

Psalm 55:13-14

"It is right for me to feel this way about all of you, since I have you in my heart; for whether I am in chains or defending and confirming the gospel, all of you share in God's grace with me. God can testify how I long for all of you with the affection of Jesus Christ."

Philippians 1:7-8

"As apostles of Christ we could have been a burden to you, but we were gentle among you, like a mother caring for her children. We loved you so much that we were delighted to share with you not only the gospel of God but our lives as well, because you have become so dear to us."

1 Thessalonians 2:7-8

"Above all, love each other deeply, because love covers over a multitude of sins."

1 Peter 4:8

"Greet one another with a kiss of love. Peace to all of you who are in Christ."

1 Peter 5:14

When the senior high youth of our church go on the mission trips to Appalachia to rebuild homes, one of the favorite activities we do while there is to make "warm fuzzy bags." Warm fuzzy bags are paper bags with our names written on them that are taped on the wall. Everyone is encouraged to write each other "warm fuzzy" notes. "Warm fuzzies" are words of encouragement, appreciation and love for each other.

On one of our trips, we worked at a site with another team from Illinois. There were a total of eighteen of us working at the site and, as a result, we got very close to each other. Two girls from our team noticed that Gene, the male leader from Illinois, did not have a warm fuzzy bag. The girls thought they would surprise him by making him a bag and putting a large sign next to it making sure he knew that he now had one. Little did they know the impact this gesture would have on him.

The mornings at ASP are very busy with getting the supplies you'll need for the day, packing lunches and just trying to get teenagers moving at 6:30 in the morning. Gene had been at the hardware store helping the staff obtain the needed supplies for the day. When he returned I told him to be sure to check in the cafeteria for a surprise. A few minutes later he stopped our van as we were leaving. With tears in his eyes, he told us that although he's been coming to ASP (Appalachia Service Project) for eight years, he had never had a warm fuzzy bag and we had no idea how much this meant to him. (We made sure that he got a lot of warm fuzzies that week.)

It is a basic human desire to feel loved and appreciated. When these feelings are denied, it often results in rejection that often creates a calloused and sometimes hateful heart. I make it a point to create warm fuzzies as often as I can: maybe by writing to a nephew in prison, visiting a shut-in that many people may have forgotten about, giving a compliment to someone doing a seemingly mundane job, or just by smiling or joking with people that I encounter during the day to make their day a little lighter.

My daughter was going through some stressful times at college and was in need of some warm fuzzies. In an effort to make her feel better, I wrote down a month's worth of special memories and reasons why I thought she was special, put them in a warm fuzzy bag and mailed them to her. The directions stated that she was to read only one a day. She often told me how these got her through the day.

Have you received or given any warm fuzzies lately? Possibly by taking food to someone who is ill or someone who has had a death in the family, listening to someone who has a problem, or visiting someone who is lonely or sending a card to let someone know you're thinking about them. There are so many ways to make people feel loved and appreciated.

Paul sent many "warm fuzzies" to the churches that were having difficulty in remaining faithful when Christianity was beginning. Those first churches needed lots of encouragement during this time. In the face of death and persecution, they needed someone to constantly remind them that they were loved and to encourage them to remain faithful. Although Christians are not being persecuted today (at least in the United States), we still need to hear this message: A message of love and encouragement to both those new in the faith and those who have grown stagnant in their faith.

Do you know someone that could use a warm fuzzy bag? Be aware of those who may need a word of encouragement and know that someone cares. Do nice things for people, even those who may be mean and grumpy and irritable. They are the ones that most likely need it the most.

Prayer: *God, thank You for the warm fuzzies You give us every day. If we had a bag with all Your blessings, it would be constantly overflowing. Let us share warm fuzzies with those who need it the most—the lost, the lonely and the forgotten. What a privilege to touch someone's life in a way that they can feel Your love in a lost world. Use us as we are needed. Let the messages we share be ones that will uplift the weak in spirit and help them feel Your love.*

Chapter 48
Does God Change?

"The Lord saw how great man's wickedness on earth had become, and that every inclination of the thoughts of his heart was only evil all the time. The Lord was grieved that he had made man on earth, and his heart was filled with pain. So the Lord said, 'I will wipe out mankind, whom I have created, from the face of the earth.'" (Thus came the flood)

Genesis 6: 5-6

"The Lord said to Moses, 'How long will these people treat me with contempt? How long will they refuse to believe in me, in spite of all the miraculous signs I have performed among them? I will strike them down with a plague and destroy them, but I will make you a nation greater and stronger than they.'"

Numbers 14: 11-12

(Moses convinces God not to destroy everyone)

"Then Isaiah said, 'Hear now, you house of David! Is it not enough to try the patience of men? Will you try the patience of God also? Therefore the Lord himself will give you a sign: The virgin will be with child and will give birth to a son, and will call him Immanuel. He will eat curds and honey when he knows enough to reject the wrong and choose the right. But before the boy knows enough to reject the wrong and choose the right, the land of the two kings you dread will be laid waste.'"

Isaiah 7: 13-16

(Thus came Jesus)

The more I read and know about the Bible, it seems that the God from the Old Testament and the God of the New Testament are different in many ways. It makes you wonder, "Did He have to change because the people kept sinning again and again?"

In many cases, it appears that God bit off more than He could chew when He created humans. No matter how much He has done for them throughout Old Testament history, and even though many of them actually witnessed unbelievable miracles and could see His presence in the pillar of fire as He lead the Israelites out of Egypt, they continued to sin and fall away. Just as with a parent raising a child, He often had to punish them to get them back on track. This seems to happen many times up until Jesus' birth.

In sending Jesus, instead of appearing in another form, He comes as flesh and blood. This was too hard for many people of that day to comprehend—God coming down to earth as an ordinary, plain man that can see, feel, think and touch just as we do. Until then, I wonder if God really understood how easy it is for humans to sin? He knew that Jesus could reject sin, but I'm not so sure He truly understood how difficult it would be even for Him.

In the Old Testament we see punishment after punishment, but people keep falling back into the same old habits. Could it be that God re-evaluated the situation and realized He had to do something different? Parents need to use different disciplines with each of their children. One child may only need a stern word or look and that ends the misbehavior. Another may only seem to respond to spanking. Another may completely rebel to physical punishment and the parent may try many types of rewards and punishments to see which works best.

The best solution He came up with to deal with us, a sinful people, was love. He loved us so much that He sent His only son to die a terrible death to be a perfect example for us. Could you do that? Would you be willing to offer one of your children to die a terrible death to save the world? I don't know that I could. I might be willing to die for others myself, but I couldn't offer my children. That is why we fall short and can't even come close to being God. Can you imagine God and Jesus working out this plan before He sent Jesus? Even for God, it had to have been a gut wrenching decision but one He knew Satan couldn't foil.

Many people would disagree with me, but I do believe that God started with a plan for us and as it started to go haywire, He had to keep readjusting those plans as humans kept rebelling and disobeying. Thank goodness He loves us enough not to give up on us too easily or we would have been left behind long ago with no hope of spending eternity with Him.

Won't you open your heart and follow the plan He has for you today? He has made many changes for you. Won't you make one big change in your life to accept Him?

Prayer: *Father, You have done so much for us yet we continue to disobey. Thank You for loving us so much that You're willing to try whatever it takes to bring us to You. As with the example of a parent with a child, some may just need to hear Your stern warning, but others need to be knocked down over and over again to get the message. Keep us strong to resist the many temptations in the world. Thank You for the best plan of all to make us change out of love, Your son!*

Chapter 49
Know You by Name

"'If you are pleased with me, teach me your ways so I may know you and continue to find favor with you. Remember that this nation is your people.'
The Lord replied, 'My presence will go with you, and I will give you rest.'
Then Moses said to Him, 'If your presence does not go with us, do not send us up from here. How will anyone know that you are pleased with me and with your people unless you go with us? What else will distinguish me and your people from all the other people on the face of the earth?'
And the Lord said to Moses, 'I will do the very thing you have asked, because I am pleased with you and I know you by name.'"

Exodus 33:13-17

"A good name is more desirable than great riches; to be esteemed better than silver or gold."

Proverbs 22:1

"After he had provided purification for sins, he sat down at the majesty in Heaven. So he became as much superior to the angels as the name he has inherited is superior to theirs."

Hebrews 1:3-4

*****

There are some people with the gift of remembering the name of everyone they meet the first time. I am not one of these. When my children were young I often called them each other's names. Then as they got older and we adopted dogs, I even began calling them the dog's names or the dogs the kid's names.

When I refer to one of my three brothers, I often say the wrong name for each of them. I seriously think I have a problem.

Since I taught preschool for sixteen years, I have met hundreds of children and their parents. It's very embarrassing when I meet one of my students a few years later and can't remember their name or see a parent and can't remember what child is theirs.

Sometimes I'll even momentarily forget someone's name I know well. I honestly fear this is an early sign of Alzheimer's. This can be very embarrassing since knowing someone by name indicates how interested you are in him or her. In most cases, I'll just carry on a conversation without having to use their name so as not to make a fool of myself until it finally comes to me.

We live in a society where names are of great importance. Names are used to carry on a family name for many generations. Since girls' names are usually changed to their husband's last name, having a boy to carry on the family name is very important. Some women may hyphenate their name so they don't lose their family heritage. Also, putting titles on names makes a person's value or status clearer. (Mr., Mrs. Dr., Rev., etc.) Movie stars, singers, and authors place great importance in a name that sounds good, often changing their stage or writing name to one that has an appealing sound to it.

God places great emphasis on names also. His name alone is very important and many names are given to Him in the Bible: Lord, Yahweh, The Almighty, I Am, The Way, The Word, The Alpha and the Omega, and many more. God also changes many people's names to indicate they have been changed through following Him: Abram becomes Abraham, Jacob becomes Israel, Simon becomes Peter, Saul becomes Paul, etc. With changed hearts come changed names.

Many of us give nicknames to our children or loved ones that resemble a personality trait they have or maybe something that rhymes with their name, but with a twist. Many close friends and family call me "Sis," and we have named our children silly names such as "Ruby" for Robyn, "Caseby" for Cassie, and "Jacobphine" for Jake. When you move away and no one calls you that name for a long time and then you come home again, it's comforting to know people still remember that special name that only a few insiders had the privilege of knowing.

I am impressed with our minister's ability to remember people's names. In most cases, after meeting a person once, he'll have a name memorized. This is important for someone in that profession since everyone wants to feel like their pastor cares enough about them to know them by name.

In the same way, it's comforting to know that God knows each of us by name. It's interesting how God stresses this to Moses in Exodus 33 mentioned earlier. *"I will do this very thing you have asked because I am pleased with you and I know you by name."* (Exodus 33:17) In doing this, He's indicating a close relationship with Moses.

Do you think God knows you by name? When He hears your name or thinks of you, what characteristics do you think are standing out in His mind? As a kind, giving, loving person; a determined, caring, devoted person; someone who truly desires a close relationship with Him and shows it in many ways? He desires to know each and every one of us personally. If you don't know Him yet, start today. Read His Word, go to church, and join the fellowship of believers to do His work. He's a really nice guy and He'll never let you down. It's a friendship that will take you down many roads you never dreamed you'd travel and He'll be calling your name along the way.

Prayer: *God, everything good on this earth bears Your name. Your name takes many forms with the many roles You play. Create in us a desire to know You and to do Your will. In so doing, our name is a pleasing sound to Your lips—a name You know well and will call upon to accomplish Your work.*

Chapter 50
Suffering

"Come to me, all you who are weary and burdened, and I will give you rest. Take my yoke upon you and learn from me, for I am gentle and humble in heart, and you will find rest for your souls."

Matthew 11:28-29

"Therefore we do not lose heart. Though outwardly we are wasting away, yet inwardly we are being renewed day by day. For our light and momentary troubles are achieving for us an eternal glory that far outweighs them all."

2 Corinthians 4:16-17

"Therefore, since Christ suffered in his body, arm yourselves also with the same attitude, because he who has suffered in his body is done with sin. As a result, he does not live the rest of his earthly life for evil human desires, but rather for the will of God."

1 Peter 4:1-2

"He will wipe away every tear from their eyes. There will be no more death or mourning or crying or pain, for the old order of things has passed away."

Revelations 21:4

"For he that is the least among you—he is the greatest."

Luke 9:48

Nobody likes to suffer, but after we've survived and incident where we have suffered—it becomes a time of learning and maturity. You may even hear people brag about how they survived a bad experience, it then becomes the source of books that are written. Or they may even get T-shirts made to proclaim that they survived the incident: earthquakes, hurricanes, a very hot summer, a certain boss, etc.

There are two types of suffering—physical and emotional. Depending on the circumstance, one can be as painful as the other. In both instances, you can come out of these bad experiences either with a stronger character, or scarred for life. With a stronger character you are better able to handle other difficult life situations and help others that have shared the same bad experience. If you come out scarred, you may no longer be able to function in society and be left with a mental illness. How people respond so differently to similar situations and why bad things happen to good people, only God knows.

Those that have been able to overcome great odds or misfortunes come through it with a different perspective on life. They appreciate little things more and are able to see things with a clearer, more mature attitude. This must be what Paul is referring to when he says, *"There was given me a thorn in my flesh, a messenger of Satan, to torment me. Three times I pleaded with the Lord to take it away from me. But he said to me, 'My grace is sufficient for you, for my power is made perfect in weakness.'"* (2 Corinthians 12: 7-9) When you have suffered, you lose your arrogance, you are more compassionate of others who are experiencing pain, and you realize how little control you really have in your life. Most importantly, you realize your need for God. Maybe the reason those that end up scarred for life from bad situations is because they never acknowledge their need for God. Unfortunately, suffering is what it takes for many to come to Christ. Until then, we think we have complete control of our lives and don't need a higher being. Matthew 11: 28-29 says it well when Jesus tells us, *"Take my yoke upon you and learn from me, for I am gentle and humble in heart, and you will find rest for your souls."* Oh, the joy we experience when we truly do find rest for our souls.

Is it necessary to experience rough times to be able to know joy? What would you have to look forward to if you only experienced joy all the time? Another important factor is what brings you joy? If it's earthly desires—you will find this type of joy is only temporary. If it's a joy from doing God's work and following His path, you will find the everlasting joy that He has planned for you.

You may wonder, "What kind of God would want us to suffer to come to Him?" He doesn't want you to suffer, but He knows the suffering that awaits you after death without Him is so much greater. Unfortunately, some will only come to Him through suffering. He does require a humble and obedient heart. To acquire that, many of us need to experience suffering.

Does God know what our suffering feels like? If He didn't before, He certainly did after He let His Son die for us. By Jesus' great suffering He proves His never-ending love for us.

The worst suffering I can imagine would be to see a terrible death of my own child. Can you imagine witnessing Jesus' death as a parent?

Secondly, by suffering such a horrible death, He is able to feel any kind of pain you could possibly experience. You may say, "Yeah, but why did I suffer so much when I didn't do anything?" Guess what? Jesus didn't do anything either. He never sinned, never did anything wrong, but was killed as if one of the worse criminals of the time. He did this so you will know; Yes, He does understand what you're suffering. He does know your pain. And He knows if you persevere till the end, *"He will wipe away every tear from your eyes. There will be no more death or mourning or crying or pain for the old order of things will pass away."* (Revelations 21: 4)

Just today my husband and I attended a funeral of a twenty-three-year-old young man. Within two months of being diagnosed with cancer he was dead. This young man was so fortunate to be surrounded with a family of very loving and faithful people. His father was a preacher and his grandmother and mother came to his bedside every day reading him scripture to keep his spirit strong. The doctors and nurses were overwhelmed with the strength and faith of this family. He died in peace and without fear. Now try to imagine another family experiencing the same situation that doesn't know God. What a sad thought! Don't be the second family. Come to God today!

Prayer: *God, if it takes a thorn in my side to bring me to You, give it to me now. Much better a thorn than a life without You on the other side of the abyss. Help us to know that whatever we may suffer in this world is insignificant to the joy we will experience when we reach Your kingdom.*

Chapter 51
What the World Needs Now/Love

"I may speak in different languages of people or even angels. But if I do not have love, I am only a noisy bell or a crashing cymbal."

1 Corinthians 13: 1

"Love is patient and kind. Love is not jealous, it does not brag, and it is not proud. Love is not rude, is not selfish, and does not get upset with others. Love does not count up wrongs that have been done. Love is not happy with evil but is happy with the truth. Love patiently accepts all things. It always trust, always hopes, and always remains strong."

1 Corinthians 13: 4-7

"Show mercy to others, be kind, humble, gentle, and patient. Get along with each other, and forgive each other. If someone does wrong to you, forgive that person because the Lord forgave you. Do all these things; but most important, love each other. Love is what holds you all together in perfect unity."

Colossians 3: 12-14

"This is how we know what real love is: Jesus gave his life for us. So we should give our lives for our brothers and sisters. Suppose someone has enough to live and sees a brother or sister in need, but does not help. Then God's love is not living in that person. My children, we should love people not only with words and talk, but by our actions and true caring."

1 John 3: 16-18

If you are a parent of more than one child, you've probably been given the guilt trip, "You love so and so more than you love me?" All three of my children have said this at one time or another.

I love all of my children just the same. However, as different needs or hardships arise between each on of them, I may give one more attention at that time.

Our dog Bailey recently had surgery on both of his knees to remove bone chips behind his knees. Since he was unable to walk for a period of time, he required a lot of my attention. He needed to be carried everywhere, I had to spoon-feed him since he wouldn't eat, and had to force ice into his mouth because he wouldn't drink due to the medications. As a result our older dog Ginger didn't like this one bit. She would get in my face and whine and lick me wanting me to give her attention too. Apparently animals have the same traits as people.

People often need to be reassured that they are loved. Husbands and wives that lead busy lives or devote much of their time to their children or work, may begin to feel neglected by the other. It's important that we take time to show others that we love them. Some may assume that the other should just know that they love them: Fathers may feel they are showing their love to their family by working long and hard hours to provide for them, yet not spending time with them or showing it in any other way. Mothers may neglect their husbands by solely devoting their time to their children.

It has been proven that babies who aren't given love at an early age do not develop normally, both physically and emotionally. Without love, people may become bitter and mean and often spend a lifetime searching for love, usually in the wrong places.

It breaks my heart to see a young child being neglected or abused. This is often the result of parents who are unable to find love themselves and often turns to drugs or alcohol to fill this void. Children from these situations either become withdrawn, act out in anger, or have emotional problems.

Loving people who are easy to love is easy. God calls us to go beyond this to love the "least of these" and to love your neighbor. This may be someone who is mean and cranky, or may even be your enemy. God's perfect plan for us is to love each other so much that we become one in mind and spirit. In doing so, we become a powerful force.

God's love is unending and ever flowing. Once you've received it, you'll be amazed how differently the world looks through the eyes of love—that person that was getting on your nerves today doesn't seem so bad after all—a wrong someone did to you is forgiven—an irritable mood is seen as someone who's having a bad day and needs a little more TLC.

The most important person you can learn to love is yourself and to know that God loves you. If someone is confident in love and feels loved, they can conquer many things in life. God wants this for all of His children. Open your hearts, let His love in. He's been waiting patiently with open arms. Be prepared for the biggest hug of your life. I can't help but sing that Dionne Warwick song, *What the world needs now, is love sweet love. No not just for some, but for everyone.*

Prayer: *Father, Your love is so freely given and yet we have such a hard time accepting it. We all soon find out it's only Your love that can fill that deep void many of us feel in our lives. The fortunate ones discover this early on, while others may take a lifetime of searching. Let me discover Your love today Lord. In return, let me be able to give it as freely as You have given it to me. Yes, the world does need love, sweet love. Not just for some, but for everyone!*

Chapter 52
Rules, Rules, Rules

And God spoke all these words:

"I am the Lord your God, who brought you out of Egypt, out of the land of slavery. You shall have no other gods before me.

You shall not make for yourself an idol in the form of anything in Heaven above or on earth beneath or in the waters below. You shall not bow down to them or worship them; for I, the Lord your God, am a jealous God, punishing the children for the sin of their fathers to the third and fourth generation of those who hate me, but showing love to a thousand generations of those who love me and keep my commandments.

You shall not misuse the name of the Lord your God, for the Lord will not hold anyone guiltless who misuses his name.

Remember the Sabbath day and keep it holy. Six days you shall labor and do all your work, but the seventh day is a Sabbath to the Lord your God. On it you shall not do any work, neither you, nor your son or daughter nor your servant, nor your animals, nor the alien within your gates. For in six days the Lord made the heavens and the earth, the sea, and all that is in them, but he rested on the 7th day. Therefore the Lord blessed the Sabbath day and made it holy.

Honor your father and your mother, so that you may live long in the land the Lord your God is giving you.

You shall not murder.

You shall not commit adultery.

You shall not steal.

You shall not give false testimony against your neighbor.

You shall not covet your neighbor's house. You shall not covet your neighbor's wife, or his manservant or maidservant, his ox or his donkey, or anything that belongs to your neighbor.

Exodus 20: 1-17

"This is the covenant I will make with the house of Israel after that time declares the Lord. I will put my law in their minds and write it on their hearts. I will be their God, and they will be my people. No longer will a man teach his neighbor, or a man his brother, saying, 'Know the Lord,' because they will know me, from the least to the greatest. Declares the Lord."

Jeremiah 31:33-34

*****

Rules are necessary for this world to have some sort of order, but sometimes I get irritated with so many rules in life. I realize rules are necessary for a civilized society, but it's not unusual for them to be taken to extremes or for people to make up stupid ones that make no sense. For example, have you ever had to park in Washington, D.C.? If so, you know how parking is hard to come by and the little parking there is has so many restrictions that it's hard to understand what you can and can't do.

My husband works for the government and has to go to D.C. at times for meetings. One day in particular he found a parking lot that had meters and a sign that said, "No Standing between 8:00-3:00." He wasn't quite sure what "standing" meant, but the meters were for two-hour periods, so he thought maybe it means no long-term parking. Well, he parked, put money in the meter, and went to his meeting. Of course when he came back he had a ticket on his car. He notched it up as a lesson learned and came home and tried to pay the ticket by phone. This was a twenty-minute process and he wasn't sure if it actually went through since the whole thing was very confusing. We then sent the $100 to pay the fine and sent it to the address indicated on the ticket.

Two months later we received a bill stating that the ticket was not paid and we now owed $200. This was very irritating, but we kept our cool and made a copy of the cancelled check and sent it to them, thinking surely this would take care of it we put it out of our mind.

Another two months later we received yet another bill. This one more threatening and saying it must be paid for at once. By now my husband was getting pretty angry. He then called the D.C. Police Dept., which wasn't an easy task since you have to go through so many recordings, and by the time he talked to an actual person he was livid. After much discussion it was discovered that he had been given two tickets during the same two-hour period. One must have blown off, causing him to be cited a second time. This did not matter to the clerk he was speaking to. They still insisted he owed $200 and continued to tell him if it wasn't paid immediately our credit would be ruined. By now my husband was beyond control and told them they could come arrest him and lock him up, but he wasn't going to pay the second ticket. We did receive several more threatening letters but threw them in the trash. The matter was eventually dropped.

This is an example of the trouble and confusion that can be caused by rules that are not clearly defined. Sometimes people at businesses make up rules because something is a pet peeve. Sometimes schools or other organizations have to go overboard in enforcing rules because a certain group has gotten out of hand or caused trouble to the point that others suffer because of these few. Rules have to be clearly defined in sports to help clear up instances where both sides see a play a different way. In addition, extra referees are added to the field to make sure plays are seen from all angles. Even at this, people still get very angry thinking a wrong call has been made.

As Christians, we do the same thing with the Ten Commandments. We try to say, "Yes, God but..." or "It really wasn't my fault. So and so made me do it." Or "But everybody else was doing it." As times change, so have laws of our country. However, over the thousands of years, God's laws have not changed. The Ten Commandments are a moral code to live by that is necessary for society, as we know it, to survive. However, as history has proven, as long as there have been laws, there have been people to break them. Satan loves rules because he knows it doesn't take too much nudging to make us break them. He helps us twist situations around in our mind to somehow convinces us that it's not really wrong.

The mistake the Pharisees and Sadducees made was to put so much emphasis on the laws, that they forgot compassion and love. When Jesus came he added this commandment: *"Love the Lord your God with all your heart and with all your soul and with all your mind and with all your strength."* (That's a lot) The second is this: *"Love your neighbor as yourself. There is no commandment greater than these."*

So, now if you're really good at loving people, you don't need to worry about all those other commandments. If you truly follow the commandment of love, all of the others will fall in place naturally.

Although many rules are stated in a negative way; No Loitering, No Speeding, No Food, No Parking, No Trespassing. In following Christ's new rule notice it's stated in a positive way; Love God, love your neighbor, be kind, be generous, share, love, love, and love some more. These are some rules I can live by.

Sometimes there is a conflict between God's rules and man's rules; Abortion is legal, but very upsetting to God (You shall not murder); We allow death in an electric chair, but God says thou shall not kill again; Stores are now opened on Sunday's when we are supposed to make the Sabbath holy. Even God took a day off. Are we better than God? What day is a family day anymore? On many of these issues, we can take a stand as Christians to not do these things and encourage those we love not to also.

We may not like all the rules that are in our society, but at least we live in a country where we can express our feelings about them. Rules can be annoying but they must be followed until they are changed. If there is a law or rule that needs to be changed, be active in bringing about that change in a loving, peaceful way. Is there a law/rule you are tempted to break? Pray for strength to not fall into temptation.

Prayer: *God, You have given us Your rules to follow. As You have promised—these are written on our hearts. Help us to remember that the greatest rule of all is to love You first and to love our neighbor. In this one rule, all can be well and good with the world. Be with us to keep us strong when Satan tries to convince us that it is okay to break rules. Let Your truth remain strong in our hearts as we try to decipher what is right and wrong in this world.*

Chapter 53
Servanthood

"Whoever tends a fig tree gets to eat its fruit, and whoever takes care of his master will receive honor. As water reflects your face, so you mind shows what kind of person you are."

Proverbs 27: 18-19

"Whoever wants to become great among you must be your servant, and whoever wants to be first must be your slave—just as the Son of Man did not come to be served, but to serve, and to give his life as a ransom for many."

Matthew 20: 26-28

"During the meal Jesus stood up and took off his outer clothing. Taking a towel, he wrapped it around his waist. Then he poured water into a bowl and began to wash the followers' feet, drying them with the towel that was wrapped around him."

John 13: 4-5

"When he had finished washing their feet, he put on his clothes and sat down again. He asked, 'Do you understand what I have just done for you? You call me 'Teacher' and 'Lord,' and you are right, because that is what I am. If I, your Lord and Teacher, have washed your feet, you also should wash each other's feet. I did this as an example so that you should do as I have done for you.'"

John 13:12-15

"You my brothers were called to be free. But do not use your freedom to indulge the sinful nature; rather, serve one another in love. The entire law is summed up in a single command: "Love your neighbor as yourself."

Galatians 5: 13-14

I have been reading a book about Mother Teresa that cites many quotes and short stories from her life. What a wonderful woman and inspiration she was to us all. To think of how one small woman who had so little could accomplish so much.

When Mother Teresa, or Agnes Bojaxhiu (her real name), was eighteen she joined a convent and taught mostly wealthy young girls in Darjuling, Calcutta. While teaching there it didn't take long for her to discover that people living outside the convent were in severe poverty. She soon left the convent to devote her life to the poor. She began to care for abandoned children and those dying on the streets. She says she had "no plan on what work needed to be done, but just worked according to people's suffering."[15]

Wouldn't it be wonderful if we all could have the heart of Mother Teresa? To feel God's call so strongly that you are able to love without fear, even those who are dying of diseases that most of us wouldn't even come close to. What an act of Christian faith! If we all had such a faith, I have no doubt the whole world would be Christian.

One of the quotes from one of her stories goes like this:

"A man, a follower of the Hindu religion, came to our home for the dying at Kalighat at a time when I was busy curing the wounds of a sick person. He watched me for a while in silence. Then he said, 'Since it gives you the strength to do what you do, I have no doubt your religion has to be true.'"[16]

I recently drove a group of women from our church to the Brethren Service Center in New Windsor, Maryland. The man that was our guide had a strong German accent and at first I thought, *Great, it's going to be hard to understand what he says.* He took us to an orientation room and explained how the organization accepts good clothing, blankets, medicines, or almost anything that the poor can use. They package it, store it in a warehouse where it is then sent to Baltimore to their shipping company to be sent to third world countries or wherever there is a need. Volunteers do most of the work done at the distribution center. As he was explaining all of this to us, he kept apologizing for his poor English, although after getting use to his accent, I found he wasn't hard to understand. At the end of the tour I was proud to hear him say how he loves America and is overwhelmed by the way Americans volunteer and reach out to others. In Germany and most European countries, people won't do anything unless you pay them for it.

I'm proud to be an American Christian. As a country and a people that are so blessed, we should never take those blessings for granted and make every effort to share them with others.

Jesus' example of washing the disciples' feet was unbelievable to them, especially to Peter at the time. Jesus' call for them to be a servant first was so different than what they had been taught and what many still believe today.

Today as I read John 13: 2-17 about this act of Jesus, although I've read it many times before, the act of him taking off his outer garments and wrapping a towel around his waist really caught my attention. Not only is He giving an example of servanthood, but humbles himself to the point that he completely bares himself to them. Can you imagine serving in nothing but you underwear? This shows great humility.

Have you been called to service? Have you felt a nudge to do something about an injustice you've noticed? Many people may see something that bothers them, but then get so caught up in life they soon forget about it. I am very fortunate that I've been able to stay home and do what my heart leads me to do this past year and a half. Most families need two incomes to support them in this day and age, yet we have managed to do so with one somehow. (Actually, I really know it's God's help) If you are serious about wanting to serve, ask for God's guidance in what you should be doing and He will show you the way.

My best friend is a teacher whose son has muscular dystrophy. She had to quit her job so she could stay home with him. Not only is she a servant to him, but she has many other servant roles she does through her home: She sends flowers and cards to the sick and grieving, takes calls for Concern Hotline (a crisis call line), cooks dinner for people who have been sick or had surgeries, and helps whenever she can with many other church projects. She is the example that Mother Teresa gives.

Reexamine your life and values. God has much for you to do. Let others know that ours is a true religion. Let them know this by your deeds.

Prayer: *God, You certainly outdid Yourself when You accomplished great deeds through a tiny woman named Mother Teresa. What an example of what can be done when Your love is too big for the human body. Let us have an ounce of that courage and love so that others will see You through us.*

Chapter 54
Love Hurts

"Praise be to the God and Father of our Lord Jesus Christ, the Father of compassion and the God of all comfort, who comforts us in all our troubles, so that we can comfort those in any troubles with the comfort we ourselves have received from God."

2 Corinthians 1:3-4

"When Jesus saw her weeping, and the Jews who had come along with her also weeping, he was deeply moved in spirit and troubled."

John 11:33

"At the sixth hour darkness came over the whole land until the ninth hour. And at the ninth hour Jesus cried out in a loud voice, 'Eloi, Eloi, lama sabachthani?'—which means, 'My God, my God, why have you forsaken me?' With a loud cry Jesus breathed his last."

Mark 15:33-34, 37

"I had confidence in all of you, that you would all share my joy. For I wrote you out of great distress and anguish of heart and with many tears, not to grieve you but to let you know the depth of my love for you."

2 Corinthians 2:3-4

*****

Love is an emotion that can cause both ecstasy and great pain. Anyone who has loved, more than likely has suffered in some way as a result of that love. The hurt may be a result of your significant other not paying enough attention to you or maybe paying too much attention to someone else or even leaving you for someone else.

As a friend, you may have been hurt by a confidence broken or rejection. Many marriages that end in divorce usually result in one person being severely and emotionally hurt. Most will agree—there is no worse pain than lost love.

Parents feel the hurt for their children when they experience the many pains the world can bring: Not being picked for a team, making mistakes or bad choices, being teased for an imperfection, trying and failing, or just when they aren't happy in general. When you truly love someone as a parent loves a child, you wish you could take their pain and bear it for them. At the same time you know that growth and maturity comes through this pain and it must be experienced to understand other people's pain.

Have you ever been hurt so badly due to lost love that you thought you would die? But you somehow survived. What brought you comfort?

Children receive comfort by being hugged and cradled by a parent. As adults we need to know someone cares and sometimes just need a listening ear—and hugs still work wonders. Emotional hurts often just need time to heal.

Think about the times you have hurt the most. Was there anyone or anything that could comfort you during that time? Just as a parent wants to comfort a child, God wants to comfort you. He offers it to you at all times. All we have to do is receive it. Can you imagine Him reaching to you with all His might, wanting so badly for you to reach back and feel His embrace? What a gratifying experience for both Him and us when we finally receive His love and comfort.

As a teenager, some of my hardest tears ever shed were from rejected love. As a parent I know some of the hardest tears my children have shed have been over broken hearts. Just like a chain reaction, I can feel their pain because I have experienced it and God can feel our pain because He has felt it too. All the hurt feelings we have felt due to love are the same feelings God feels for us. Pain we feel from failure, rejection, lost love, or injustice, hurt Him badly. But the only difference is—in many cases we are the ones that have caused Him the pain because we have rejected Him.

Those who have suffered severe pain, such as the death of a loved one, have to go through a grieving process. Through it all, if they have a relationship with Christ they are given an inner strength and peace that is beyond understanding. You can tell the difference between a living relative of someone who has died that has faith compared to someone with little or no faith. Those with faith will show sorrow, but have a sense of hope and find strength and are at peace through it all.

There are some who are so badly hurt by love that they no longer want to be a part of the world or don't want to have relationships anymore. They may become a recluse, rejecting affection or love from anyone. To them, a life with no feeling is better than taking a chance on getting hurt by love again.

Have you been hurt by love? God offers a love that is never failing. When all earthly love fails, He will always be there for you. He feels your hurt so much that He was willing to let His only Son come to earth to feel our pain. Through His Son He was able to feel the worse imaginable pain we could ever feel—Both the pain of rejection, and pain caused by human hands.

Let Him feel your pain. Let Him carry you through those unbearable times in your life. Let Him be your rock.

Prayer: *God, sometimes it hurts to love. People we love may get hurt, hurt us, leave, or die. Since you sent Jesus to become one of us, You understand our pain. Let Your Spirit fill us and give us strength during these most difficult times. Heal us Lord, carry us, and open our hearts to feel Your love so that we can love with confidence again.*

Chapter 55
Seasons of Life

"People were bringing little children to Jesus to have him touch them, but the disciples rebuked them. When Jesus saw this, he was indignant. He said to them, 'Let the children come to me, and do not hinder them, for the Kingdom of God belongs to such as these. I tell you the truth, anyone who will not receive the kingdom of God like a little child will never enter it.'"

Mark 10: 14-15

"The glory of young men is their strength, gray hair the splendor of the old."

Proverbs 20:29

"It is good for man to bear the yoke while he is young."

Lamentations 3: 27

"Oh, for the days when I was in my prime, when God's intimate friendship blessed my house, when the Almighty was with me and my children were around me."

Job 29: 4-5

"Our lifetime is seventy years or, if we are strong, eighty years. But the years are full of hard work and pain. They pass quickly, and then we are gone."

Psalm 90: 10

I can remember when I was very young and couldn't wait for many things in my life to happen. First, I couldn't wait to go to school. Then learning to ride a bike seemed like the most exciting thing in the world if only I could do it. Then, when I got in school, I couldn't wait to be a teenager—driving a car and getting a boyfriend consumed my thoughts and desires. With these major accomplishments under my belt, I was ready to tackle all the other wonderful things that life had in store for me: college, marriage, living on my own, a job, a first house, and then—children.

When the children came, they became my focus in life—their accomplishments became mine. I couldn't wait until they spoke their first word, "Mama" of course, then I couldn't wait until they walked. (Little did I know how much that stage would wear me out) Having three children in three and a half years caused my life to be very full and a seemingly unending routine of changing diapers, stopping fights, feeding people, and cleaning up messes.

As they began to grow, they each began to get involved in their own areas of interest—beginning the ceaseless era of driving kids to soccer, piano, wrestling matches, running events, basketball, 4-H and numerous other activities.

At this point I began to look forward to the day when they could drive—to relieve me of some of the endless driving excursions. Of course with the driving, comes teaching them, which may cause a nervous disorder sometimes referred to as "foot in the floorboard" syndrome. Then when they do get their license, you begin to worry yourself to death, needing to know exactly where they're going and making sure they know how to get there so you can inform them of any obstacles they may face on the way. And then the awful waiting for them to get home when they are late—imagining they are surely in a ditch somewhere and they need your help desperately.

Faster than you can bat an eye, the next thing you know—they're off to college. Now you're ready for life to slow down a little. You become apprehensive and wonder if they are ready to be on their own without you there to remind them of all the things they will forget to do. You go over and over in your mind—"Did I teach them everything they need to know to survive in this world?" Or "Oh no, I should have told them how to..." Letting go is very difficult, but with time you learn to settle into a different lifestyle revolving around graduations, paying college bills, and then getting to know your children as more of an equal rather than a child that needs to be shown the way.

At this time, my youngest is twenty-four and my oldest is twenty-eight. I have learned to wait for things in life. The oldest is married and has given me the greatest gift of all, two beautiful grandchildren; I wait patiently when the other two will find that hopefully perfect spouse; I wait patiently for eyes and ears that will go bad; aches and pains to begin and wrinkles on my face. (Okay, I already have a few.)

At this season in my life—when I look back, it seems that it has gone by so quickly. And the older I get, the quicker it seems to go. My husband and I continue to fill our lives with things to do. Him with his regular job and coaching cross country and track; and me with mission work in my church, learning a new language and beginning a picture framing business. We also do a lot of traveling to see the "kids," or to help them with a house project or with moving from place to place.

The grandchildren have now become a highlight in our lives. We relish every minute we can spend with them since we only see them once a month. This time I don't wish for them to grow up quickly. I want them be babies for a while. We bask in the joy of their youthful innocence and always look forward to when we can see them again.

Then one day the circle will change and our children will be coming to help us with the things that need to be done that we can no longer do for ourselves. They may need to help make decisions to care for us if we become ill and then begin to worry if we're okay when they haven't heard from us for a while. God has His way of bringing things full circle, doesn't He?

If you begin to contemplate on the seasons of your life too much—you can become sad. However, being stuck in any one season would become dull and we would have a strong desire for change. We need to accept each season gracefully and thank God for the many blessings He has given us along the way. As I look back, I can see the many ways He has been there for my family. So many "could have beens," yet so many lessons learned.

I've come to accept with grace the season I'm in now and am ready to move on to the final season of my life. Knowing that God will continue to be there with me every step of the way takes away any anxieties I may have. No matter what age we are, we continue to need His grace and guidance. One thing I have learned is that you never grow too old to make mistakes. Yes, He will continue to guide me and comfort me through the happy and sad times in the remaining years of my life. With His strength, I can wait patiently for what lies ahead.

Prayer: *Thank You God for this beautiful life You have given us. You have given us many blessings along with times of despair. Times of learning and becoming stronger to grow into the person You want us to be. Continue to be with us as we approach another season in our life. Each one with it's own significance and beauty. Thank You for seasons and changes to let our lives come full circle. As we look back God, we see how You have been active in our lives ever since we were in our mother's womb. As winter approaches, Lord, we will find warmth in Your love.*

Chapter 56
Hindsight

"I will remember the deeds of the Lord; yes, I will remember your miracles of long ago. I will meditate on all your works and consider all your mighty deeds."

Psalm 77:11-12

"Consider what God has done: Who can straighten what he made crooked? When times are good be happy; but when times are bad, consider: God has made the one as well as the other."

Ecclesiastes 7:13-14

"Endure hardship with us like a good soldier of Christ Jesus. No one serving as a soldier gets involved in civilian affairs—he wants to please his commanding officer. Similarly, if anyone competes as an athlete, he does not receive the victor's crown unless he competes according to the rules. The hardworking farmer should be the first to receive a share of the crops. Reflect on what I am saying, for the Lord will give you insight into all this."

2 Timothy 2:3-7

"Those who hear God's teaching and do nothing are like people who look at themselves in a mirror. They see their faces and then go away and quickly forget what they looked like. But the truly happy people are those who carefully study God's perfect law that makes people free, and they continue to study it. They do not forget what they heard, but they obey what God's teaching says. Those who do this will be made happy."

James 1:23-25

Most of us who are in the mid-life years reflect back on our life—our accomplishments, mistakes, and paths we have chosen. Through time, lessons learned from mistakes and the results from wise decisions are clearer to see. It also becomes apparent how God has worked in our life and has been there with us by either holding us up through the difficult times or by watching closely nearby as we make mistakes, hoping that we will learn from them.

As I look back on my life experiences, I can see major decisions I have made that were influenced by God's urging. Activities that I was once passionate about became more difficult, influencing me to redirect my attention to another cause that is also important. Jobs can become a mindless task or burdensome, causing a desire to change to a different calling. Events that may have seemed devastating at the time have helped me grow, and now when I look back on them—it makes more sense as to why they happened.

After much reflection you come to realize that decisions made after going to God in prayer for guidance, are the ones that have had the most pleasing results and are the least painful. Others, where you've tried to make things happen out of self-satisfaction or without regard to others, are usually the ones that have led to mistakes and sometimes lessons learned the hard way. You may even be able to see how difficult people you've encountered in your life have even played a role in the direction your life has taken. Just as God hardened many people's hearts in Old Testament days, He continues to harden people's hearts today to get certain results accomplished that may not have happened otherwise.

The secret is to be able to be aware of these seemingly bad circumstances and accept them. As we are told in Ecclesiastes 7:14, "*When times are good, be happy; but when times are bad, consider; God has made the one as well as the other.*"

No one wants to endure pain or go through hard times, but if we can look at these occurrences with a good attitude as Paul did when he was in prison, even bad situations can be accepted with grace. The more stubborn we are, the harder the lessons or experiences become. For some, all we need is a gentle nudging; others need to be hit hard—like running into a brick wall.

Yes, as I look back over my life, I can see all the good and bad things that have happened and the importance each one of them has had in forming me into the person I am today. What do you see as you look back over your life? Are you still holding grudges for a wrong done to you at some time during your life? Learn to accept this as a growing experience and move beyond it. God was probably trying to move you in a different direction.

One way of using a bad experience is by being able to comfort others that have shared the same experience. What a blessing you can become to many others. Have you been betrayed in love? Move beyond that to realize that possibly God has another plan for you. Although you may have thought your life was perfect before, like Job, He may have greater things planned for you than you may have ever imagined.

God does not promise our life as Christians to be all rosy. He does promise a better place for you if you are able to persevere and continue to follow Him to eternity. Embrace the good and bad in your life. In the end you will see how God's hand has had a part in where you are today.

Prayer: *God, thank You for both the good and bad things that happen in our lives. Even when Satan plays a part in making life miserable, You are there to turn it around for our good. Open our eyes that we can see the purpose of every experience and how we can better use these experiences to get closer to You. As I look back I can see the two sets of footprints of us walking together. Then I see only Your's—when you carried me. Thank You, God! I know there were times when I was very heavy, but no load is too great for Your great strength.*

Chapter 57
Creation

"In the beginning God created the heavens and the earth. Now the earth was formless and empty, darkness was over the surface of the deep, and the Spirit of God was hovering over the waters. And God said, 'Let there be light' and there was light."

Genesis 1: 1-3

"And God said, 'Let there be an expanse between the waters to separate water from water.'"

Genesis 1:6

"And God said, 'Let the water under the sky be gathered to one place, and let dry ground appear.'"

Genesis 1:9

"Then God said, 'Let the land produce vegetation: seed-bearing plants and trees on the land that bear fruit with seed in it according to their various kinds.'"

Genesis 1:11

"And God said, 'Let there be lights in the expanse of the sky to separate day from night, and let them serve as signs to make seasons and days and years.'"

Genesis 1:14

"And God said, 'Let the water teem with living creatures, and let birds fly above the earth across the expanse of the sky.'"

Genesis 1:20

"And God said, 'Let the land produce living creatures according to their kinds: livestock, creatures that move on the ground, and wild animals.'"

Genesis 1:24

"Then God said, 'Let us make man in our own image.'"

Genesis 1:26

"God saw all that he had made, and it was very good."

Genesis 1:31

*****

What's the last thing that you created? Creating things gives you a sense of satisfaction that most tasks don't. When you are able to see your finished project after days or months of work, there is a pride that is very pleasing.

One of my pastimes is quilting. To quilt, you have to be patient since it is a very l-o-n-g process. The first and most important decision is in deciding what pattern and materials to use. Then you cut out all the pieces, sew them together; pin the top, batting, and backing together; next you mark the pattern to quilt; and then finally the tedious quilting process begins. In the end you hope to have a beautiful masterpiece that only another seamstress or quilter could truly appreciate.

For a carpenter or builder, the steps are very similar: First you must decide on what style of house you're going to build; plans need to be drawn; permits need to be obtained; then you have to order all the materials you will need; give a crew directions on what needs to be done; oversee to ensure that everything is being done correctly, and coordinate plumbers, electricians, and dry wall people. Finally, after several months of hard work there is a finished product and final inspections need to be made.

Farmers go through the same process as they till the land, plant crops, care for the crops, pray for good weather, harvest the crops, and finally take them to market.

In all these professions, great pride is taken at the end of each project or harvest. Through the work of their hands, people accomplish great tasks.

Through the work of their hands they can create a warm blanket that can be passed down from generation to generation. They can create a home where a family will love each other, grow together, and experience many of life's hills and valleys. They can grow food so people can be fed and be satisfied at the end of a hard day's work. Yes, work done with our hands to create things brings great satisfaction.

I often wonder when God created the world, how much planning He had to do before He actually did it? Did He have to clearly think through every step as we do in most jobs, or did He just have fun and make it up as He went along? I can just imagine the fun He must have had when He was creating the animals—thinking, *Hey, this one would look cool with a long neck.* Or *I'll give this guy a real long nose and I'll make some that live in water, and some will have wings to fly and some will crawl on the land. Oh, and what will they eat? Some will eat each other and some will eat plants. Maybe I'll call that a food chain.*

Now, how can I make them procreate? I'll have to make it something fun or they might not want to have babies. Last of all, I'll make a being called man to care for all this stuff I've created. Oh, and I guess I better make something else called a woman so they can do this procreation stuff. This was after He had already made the sky, land and water. (That was another story in itself.) After six days, He finally sits back and looks at what He's made and thinks, *Hey, this looks pretty good! Not too bad for an old guy. I think I'll take a little rest now. This creation stuff can wear you out.*

Now, this was just with the world as we know it. I also wonder if He did this for each planet or each solar system He created? Surely we're not the only life out there.

Just as with things we create, when you are finished your job isn't always done. Now there is work to do for upkeep: Wash the quilt, fix things that break in the house, fertilize the fields and cut back the harvest, answer everybody's prayers.

Yes, creation is a long and ongoing process. In most cases the job is never quite finished unless the creation is destroyed. Wear and tear on quilts and houses usually result in mending and rebuilding and sometimes they need to be destroyed and a new one will take its place. God gave up on His original creation when He brought the floods. But thank goodness He didn't completely give up on us when he had Noah load the animals up two by two on a huge boat and took a handful of his family to preserve this creation.

Have you ever made something that you weren't satisfied with and couldn't get it right, so you just started over again? After making several mistakes you just put your hands up in surrender and tell yourself, "I'll know not to make the same mistake when I make the new one." God had His basic plan intact after the flood; the only problem He kept having involved attitudes and free wills. Did He really know what He was getting into when He gave these to men? I wonder how many times He sits back and watches what we're doing with His world and thinks, *Oh, I wish they wouldn't do that!*

It would be the same feeling we would have after spending months and years creating something. Imagine the feeling if a treasured gift was used improperly or neglected to the point that it was ruined. You may wish you had never given it to that particular person. But if you give something to someone that takes great care of it, you want to continue giving them more, because you know it will be cared for.

Nothing man has created can compare to the beauty and well thought out plans that God has made for us on this earth. Anything that man creates is just a small extension of what God has given us already. When we extend on His plan or become part of it, we become partners working alongside of the Great Creator. Won't you work along with Him today? Start by cleaning up that dirty roadside that people have littered. More importantly, don't litter. Recycle so you don't desecrate this precious earth. Take in an animal that is about to be put to sleep. Take care of the neighbor that needs your help. A man and woman's work is never done until you leave this world. However, God's work is never done. Never stop appreciating and taking care of this beautiful creation called earth and life that He has given us.

Prayer: *Wow God, You really did a great job when You created this world. You thought of every detail so that we could be happy. Your power and creativity leave us in AWE! Keep us ever mindful that we are stewards of this beautiful place we call earth and help us to never take it for granted. Thanks for loving us so much! You are an AWESOME God and Creator!*

Chapter 58
Stagnation

"These people honor me with their lips, but their hearts are far from me. They worship me in vain; their teachings are but rules taught by men."

Isaiah 20:9-13

"A good person who gives in to evil is like a muddy spring or a dirty well."

Proverbs 25:26

"You are the light of the world. A city on a hill cannot be hidden. Neither do people light a lamp and put it under a bowl. Instead they put it on its stand, and it gives light to everyone in the house. In the same way, let your light shine before men, that they may see your good deeds and praise your Father in Heaven."

Matthew 5: 13-16

"Be very careful, then, how you live—not as unwise but as wise, making the most of every opportunity, because the days are evil."

Ephesians 5: 15-16

"It is now time for you to wake up from your sleep, because our salvation is nearer now than when we first believed. The 'night' is almost finished, and the 'day' is almost here. So we should stop doing things that belong to darkness and take up the weapons used for fighting in the light. Let us live in a right way, like people who belong to the day."

Romans 13: 11-13

Have you ever observed a lake or pond that doesn't have new water flowing into it or has no place for the standing water to go? It develops green "gunk" and eventually turns stagnant. When the heavy rains come, if the water has a place to overflow to—it will eventually wash the "gunk" out and it will temporarily look fresh again.

Christians can also become like a stagnant pond and start to accumulate "gunk." We may get Bible learning once a week when we go to church and think we are doing our Christian duty. After all, we're going to church. A lot of our neighbors don't even do that. For many, other than going to church once a week, there are no other signs of being a Christian. Webster's Dictionary describes stagnant as: ceasing to flow, motionless, dull. In the Christian life, we can become dull.

Like the pond, we need a constant flow of living water: God's word, fellowship with other believers, opportunities to serve and share Christ's love so that we don't become stagnant. Throughout our lives as Christians, ideally we mature and experience Christ more intimately; our ideas and feelings begin to change. Things that used to be of major importance now don't seem so important. Likewise, things that weren't important now take on new meaning and are of great importance.

We all know people that are very set in their ways; keeping the same routine every day, who are very closed minded—thinking their way of thinking is the only way, and are very rigid in their beliefs. Any change in their routine or threat to their way of thinking is a great source of anxiety and stress for them.

From what we read in the Old Testament, this seems to be what happened to the Pharisees and Sadducees. They had a very strict set of laws and rituals they followed and any deviation from these became a sin. It got so bad that they kept adding more laws and soon it seemed almost everything anyone did was a sin and therefore sin offerings had to be burnt continually. The key component they were missing (the fresh water) was love and compassion. No matter how desperate a need was; to deviate from the "law" was forbidden. "Don't dare heal someone on a Sabbath day." (Luke 13:10-17)

Then Jesus came to show us a new way. A refreshing way where the only law was the law of love and compassion. Of course this "law" wasn't written in the Pharisees and Sadducees rule book so it caused them great stress and anger that anyone would dare challenge what they "knew" to be true. Love had become so far from their understanding in dealing with people, that they couldn't even comprehend what Jesus was teaching. As Matthew 5 vs. 13-14 mentions, we are to be a "light to the world." We're not to hide it under a bowl.

God doesn't want you to be lukewarm in your relationship with Him. If you accept and know Him, you will lead a life that shows beyond a shadow of a doubt that He is active in your daily life. Don't sit at home being your good little self, thinking that your not breaking any of the Ten Commandments, so you must be a Godly person. When you truly know Him you have to become a doer. He won't let you sit still feeling cozy about yourself.

It can be very easy to become complacent with our lives when we are so comfortable. It's easy to forget about the homeless person on the street while we sit in our comfortable warm homes with plenty to eat. It's easy to forget about the family that can't afford to buy their children decent clothing. It's easy to forget about the lonely person in the nursing home that has no one to visit while we have a loving family that surrounds us. In many cases what we don't do becomes as much of a sin as what we do wrong intentionally.

How much "gunk" do you have built up in your life? Do you lead the same sinless routine every day, but don't do anything to help your neighbor either. Is your stagnation getting so bad you can't see clearly anymore? No new ideas or thoughts, especially concerning God, coming into your life lately? Don't let your gunk get too thick. Let Christ's living water come into your life to wash all of it away. With each act of kindness and love—your life will become cleaner and fresher, allowing the same living water to overflow into other people's lives.

Prayer: *God, You know that one of Satan's greatest pleasures is for us to become stagnant: such a simple, subtle tactic. Before we knew You, our goal in life was to lead a comfortable, easy life. After knowing You, we learn that true pleasure comes from the love You give to us so abundantly that if overflows into everyone's life that we touch. Wash away my stagnation today Lord. Let everyone see a new, refreshed me that glorifies You.*

Chapter 59
Like a Child

"Lord, my heart is not proud; I don't look down on others. I don't do great things, and I can't do miracles. But I am calm and quiet, like a baby with its mother. I am at peace, like a baby with its mother."

Psalm 131:1-3

"At that time Jesus said, 'I praise you Father, Lord of Heaven and earth, because you have hidden these things from the wise and learned, and revealed them to little children.'"

Matthew 11:25

"Jesus said, 'Let the children come to me, and do not hinder them, for the Kingdom of God belongs to such as these. I tell you the truth, anyone who will not receive the Kingdom of God like a little child will never enter it.'"

Mark 10:14-15

"He took a little child and had him stand among them. Taking him in his arms, he said to them, 'Whoever welcomes one of these little children in my name, welcomes me; and whoever welcomes me does not welcome me but the one who sent me.'"

Mark 9:36-37

*****

Children are my specialty. I have taught preschool age children for sixteen years. Their innocence and the way they see the world fascinates me. I wish I had written down the many funny and touching things they have said to me in the past, but here are a few:

One day after we worked on a big project and ran out of time to go outside to play, I told the children, "Sorry, guys, we ran out of time to go outside."

One of the children responded, "Mrs. Ritter, I'm going to have to buy you a new watch."

Another time we were studying weather and had read a book on how water evaporates and forms clouds. I told them when the clouds get heavy the water comes down as rain. Later, they were to draw clouds and dictate to me how they were formed. I was testing to see if they comprehended what we read. Some of them were able to remember what I told them, but one little girl said, "God made the clouds and rain and the rainbows." Since I was doing dictation, I wrote down exactly what she said with pride, being the Christian that I am. It so happened that this was during a time that our school was being audited by the Head Start "Big Wigs" to make sure we were doing things right. When one of them saw her paper, I was questioned about it since we aren't allowed to teach religion. They were satisfied with the explanation that it was dictation, but gave me a raised eyebrow look as I was explaining.

There was another little boy who had a difficult time allowing enough time to stop playing in time to go the bathroom. As many times before, he began jumping up and down and yelling, "Mrs. Ritter, I have to go to the bathroom!" Seeing it was an emergency, I tried to get him there as soon as possible, but it wasn't soon enough. As I was changing him, he asked me, "Aren't you going to spank me?"

I immediately felt a sense of compassion for him—knowing that this is what happens at home. I said, "No, Johnny, I would never spank you."(Not his real name)

If you listen to children and watch them explore the world, you notice that they see things differently than adults. They haven't been tarnished by life yet and are able to see things with the wonderment and simplicity that we have lost over the years. I love being able to let myself look at things through a child's eyes: The amazement of a lightning bug, picking flowers (sometimes weeds), openly describing what makes them happy or sad. Yes, I know what Jesus meant when he said, *"Anyone who will not receive the Kingdom of God like a little child will never enter it."'*

Children are so loving and trusting. Even if you break that trust in some way, they are willing to continue trusting you over and over again. They don't need miracles to prove something to them, you can simply tell them and they will believe. As they grow and begin to realize that many things they have learned aren't true (Santa, Easter Bunny, the Tooth Fairy), then they begin to doubt that everything they hear isn't true. Then they turn into teenagers and don't believe anything you say. We're just old people who don't know what we're talking about and now they know everything.

Have you noticed how differently people act when they talk to babies? We use baby talk and sing lullabies and make funny faces. There's nothing more rewarding than when a baby looks at you with total amazement and wonder as they are experiencing the world for the first time. In playing with toddlers and young children it's fun to get down to their level and let your imagination wander, as if you were that age again. A common game my preschoolers would play was pretending to be dogs or cats and superhero people. It was fun to watch them play the role so well—to break that train of thought would take them away from that perfect place they had worked so hard to create.

When was the last time you were able to be like a child? Can you believe in things that are unbelievable? Are you able to totally trust God like a child and just believe? Dare to think like a child! Jesus is saving a special spot on His lap just for you.

Prayer: *God, what a perfect plan You had for us when You created us as little beings that feel, learn, grow, experience the world, and eventually are able to think for ourselves. Thank You for not making us clones with no emotions or reasoning skills of our own. Let us learn life lessons from the beautiful children You have given us. Let us be able to trust You totally and be in awe of these amazing beings You have created called children. Help us to think like a child again.*

Chapter 60
Contentment/or Lack Of

"The Lord is my shepherd, I shall not be in want. He makes me lie down in green pastures, he leads me beside quiet waters, he restores my soul."

Psalm 23: 1-3

"Praise the Lord, O my soul; who satisfies your desire with good things so that your youth is renewed like the eagle's."

Psalm 103: 1,5

"A heart of peace gives life to the body, but envy rots the bones."

Proverbs 14:30

"As water reflects your face, so your mind shows what kind of person you are. People will never stop dying and being destroyed, and they will never stop wanting more than they have."

Proverbs 27:19-20

"I denied myself nothing my eyes desired; I refused my heart no pleasure. My heart took delight in all my work, and this was the reward for all my labor. Yet when I surveyed all that my hands had done and what I had toiled to achieve, everything was meaningless, a chasing after the wind;"

Ecclesiastes 2: 10-11

*****

My husband I have reached an unusual milestone for this day and age—thirty-some years of marriage. It hasn't all been "wine and roses," but we have survived many peaks and valleys.

We began our marriage on very meager wages of $6,000 a year for the first two years while he was in the Air Force. We started with a furnished apartment until we could afford to buy our first, very cheap furniture. Our car was a very cool Gremlin that had a quite a few miles on it. Although we didn't have much, we were very content with our lives.

Through the years we have had our battles, usually over insignificant things, but we always made up eventually. After seventeen years of marriage, things seemed to change. Our children were getting older and we seemed to be drifting apart. He was very distant, we didn't communicate well without it turning into an argument, and we didn't even like each other very much. It seemed like we were in competition as to who did the most work or who was right or wrong. This went on for about six years. I was very discontented with our life together, and I'm sure he was too. During this time I desperately desired love and affection from him. I would see other couples who seemed to be madly in love and ached inside to have those feelings again.

At one point I knew things had to change or I was going to leave. He sensed this and we eventually had a terrible fight, both expressing our feelings. Things seemed to change after that. We were more aware of each other's needs and were able to see the good points in each other again. When it came down to it, we knew we still loved each other.

Since this occurred while we were in our early forties, I feel it could have been what many refer to as a mid-life crisis. It seems like at mid-life we stop to re-examine our life to see if we are satisfied with what we have and what we've accomplished. This is spoken well in the verse from Ecclesiastes 2:11 where it says, *"Yet when I surveyed all that my hands had done and what I toiled to achieve, everything was meaningless, a chasing after the wind."*

For me, after going through many years of totally giving myself to my children, I now realized I needed and craved love for myself. I felt like I needed to feel it again as I did when we were first in love.

Discontentment doesn't have to be a bad thing. Out of discontentment many good changes can occur, but no one should be content with a bad relationship. I'm not saying that you should get a divorce, but try to make your marriage better. However, if abuse is involved, you need to get away from the situation.

Governments and societies have been changed out of discontentment, especially those where the people are being oppressed. As with the author of

Ecclesiastes, many people finally come to Christ out of discontentment resulting from a feeling of meaninglessness of what they've achieved in life thus far.

During discontentment, choices are made—some good, some bad. Many do end up in divorce: more than half of the population in the United States has been married twice. I wonder out of all those divorces, how many wish they had stayed with the first mate? My guess is that some of the same problems they experienced with the first spouse are repeated with the second. The fortunate ones have learned from the first and can lead a happier life with another. The sad part is when children are involved, their need for love and affection is neglected during this time of turmoil and they may grow up with confusion about relationships.

Contentment can involve many areas of our lives: relationships, careers, houses, cars, clothes, things, and more things. We never seem to be content with what we have and always want more. I look back to those beginning days of our marriage and wonder what is missing now? Why was I so content with so little then? I've come to realize it was because we were starting fresh and just beginning to build our life together. We loved each other and everything we acquired was new and exciting and OURS. Although, what we had weren't quality things, we were proud of them. We were even proud of the old station wagon we got that had air conditioning but broke down quite often, and the black and white television we used the first seven years of our marriage.

The secret is that you can be happy and content with life when you know you are loved. The problem with human relationships is that they oftentimes fail us. However, a relationship with Christ will never fail you. This is why so many that truly do have a relationship with Christ, can be happier with less. They realize the treasures of this world are of no importance. It's the treasure they store up in Heaven that counts: loving God, loving others, and sharing blessings.

Are you satisfied with your life? Are you content with the way it has turned out, or is there something missing? Don't spend a lifetime of discontentment to realize that God is what has been missing all along. A good life is one with no regrets. A life with Christ is a life that is satisfied even when things aren't going well, even when disasters strike. This is obtained because you know you are loved no matter what. Knowing this makes it easier to weather any storm. Be content with your life today. Choose Christ!

Prayer: *God You put us in this world giving us a free will and a mind of our own. With that freedom comes emotions that enable us to think, feel, and desire. Help us to not listen to that voice that tells us we're not satisfied with what we have. Also help us to be willing to make changes when they need to be made. As The Serenity prayer reminds us:*
"God, grant me the serenity to accept the things I cannot change; courage to change the things I can; and wisdom to know the difference."

Chapter 61
The Church

"How lovely is your dwelling place, O Lord Almighty! My soul yearns, even faints, for the courts of the Lord."

Psalm 84: 1-2

"Blessed are those who dwell in your house; they are ever praising you."
Psalm 84: 4

"I will put a stone in the ground in Jerusalem. Everything will be built on this important and precious rock. Anyone who trusts in him will never be disappointed."

Isaiah 28:16

"This stone is worth much to you who believe. But to the people who do not believe, the stone that the builders rejected has become the cornerstone."

Psalm 118:22

"And I tell you that you are Peter, and on this rock I will build my church, and the gates of Hades will not overcome it."

Matthew 16: 18

"You are no longer foreigners and aliens, but fellow citizens with God's people and members of God's household, built on the foundation of the apostles and prophets, with Jesus Christ Himself the chief cornerstone. In him the whole building rises together and rises to become a holy temple in the Lord. And in him you too are being built together to become a dwelling in which God lives by his spirit."

Ephesians 2: 19-22

For those of you who like controversy or a good argument, that can easily be remedied by starting a building campaign in a church. We recently went through such a scenario and I'm thankful to say—we survived. In fact, after surviving this, a group of us came up with an idea to sell t-shirts with the slogan, "I Survived the Building Project" to other churches undergoing building projects. Maybe we could we could make millions to pay off our debt. (Just kidding.)

Going through a building project in a church is a very emotional time for many people because everyone feels like it is their church. If you've ever built a home of your own, you can understand all the decision-making that goes into building a home with one family occupying it. The agreement process that must take place between a husband and wife; choosing cabinets, rugs, linoleum, and colors can create many disagreements. You can only imagine how difficult the task might become when hundreds of people are involved.

For many, this is the church where they; grew up in, got baptized, were confirmed, got married in, sang in the choir, attended youth group, and attended many funerals of loved ones. The thought of moving to a different location brought tears to many peoples eyes. To move would have caused a great feeling of loss for many. Change in a church is very difficult.

The decision was finally made that we would stay in our present location and then we did what all good Methodists do—formed a Building Committee, Transition Committee, and a Fund Raising Committee. We were very fortunate to have had a wonderful minister through this process that had a gift of keeping the peace and letting everyone voice their opinion and yet come together in agreement. The building phase got a little tricky, since Sunday School classes got scattered all over town, meeting in places such as the local funeral home, fire station, the choir loft and vacant houses. It was a true test of all of our patience!

We're happy to say the building is now completed and is beautiful. At the Open House, "Oohs" and "Aahs" were heard all around. (At least for a little while. Then it turned into, "Why didn't they do it this way or that way?"). Another large "Ooh!" was when we got was the large mortgage payment we were left with. However, so far we've met all the payments and things are going well.

After the building was finished and things started settling down, then it was time to continue doing God's work. (It did continue during the process, but slowed down somewhat.) God calls us to go out and serve and help those in need. He didn't place much emphasis during His time on earth on building new buildings. As mentioned in the verse from Ephesians: *"We are members of God's household, built on the foundation of the apostles and prophets, with Jesus Christ himself the cornerstone."* (Ephesians 2:19). He shows us this by the example He gave us. If we could put one word on the cornerstone of the church that would exemplify Christ, what would it be? *Servant*. He came as a servant, not as one who lived in luxury and demanded to be waited on.

What is the definition of a church? Is it the building we worship in or is it the people that come to praise, worship, and serve Christ? Ephesians 2:22 describes it well.

"And in him you too are being built together to become a dwelling in which God lives by his spirit." If the church were destroyed by a hurricane or fire would that be the end of the church? No, the church is the people. We become the church by letting Christ dwell in us.

You may be familiar with the children's song, *"I am the church. You are the church. We are the church together."* Yes, we are the church. Many things are accomplished through "the church." Each of us is a part of the body of Christ. When one of us is hurting, the others hurt with us. When one of us is joyful, the others are joyful with us. When there is a need, different members come together to meet the need. No part is more important than the others. They are equally important.

In 1 Corinthians 1:21-22 we are told: *"The eye cannot say to the hand, 'I don't need you!' and the head cannot say to the feet, 'I don't need you!' On the contrary, those parts of the body that seem to be weaker are indispensable."* Everyone from the minister to the nursery worker to the custodian is of equal value.

Some people don't feel the need to go to a church. They feel they can simply read the Bible at home occasionally, say their prayers when they need something and they are satisfied. Fellowship with other believers is important because we give each other support in times of need. If one part of the body (us) becomes weaker or fails to function, the other parts (other believers) make up for it. For example, if you become blind, your senses of hearing, smell and touch become stronger; if you lose a leg or arm, your other parts become stronger to make up for the loss. Within a fellowship of believers, when we are hurting, others help to pick us up and support us. How sad it is for those who don't become a part of the Body of Christ to know the strength and love gained from it.

The structural building that makes a church is important in that it makes it easier to accomplish our goals and gives us a place to meet. But the real church is the people that make it alive—you and me. What part of the Body are you serving? Whether the eye, hand, foot, nose or finger—it is important that you do your part.

Prayer: *God, help us to realize the real church is within each of us. What we do with our gifts will determine what will become of our "church." Let all churches/people come together to help build up the whole Body so that You can become a beacon to the world. A beacon of hope and love to all.*

Chapter 62
The Tower of Babel: Different Cultures

"Do not abhor an Edomite, for he is your brother. Do not abhor an Egyptian, because you lived as an alien in his country. The third generation of children born to them may enter into the assembly of the Lord."

Deuteronomy 23: 7-8

"Now the whole world had one language and a common speech. As men moved eastward, they found a plain in Shivar and settled there. They said to each other, 'Come let's make bricks and bake them thoroughly.' They used bricks instead of stone and tar for mortar. Then they said, 'Come let us build ourselves a city, with a tower that reaches to the heavens, so that we may make a name for ourselves and not be scattered over the face of the whole earth.'

But the Lord came down to see the tower and the city the men were building. The Lord said, 'If as one people speaking the same language they have begun to do this, then nothing they plan to do will be impossible for them. Come let us go down and confuse their language so they will not understand each other.'

So the Lord scattered them from there over all the earth, and they stopped building the city. That is why it was called Babel—because there the Lord confused the language of the whole world. From there the Lord scattered them over the face of the whole earth."

Genesis 11: 1-9

*****

Can you imagine a world where all speak the same language? Does speaking the same language make you of one mind? In this story of the Tower of Babel, everyone speaking the same language apparently did make the people stronger and of one mind. So much so that it causes them to want to compete with God rather than serve Him.

In the story, God comes down and sees what the people are doing and decides to confuse them because, "nothing they plan to do will be impossible for them."

Have you ever been in a situation where you were the only, or one of few people that didn't speak the same language as everyone else? It makes you feel like you're not very smart and frustrates you because you want to be able to communicate with everyone else. If you know there is someone else in the room that speaks your language you are immediately attracted to each other and you bond with a common thread.

When learning a new language you soon find out that it takes several years of studying and using the language for a purpose to become fluent. People often criticize other people that come to the United States for not learning our language right away. I can tell you from experience that after studying Spanish for several years, when it came to understanding it and speaking it fluently—that was another story. I wonder if those critics have tried to learn a new language themselves?

Several other ladies and myself started a Hispanic ministry at our church to teach Hispanic ladies to speak English. After working with this community of people in other ways, we found that the fathers were learning English at work, the children were learning at school, but the stay at home mothers were not getting the chance to learn. As we are teaching them English, we are also trying to learn Spanish. It helps them feel more comfortable struggling with our language when they can see that we are struggling with theirs also. It helps us both see that it isn't because we aren't smart or because we're inadequate that makes it difficult, but simply because it's so different from what we're familiar with.

When we first began this ministry, I wasn't passionate about it. But as I got to know these wonderful people and could see all the similarities we have and their uniqueness, I soon became very passionate about it. You can help people by giving them money to help pay their bills or fix homes to make them more comfortable, but these are only temporary. If you can teach a person a language, helping them to become productive citizens, you have helped to open doors for them for a lifetime. In addition, you are showing a people from a different country that the United States is a caring country that accepts other people. It is especially important for Christian communities to portray this, showing Christ's love for all.

I'll never forget an elderly mother of one of my students that was here visiting from Mexico. We always started class by doing the "Hokey Pokey" to learn body parts. She didn't understand one word of English, but joined in, joyfully mimicking what we did. It was so touching to see her smiling and laughing as she tried to sing along and do the motions. When class was over and she got in the van to leave, she grabbed both of my hands and looked into my eyes—saying something in Spanish. I didn't understand her words, but it didn't matter because I understood her feelings of thankfulness and pure love.

We sometimes forget that the United States is the melting pot of the world. None of us can claim this country as our own except for the Indians. Those who came here were from all parts of the world. Since the English came first, that became our native language. It's amazing to think that after all these years of so many different nationalities coming to this great nation, that English has still remained the main language. Being of the same language and all having a strong desire for freedom and justice for all has made us the strong country we are today. So powerful and desirable in fact, that many other countries teach their children English at an early age in school.

We need to take caution not to become like the people building the Tower of Babel, to not become proud, thinking we are all-powerful and can survive without God's help. Unfortunately, with power often comes pride and arrogance. We need to continue to reach out to others by being willing to meet them halfway. Try to learn other languages, help new people coming to our country get on their feet, and welcome them with open arms. (I know immigration is a hot topic right now. That's another chapter.)

One year as I was teaching about missions during Bible school, I began the class by giving the children a piece of paper and told them to do exactly as I said. Then I began giving them instructions how to draw a house speaking in Spanish. When they looked at me confused I said, "What's wrong? I'm telling you exactly what to do, now please follow my directions." As I continued, they got very frustrated. At one point a kindergartener said "You're not talking right." It was my goal to help them understand how hard it is for those that don't know our language and are trying to start over in a new and strange society. It is a very scary feeling and makes you feel inferior.

God loves all people and can speak to each of us in a universal language, the language of love. In return, He expects us to share that language with others. Start today by telling your neighbor Te quiero. I love you!

Prayer: *God, help us not to be so comfortable with this beautiful, wonderful country that we ignore the struggles that other people experience in other countries. Thank You for the uniqueness of each country. How much more interesting this world is by having so many different languages and cultures rather than everyone being the same. No matter what language we speak, let us always speak the language of love to those that need it most; strangers from other lands, our neighbor, that difficult person at work, or even a member of our family that is difficult to love. We have all been one of these people at some time in our life and yet You continue to show Your love to us unconditionally. Continue to be with us as we strive to love others the way we want to be loved.*

Chapter 63
I Hope You Dance

"When the men carrying the Ark of the Lord had walked six steps, David sacrificed a bull and a fat calf. Then David danced with all his might before the Lord. He had on a holy linen vest. David and all the Israelites shouted with joy and blew the trumpets as they brought the Ark of the Lord to the city."

2 Samuel 6: 13-15

"You turned my wailing into dancing; you removed my sackcloth and clothed me with joy, that my heart may sing to you and not be silent. O Lord my God, I will give you thanks forever."

Psalm 30: 11-12

"There is a time for everything, a season for every activity under Heaven: a time to mourn and a time to dance."

Ecclesiastes 3: 1,4

"To what can I compare this generation? They are like children sitting in the marketplace and calling out to others: 'We played the flute for you, and you did not dance; we sang a dirge and you did not mourn.'"

Matthew 11: 16-17

*****

There's nothing more precious than to see a very young child bounce or dance in joy to a beat. My children would move their body to music by bouncing up and down before they could talk or walk. For children to do this instinctively at such an early age proves that it must be inborn.

As early as in Exodus and in many verses in Psalms and Ecclesiastes, joy is demonstrated through dancing. David was known for expressing his joy through dance as shown in many verses in Psalms.

Dancing is one of those things that people either love or hate. If you have rhythm and can carry a beat, you probably enjoy it. However, if you trip over your own two feet just walking, dancing is probably not one of your favorite activities. Since I enjoy both exercising and music, I have found the perfect outlet; an exercise group called *Curves*. At *Curves* you exercise on different types of machines that work all the parts of the body. In between the machines you move to padded "recovery stations" to maintain an increased heart rate. During the entire time there is upbeat Christian music playing for you to move along to. You feel as if you are dancing as you exercise to the beat.

When dancing with a partner, you need to be extra talented since one person needs to lead and another needs to follow. If two people try to lead, it just doesn't work since they are not in sync with each other. This could lead to a dancing disaster and some sore toes.

Dancing is a good example of what it's like to be completely in tune with God. If you have a close relationship with Him you can dance a beautiful dance together. As the perfect partner He knows just the right moves. He loves to dip and turn and do the two-step. Sometimes He likes to slow dance and sometimes He likes to speed things up.

Line dancing is a good example of many Christians moving in sync with each other, doing the same dance: Loving God and others. To learn a Line Dance takes practice. First you learn the steps, and then you need to learn to do them smoothly and in step with everyone else.

Having a relationship with Christ requires learning God's Word and practicing it. For some it may come easily and naturally and others may need to work harder at it, as temptations will try to persuade you otherwise. Just as Curves helps keep me physically fit, knowing God's Word and acting on His love keeps me spiritually fit.

David's joy in God was so great, he is portrayed as dancing almost wildly. His love was so exuberant; he didn't feel inhibited by what others thought of him. Think of how you would react to the most exciting news you could imagine: Maybe a loved one coming back to life; winning the lottery; the love of your life proposes to you; you are told you are going to have a baby after years of trying; your cancer is gone; your handicapped child is well again. How would you react? Some may cry with joy, some may jump up and down, some may run around kissing and hugging everyone in sight. . .and some may dance.

When each person turns to Christ, this is the joy He feels. When someone is truly forgiven of sins that he has carried for a lifetime, this is how he feels. When someone has been lost all her life and have felt unloved, and then find Christ, this is how she feels.

Do you feel like learning a new dance today? Let God lead. The steps are easy and the beat is irresistible. As Leann Womack's song says, "I Hope You Dance!" and so does God.

Prayer: *God, the music of Your love is playing. Some hear and want to join the dance while others stand in the crowd, watching, wondering; "What is this dance about?" "Should I join in or will I look foolish?" Those who have joined the dance, wait anxiously for all to join in. In this dance, if you stumble and fall, others are waiting to pick you up and let you start over again until all are in perfect harmony. Let the music begin as we all join the dance today!*

Chapter 64
Peace vs. War

"There's is a time for everything, and a season for every activity under Heaven."

Ecclesiastes 3:1

"A time for war and a time for peace."

Ecclesiastes 3:8

"Though one may be overpowered, two can defend themselves. A cord of three strands is not quickly broken."

Ecclesiastes 4:12

"Is not this the kind of fasting I have chosen: to loose the chains of injustice and untie the cords of the yoke, to set the oppressed free and break every yoke?"

Isaiah 58:6

"When you hear about wars and stories of wars that are coming, don't be afraid. These things must happen before the end comes. Nations will fight against other nations, and kingdoms against other kingdoms. There will be earthquakes in different places, and there will be times when there is no food for people to eat. These things are like the first pains when something new is about to be born."

Mark 13: 7-8

"Peace isn't the absence of war, it's the presence of justice and equality for all humankind."

Martin Luther King, Jr.

The quote above from Martin Luther King Jr. touched me so much that I bought a t-shirt with the quote on it. In a nutshell it describes how I feel about war.

Since I've begun to have a closer walk with God, I've been confused about what our stance as Christians should be concerning war. Peace sounds like such a good word, bringing to mind images of love and happiness. Yet how can you be at peace when there is so much injustice and oppression in the world? You see peace activists marching against war, but they offer no solutions as how to obtain justice. What should our response be when there is a tyrant running a country of mostly very poor people that are killed by the thousands if they don't go along with his way of thinking? All the while he sits in his palace of extreme luxury. Should we just sit back and place sanction upon sanction on them, which in effect only hurts the poor people more? Should we just sit silently by and pray for peace? Should we just take the attitude they will have to take care of it themselves? At what point does God want us to intervene?

In the Old Testament times God used war on many occasions to bring about change and punishment. But after Christ came, it seems that His strategy has changed.

When I decided to write on this subject, I searched the scriptures diligently looking for verses in the New Testament to support or not support war. There are many about turning the other cheek, loving your neighbor and enemy and persevering, but no black and white answers. It might be easier to turn the other cheek when you are the one being mistreated, but when you see thousands of innocent people being persecuted it's more difficult. I wish Jesus had addressed this while He was on this earth. I can't think of any example where He just sat back and watched people be killed or die of starvation.

How can you love your enemy when they are killing people by the thousands? The attacks of September 11th have caused us to reevaluate our thoughts on these issues.

It seems our response should be to help those who are denied justice. However, always nagging in the back of my mind is, "Is it what God would want us to do?" I still don't know the answer. What I do know is that I thank God every day that I was blessed to be born in this great country of ours. It's not perfect, but we have freedom that many people in other countries have never known. We have a voice for and against what we believe in; we don't have to worry about being killed for thinking differently than our leaders; those in the worse circumstances are able to receive food and medical help when in need. Where the government fails, churches pick up the pieces to help.

The only way I have been able to resolve this issue in my mind is to pray for the President and our leaders in hopes that they are asking God for guidance and wisdom to make the right decisions. It is my hope and desire that our efforts in Iraq will in some way be the beginning of bringing about justice and democracy to that part of the world. When you continue to read reports of how the people in that area of the world think so differently than us, it's easy to get discouraged. As we know, "Through God all things are possible."

Let's continue to pray for the people of the many other countries that don't have the freedom that we take for granted. And especially pray for wisdom for the President and leaders that make important decisions daily that affect many people's lives. As President Bush himself has said, the only way we'll know if what we did was right will be by the history books. I pray that we will one day read that our intercession in this war was a good thing and will bring about positive change for that part of the world. But as we have learned, "Let it be Your will Lord, not ours, be done."

Prayer: *God, Satan loves to breed fear, hatred, oppression, and injustice in the world. If You could only put it in our hearts as to how we are to react to these terrible things. We know that Your thoughts are not our thoughts. Many times it's hard to discern what is the right thing to do. Sometimes we need the answers spelled out in black and white Lord. You give us Your Word, but still we don't know. Be with our leaders to help them make wise choices so that our country will be an example to the world of freedom and justice for all with You as our true Leader. Also be with the brave soldiers who are willing to die for our freedom and the freedom of others. Keep them safe and let them feel Your love surrounding them in times of danger and distress.*

Chapter 65
Have You Heard? Spreading the Word

"'Come follow me,' Jesus said, 'and I will make you fishers of men! At once they left their nets and followed him."

Matthew 4: 19

The Great Commission

"Then Jesus came to them and said, 'All authority in Heaven and on earth has been given to me. Therefore go and make disciples of all nations, baptizing them in the name of the Father and of the Son and of the Holy Spirit, and teaching them to obey everything I have commanded you. And surely I am with you always, to the very end of the age.'"

Matthew 28: 16-20

"But thanks be to God, who always leads us in triumphal procession in Christ and through us spreads everywhere the fragrance of the knowledge of him. For we are to God the aroma of Christ among those who are being saved and those who are perishing. To the one we are the smell of death; to the other, the fragrance of life. And who is equal to such a task? Unlike so many, we do not peddle the word of God for profit. On the contrary, in Christ we speak before God with sincerity, like men sent from God."

2 Corinthians 2:14-17

"As they were looking on, (Jesus) was lifted up, and a cloud took him out of their sight."

Acts 1:9

Can you imagine Jesus approaching you as He did Peter and Andrew when they were fishing and telling them to, "Come follow me and I will make you fishers of men?" What was it about Jesus that would attract two rough, tough fishermen to drop everything and to come follow Him immediately? God certainly must have been working on their hearts.

In Corrie Ten Boom's devotional, *Each New Day*, there's a great legend about the angels asking Jesus questions upon His return to Heaven after the "Great Commission" mentioned in Matthew 28.

It's interesting how the author portrays the angels as being bewildered as to how Jesus could have left only twelve men to evangelize the world. Jesus assures them that He is confident that this small handful can get the job done.[17]

Isn't it amazing that Christianity has spread through the whole world through the original 11, later 12 (after Judas was replaced), Disciples? Then later, Paul joins the bandwagon after his experience on the road to Damascus. (Acts 9: 1-31)

Many early Christians went through much persecution and torture because they spread God's Word, and yet the Word still survived. We should be eternally grateful for these Saints. Thank goodness we live in a country where we can pray and worship freely.

Do you think the work is finished, or do we as Christians have a role to play in continuing to spread His Word? There are still many who do not know Christ. They live in other countries, other states, your state, and even in our homes and neighborhoods.

A very interesting lady named Ludmila Bird from Russia came to speak at our church about her life growing up in Russia when Christianity was not allowed and how life is slowly changing there today. I was amazed to hear her say that many Russians have seen the painting of Christ in the manger at His birth and yet many don't even know the story behind it. In how many other parts of the world or even in our own country could this story be true?

In our country it's easy to get so comfortable with our lives that we don't feel a need for God. We get a false sense of security that we can do everything on our own, without God. Those with a false sense of security are the hardest to reach. On the other hand, when you have nothing, it's much easier to let yourself depend on a higher being.

"I'm not a preacher," you may say. "How can I tell others about Christ when I'm still learning myself?" I recall Moses trying to convince God that he couldn't speak well.

"Please send someone else, God!" (Exodus 4:1) And then there's Jonah who didn't want to go to Nineveh to preach to those "heathens." He tried to run away to get out of it and ends up in a whale's belly and then is spit out on the shores of Nineveh. (Jonah 3-4) Sometimes God uses unlikely people; those who aren't of eloquent speech; those who aren't well educated; and those that aren't as "holy" as those trained in the Bible.

You don't have to be a missionary or go to other countries to spread God's Word. You can witness to people you know—by just talking about things that your church is doing; inviting them to church or a fun church sponsored event; comforting them when they are hurting; helping people in times of distress or need. If the time does come and you don't know what to say, let the Holy Spirit say it for you. The good news is that you won't be burned at the stakes or fed to the lions for doing this. Matter of fact it won't even hurt. So what's stopping you?

God's Kingdom has enough room for every single person in the world. Each room can be filled sheep by sheep. Won't you be the shepherd that helps bring others to God's flock? When He's working in you, you'll do things you never thought were possible. If you refuse…watch out for those whales!

Prayer: *God, so many are living a Hell here on earth simply because they don't know You. When we do accept You it doesn't mean we will have a life without pain, but we will know love and know how to give love in return. Help us to get the invitations ready to invite our neighbor, friend, or the stranger that needs a church family, to be a part of Your great house. Let them see You through me.*

Chapter 66
Guilt

"When Aaron has finished making atonement for the Most Holy Place, the Tent of Meeting and the altar, he shall bring forward the live goat. He is to lay both hands on the live goat and confess over it all the wickedness and rebellion of the Israelites-all their sins-and put them on the goat's head. He shall send the goat away into the desert in the care of a man appointed for the task. The goat will carry on itself all their sins to a solitary place; and the man shall release it to the desert."

Leviticus 16:20-22

"My guilt has overwhelmed me like a burden too heavy to bear."

Psalm 38:4

"A man tormented by the guilt of murder will be a fugitive till death; let no one support him."

Proverbs 28:17

"Acquitting the guilty and condemning the innocent—the Lord detests them both."

Proverbs 17:15

"Therefore, I tell you, her many sins have been forgiven-for she loved much. But he who has been forgiven little loves little."

Luke 7:47

(The story of the woman washing Jesus' feet with oil)

As you become familiar with the Bible, you soon come to realize that many phrases used today actually originated from the Bible.

We have often heard of people finding a "scapegoat" to take the blame for a mistake they have made. In Leviticus 16:20-22 we find the origin of that phrase. Aaron is told to "place his hands on the goat's head proclaiming the sins of the Israelites and then release it to the desert. The sins will then be released at a solitary place along with the goat." It seems this was something that God required to help rid His people of their sins. What strange customs they had in Bible days!

Today we still try many means of ridding ourselves of guilt and not actually taking the responsibility for the mistakes we've made. Until you are willing to accept the consequences of your sins and be responsible for your decisions, you will never be able to grow into a responsible and productive adult. Blaming others in our society has become very prevalent. Excuses are made in an effort to make ourselves look like the victim of a barrage of unfortunate circumstances in an effort to get rich quick. Suing has become so prevalent that activities that were once everyday happenings are no longer offered due to fear of being sued. I am very pleased that a large church in our area that has a steep hill that covers several acres, still allows the community to sled ride there. There have been some broken bones but to date no one has sued. This church should be commended for their courage.

Catholics can rid themselves of guilt by going to confession and telling a priest all of their sins. There can be some merit in this from knowing your secret won't be revealed and it actually makes people admit their sins. If this is done in true sincerity it can be of some benefit. Prayers are then offered to excuse them of these sins and then they start with a clean slate until they sin again. Since we are all incapable of not sinning, visits to confessionals or just confessing to God in our prayers is a never ending cycle.

Maybe the Catholics are on the right track by offering a confessional. Many Protestant clergy have people come to them revealing secrets that have been haunting them for years. Something that they have to tell someone they can trust and know it won't be repeated and who can offer some advise as to how to rid themselves of this heavy burden. God's plan, if you are sincere, is to be able to experience forgiveness for our sins, then move on with our lives.

Through a close relationship with Christ, we realize we don't need to go through man to be forgiven. We can go directly to God. This is called blessed assurance. When you have a close relationship with Him you know you are forgiven. This doesn't mean you won't have to suffer consequences because of what you have done, only that you are forgiven and still loved—now you can make a new start in life.

I know a young man in prison who had a rough childhood due to his mother leaving when he was only eighteen months old. His grandparents and father raised him the best they could, but he always felt a void in his life without a mother's nurturing and love. He has done some things that warrant him to be in prison and is in constant denial of wrongs he has committed. It was always somebody else's fault and everybody was out to get him. He's made steady progress during his time in prison: He's gotten his GED, he's learning the plumbing trade, and attends Bible study from time to time. Prison will either make or break him. If he will accept responsibility for what he's done and can find forgiveness toward others and himself, he will do well. He'll be getting out soon and I pray that he will have grown through his experiences there.

Feelings of guilt and remorse are good in that they are needed for forgiveness. It's important to desire forgiveness. Unless we forgive ourselves and feel God's forgiveness, it is difficult to have relationships with others.

Guilt moves people to correct things that may be wrong in their life. Sitting in a comfortable home and seeing homeless people on the streets moves us to help them. Concerns about the environment and the guilt caused by trashing it, moves us to recycle and dispose of waste responsibly.

How's your guilt meter? What are you feeling guilty about? Maybe for not visiting a loved one as often as you should. Maybe for spreading some gossip that will stir up trouble; maybe for not helping the elderly person in your neighborhood that needs your help.

Is it possible that God gave us guilt to make us act on things that need our attention and so that we can come to peace within ourselves. What a perfect plan He had for us all when He created us. He left no stone unturned. Act on your guilt today!

Prayer: *God, once You become a part of our life, the rights and wrongs of the world become more profound and noticeable. Help us to use our guilt to fix something that is wrong in our homes, communities, or workplace today. Help us to not use scapegoats to relieve us of our guilt, but to take responsibility for it ourselves. Thanks for guilt. Without it we wouldn't want to fix what's wrong in our lives. In Your name we pray. Amen*

Chapter 67
Chasing God

"Yet if you devote your heart to him and stretch out your hands to him, if you put away the sin that is in your hand and allow no evil to dwell in your tent, then you will lift up your face without shame; you will stand firm and without fear. You will surely forget your trouble recalling it only as waters gone by. Life will be brighter than noonday and darkness will become like morning. You will be secure, because there is hope."

Job 11: 13-18

"Ask, and God will give to you. Search, and you will find. Knock, and the door will open for you. Yes, everyone who asks will receive. Everyone who searches will find. And everyone who knocks will have the door opened."

Matthew 7: 7-8

"O God, you are my God, earnestly I seek you; my soul thirst for you, my body longs for you, in a dry weary land where there is no water."

Psalm 63: 1

"God is honored for what he keeps secret. Kings are honored for what they can discover. No one can measure the height of the skies or the depth of the earth. So also no one can understand the mind of a king."

Proverbs 25:2-3

*****

Remember playing that favorite childhood game, Hide and Seek? (And to think it didn't even cost anything.) The game begins at an early age. When children are babies, parents play "Peek a Boo" by hiding their face with their hands or a blanket, and then magically appearing and disappearing—much to the delight of the infant.

When they become toddlers, the game gets a little more sophisticated when the adult hides behind a couch or chair and jumps out to surprise them, still to the endless delight of the child.

It becomes the ultimate game once you are one of the "bigger kids" and it's a neighborhood game, best played at dusk. Now as you hide, the goal is to become the master of not being found. The excitement of "It" getting so close that you could touch him, but not finding you is so thrilling it's hard to contain your glee as he walks right past you. Then comes the final victory of hearing "Ollie, Ollie, Oxen Free" as "It" finally gives up. (How they came up with that phrase I'll never know.)

However, if you're "It," you find delight in catching each person, taking pride in each catch, but at the same time experiencing frustration with the ones you can't find. As a seeker, you also have the difficult task of finding them before they make it to home base without you catching them.

God loves to play Hide and Seek too. The only difference in His game is that He wants to be found. Just as we experienced the delight of someone taking the effort to search for us, God takes delight in knowing He is being sought after and is especially joyful when we find Him. Finding Him takes a deliberate effort on our part without giving up. Since there are so many obstacles in the way (Satan), it's not always so easy to find Him.

During my faith journey there have been times when I have gotten close to finding God, experiencing His warmth and peace. Then there have been times when I have felt that I couldn't find Him—that he had left my presence and was no where to be found. When the feeling of His closeness wasn't there, I wondered, "What have I done wrong?" and felt empty inside.

In the book *A Purpose Driven Life*, Rick Warren tells us, "The biggest mistake we make as Christians is seeking an experience rather than seeking God." He tells us that "God wants us to sense His presence, but He's more concerned that you trust Him rather than feel Him."[18] I think the problem is that just getting near Him causes such a great sense of warmth that we think that is what we've been searching for. We don't try to pursue Him any farther because this alone is such a rewarding feeling we think we have reached closeness with Him. God wants us to go the extra yard by continuing to want to know Him even more—to know every detail about Him. To know Him so well that we know what He wants us to do, even when He's not there to show us how.

There are many examples in the Bible where it says that God hides His face. He did it with Job and He did it with David. Warren says that, "The feeling of abandonment from God often has nothing to do with sin. It is a test of faith—one we must all face." He asks, "Will you continue to love, trust, obey, and worship God, even when you have no sense of His presence or visible evidence of His work in your life?"[19]

During times of despair in my life, when I couldn't "feel" God, I would go to my church and pray at the altar, thinking surely I could feel Him again if I went to His house. Going to Him on my knees did give me more of a sense of His presence, and I was able to eventually feel Him again in my daily life. Warren says that beyond feeling Him, we have to trust that He will be there. Even in bad times we need to have faith that in the end, He will not fail us and will do what is best.

In a marriage a husband and wife go through many "dry" times where they can't feel the love from or for their partner. With the busyness we fill our lives with—it's easy to drift apart. However, when we get through these times and begin to feel the closeness again, it's like new love all over again and makes the waiting worthwhile.

Yes, there are times in your life when you will find God, but be prepared for Him to hide from you. Can your faith remain firm? He especially likes the game if you can persevere to the end, you will hear that familiar phrase, "Ollie, Ollie, Oxen Free" when He calls you home.

Prayer: *God, like a child we take delight in every time we see Your face. In our walk with You, help us to grow in confidence that although You can't always be seen—we can trust that You are still there. Help us to know You that well. God, if You must hide, please don't let it be for too long. I look forward to the day when I will see Your beautiful face when I finally do reach "home."*

Chapter 68
No Fear

"David said to Saul, 'Let no one lose heart on account of this Philistine; your servant will go and fight him.' Saul replied, 'You are not able to go out against this Philistine and fight him; you are only a boy, and he has been fighting man from his youth.'"

1 Samuel 17:32-33

"Don't be afraid of people, who can kill the body but cannot kill the soul. The only one you should fear is the one who can destroy the soul and the body in Hell. Two sparrows cost only a penny, but not even one of them can die without you Father's knowing it. God even knows how many hairs are on your head. So don't be afraid. You are worth much more than many sparrows."

Matthew 10:28-31

"Jesus said, 'Come.' And Peter left the boat and walked on the water to Jesus. But when Peter saw the wind and the waves, he became afraid and began to sink. He shouted, 'Lord, save me!' Immediately Jesus reached out his hand and caught Peter, Jesus said, 'Your faith is small. Why did you doubt?'"

Matthew 14:29-31

"The Lord sees the good people and listens to their prayers. But the Lord is against those who do evil. If you are trying hard to do good, no one can really hurt you. But even if you suffer for doing right, you are blessed. 'Don't be afraid of what they fear; do not dread those things.'"

1 Peter 3:12-14

Many of us "Baby Boomers" have gone through the "No Fear" era. No fear of dangerous sports made even more dangerous such as skate boarding, snow boarding, bungee jumping, skydiving, rock climbing, mountain biking or any sport taken to an extreme. When you are young, you think you are invincible.

One of Satan's best weapons is fear. He knows that out of fear we will do things we normally wouldn't do. Out of fear someone might shoot someone. Out of fear different cultures and races will be prejudice toward the other. Out of fear people are afraid to reach out of to other people and find love. Lastly, out of fear a country will follow a leader who is cruel and violent in hopes of saving their lives. However, as usual, God is able to turn this fear around and make people courageous for Him through His Spirit.

There are many Bible stories that tell of God's people defying unbelievable odds with no fear. One story we are all familiar with is that of David and Goliath. One of the most remarkable stories is of David, a young boy who defeats the giant Goliath with a slingshot. Before that is the story of Jonathan, David's friend and Saul's son who defeated a small Philistine army single handedly. Another familiar favorite is the story of Daniel in the lion's den—although hungry, the lions did not harm him since God had shut their mouths. And then in the New Testament you hear numerous stories of people such as John the Baptist, Peter, the disciples, Paul, and many others who, after receiving the Holy Spirit, are unstoppable in spreading the Word, even to death.

What causes people to be so bold for God?—the Holy Spirit. Once you accept Christ and the Holy Spirit enters into you—you ARE unstoppable. You have a sense of "No Fear" regardless of what may happen to you. You often hear stories of great courage even today, where people do heroic acts and don't realize until that moment, what they are capable of.

After the terrorist attack of September 11th, many people found courage they didn't know they had to help save the lives of other people. For example, the great number of firemen that lost their lives that day, and the brave people who overtook the highjackers on the plane over Pennsylvania. These brave people purposely crashed the plane into a field knowing that it was headed for the White House. The list goes on with story after story. For awhile at least, this horrible incident brought the nation together and brought out the best qualities in people in a city that is usually too busy to notice the needs of their neighbor.

A childhood story where I was able to defend my brother at seemingly unlikely odds isn't near as dramatic, but helps me understand obtaining unnatural power in a time of need:

When my brother and I were in 2nd and 3rd grade (he was the older), we temporarily lived in a neighborhood that was considered to be a rough part of town. One day I saw a group of boys circled around my brother trying to beat him up. I immediately picked up a very large branch and ran after them swinging it ferociously. Believe it or not—the whole group ran away in fear. (They were bigger and older.)

All of us, especially when it comes to protecting someone we love, have the ability to have great courage. If you can come to know and love God as much as you love your child or any loved one, the strength you obtain from being full of His Spirit is what some might consider supernatural and God's plans will get accomplished through you.

You hear of missionaries that go into war-torn countries risking their lives, and sometimes losing them, to spread God's message of love. I recently read about Liberia and how unruliness and constant violence has been a part of their lives for 200 years. Could a group of missionaries, or anyone, make a difference in a place such as this?

Have you heard the song "Pass It On?" The chorus goes like this: *"It only takes a spark, to get a fire going. And soon all those around, can warm up in it's glowing. That's how it is with God's love, once you've experienced it. You spread His love, to everyone, you want to pass it on."*

Many a spark has caught a forest on fire. That may be hard for someone to believe who has tried to start a fire before, and has had to work for hours to get it going to a blaze. But it's that initial spark that is so important. (The movie *Castaway* is a good example of this.)

Could you be a spark in a life-threatening environment? You might say no now, but once God starts working in your life, you don't know where He may lead you. And we may even react like Moses, Peter and Jonah who said, "Okay, God, but I don't know how to ..." "I don't like them!" "I don't want to..."—then suddenly the Holy Spirit strikes and there's no stopping you. The Holy Spirit is a powerful force.

How brave are you—really? Are you willing to get that fire going? Who knows what giants, cities, or whales God might have in store for you.

Prayer: *God, Satan would love for us to live our lives in fear not knowing You and afraid to do Your work. He also knows that with Your Spirit we are a force to be reckoned with. That's why he works so hard to keep us from You. Because of Your great love we can overcome him through Your Spirit. Continue to let Your Spirit move in those You have chosen to do Your work. If it is I Lord, let it be me! No fear will overcome me with You by my side.*

Chapter 69
Father, Son, Holy Spirit

"For in Christ the fullness of the Deity lives in bodily form, and you have been given fullness in Christ, who is the head over every power and authority."

2 Colossians 9-10

"May the Lord direct your hearts into God's love and Christ's perseverance."

2 Thessalonians 3: 5

"This is the one who came by water and blood—Jesus Christ. He did not come by water only, but by water and blood. And it is the Spirit who testifies, because the Spirit is the truth. For there are three that testify: the Spirit, the water and the blood; and the three are in agreement."

1 John 5: 6-8

"When the Counselor comes, whom I will send to you from the Father, the Spirit of truth who goes out from the Father, he will testify about me."

John 15:26

"The grace of the Lord Jesus Christ, the love of God, and the fellowship of the Holy Spirit be with you all."

2 Corinthians 13:14

*****

For most people, the Trinity (Father, Son, and Holy Spirit in One) is difficult to understand. In trying to explain this concept to my senior high Sunday school class, I portrayed it by adding an ice cube to a cup of hot water. After adding the ice—steam rose from the cup. The water represented God, the ice Jesus, the steam the Holy Spirit. You need the water to make ice and water needs to be boiled to create steam. All three are reliant on the other to reach their full potential. If you simply had cold water, it would serve many purposes: drinking, washing, and nourishment for plant life. With the formation of ice you add another dimension: coolness for drinks and preservation. When steam is created, you now complete the cycle by having evaporation, accumulation, and then it falls again in a pure form. Each form is as important as the others and dependent on the conditions that surround it.

In human terms, you could think of it as the mind, the body, and the heart. Your mind controls your body, but without a connection (nerves) your body couldn't respond to the command. Then when you heart is involved, you now add love and compassion to these other functions to make them operate for good purposes—at their full potential.

Although the Trinity represents the Father, Son, and Holy Spirit as one, when I pray I may have one particular form of the Trinity in mind for each situation I'm praying about. For example, for praise and thanksgiving, huge problems in the world, and intervention for people in need, I am usually thinking of God in prayer. For situations that I know Christ has shared with us when He become man (suffering, love) I think of Jesus. When I need strength to endure a situation or guidance as to how to react to situations, I think of the Holy Spirit.

Just as God's power reaches it's full potential in the combination of these three, we have the potential of working toward fullness in Christ. You can be a person who survives in the world by just doing what needs to be done to get by. This type doesn't go to any effort to help others or make a difference in the world.

You can then go to a higher level by not just caring for your own needs, but by reaching out to others to help meet their needs as well.

Then, ultimately, if you let the Spirit be your partner and work within you, you can reach your full potential with an unlimited amount of ability to accomplish great things through Christ. At this point you have reached the "fullness of Christ."

When I was a Catholic, I used to make the sign of the cross after each prayer. In doing this you touch your forehead, heart, and each shoulder. I never completely understood the meaning of this as a child until I truly understood the meaning of the Trinity. It also is a reminder that we must be mindful of God in our thoughts, hearts, and actions. All aspects of Him should be present in our everyday lives.

Today I am a Methodist, but, most importantly, a Christian. As Methodists we don't make the sign of the cross, but, more importantly, I have internalized the meaning of the cross.

Are the Father, Son, and Holy Spirit ALL a part of your life? With all three working through you, you will be able to reach your full potential. Don't settle for half commitments or partial Christianity. Reach for the unlimited source of life that can be achieved only through the Trinity.

Prayer: *God, in Your awesomeness You have thought of every possible way of reaching us, loving us, and strengthening us. Let Your power, Jesus' example, and Your Spirit guide us through life so that Your presence will be seen in our thoughts, hearts, and actions.*

Chapter 70
Temptation

"The woman answered the snake, 'We may eat fruit from the trees in the garden. But God told us, 'You must not eat fruit from the tree that is in the middle of the garden. You must not even touch it, or you will die.' But the snake said to the woman, 'You will not die. God knows that if you eat the fruit from that tree, you will learn about good and evil and you will be like God!' The woman saw that the tree was beautiful, that its fruit was good to eat, and that it would make her wise."

Genesis 3:2-6

"Jesus, filled with the Holy Spirit, returned from the Jordan River. The Spirit led Jesus into the desert where the devil tempted Jesus for forty days. Jesus ate nothing during that time, and when those days were ended, he was very hungry. The devil said to Jesus, 'If you are the Son of God, tell this rock to become bread.'"

Luke 4:1-3

"When tempted, no one should say, 'God is tempting me.' For God cannot be tempted by evil, nor does he tempt anyone; but each one is tempted when, by his own evil desire, he is dragged away and enticed. Then, after desire has conceived, it gives birth to sin; and sin when it is full grown, gives birth to death."

James 1:13-15

"No temptation has seized you except what is common to man. And God is faithful; he will not let you be tempted beyond what you can bear. But when you are tempted he will also provide a way out so that you can stand under it."

1 Cor.10:13

God's statement in I Corinthians 10:13 is a simple but powerful one *"No temptation has seized you except what is common to man. And God is faithful; he will not let you be tempted beyond what you can bear."* Why is it that some of us can resist temptation easier than others? And then some of us cave into temptation so easily. Society has made just about anything that you want to do okay. Therefore, the need to know God is very important to give us the strength and knowledge to overcome this.

Is it possible to master temptation? Temptation is a struggle we will deal with all of our lives. Satan is very good at disguising sin and convincing us that something isn't really wrong—just like he did with Eve and the fruit from the tree of "Knowledge of Good and Evil." He tells her that *"God just doesn't want you to eat it because then you'll know as much as He does."* (Genesis 3:5)

We are masters at rationalizing things in our minds to make a sin we are about to commit okay: I need to talk about so and so to get this off my chest; everyone else is doing it so it must be okay; they didn't really need this item anyway so they won't miss it if I take it; so and so hurt me and as they say—an eye for an eye; if I don't cheat on this test, I'll fail the class and my parents will kill me; I need a drink because I had a bad day. I could come up with more but this story may never end.

Gossip is a temptation many of us indulge in that we often convince ourselves that it's acceptable. We may try to justify it by saying we wanted to hear it because we are concerned about the person or want to warn another person about what someone else is saying or doing. Someone may have wronged us so we want to get other people on our side so that they will dislike that person too. Our interpretation of someone's actions may be wrong, so the information we pass on may be wrong. What a sinful people we are! Maybe if we can make somebody else look bad it will make us look better.

Stealing and cheating have become a way of life for many people. The thinking seems to be if something's not locked up or if it's left behind, it's fair game and okay to be taken. Some think the only way to get ahead in this world is by cheating people and not being honest. If others fall for their lies, it's their own stupidity. (Loser)

We are always coveting what others have—a new car, a new house, the cool style of clothes, flat screened televisions and all the newest technological gadgets, other people's husbands and wives and on and on. We never seem to be content.

God understands our temptations. Jesus was tempted for forty days in the desert. God allowed Him to go through this so He could truly understand our temptations and prove to the world that He knows what we're going through. The only way Jesus could withstand these great temptations of Satan was to know scripture so well that He could contradict every offer Satan made to Him by quoting scripture. We will never be able to resist temptation as well as Jesus, but if we try to memorize scripture or at least become very familiar with it, decisions on what is right or wrong are easier. If we are not familiar with the Bible at all, we may not even be aware that we are sinning.

Many people don't want to know God's Word because this way they can claim ignorance. In their mind they aren't bad if they didn't know that it was wrong. Some don't want to know because Godliness has too many restrictions. However, if they only knew that when you do have a relationship with Christ, you'll find you have more freedom than you've ever had before and your life becomes so much easier.

Are there temptations in your life that you feel you just can't get under control? You've tried and failed several times to overcome them? If it is a great temptation, you can't do it alone. Ask for God's help. He's just waiting to hear the words. Don't just ask Him once; ask over and over again until you have mastered the temptation. Know scripture so you know how to counteract it and why it is wrong. Through your lifetime you will cave into many temptations. But know that just like a baby, God will pick you up and let you start over as many times as you need until you can do it alone.

Prayer: *God, we all face sooo many temptations every day. Sometimes we wonder why You didn't just program us with a "no sin" mode, but instead you have given us a free will. Many times, things we see look so good it's hard to see the harm in having it, like the apple. God, You know that Satan is a very convincing fellow. As you have told us, "he is crouching at our door waiting for us." Please be with us to keep us strong enough to resist his crafty temptations.*

Chapter 71
No Crib for a Bed

"In those days Caesar Augustus issued a decree that a census should be taken of the entire Roman world. (This was the first census that took place while Quirinius was governor of Syria.) And everyone went to his own town to register.

"So Joseph also went up from the town of Nazareth in Galilee to Judea, to Bethlehem the town of David, because he belonged to the house and the line of David. He went there to register with Mary, who was pledged to be married to him and was expecting a child. While they were there, the time came for the baby to be born, and she gave birth to her firstborn, a son. She wrapped him in cloths and placed him in a manger, because there was no room for them in the inn."

Luke 2: 1-7

Angels to the Shepherds:

"Today your Savior was born in the town of David. He is Christ, the Lord. This is how you will know him: You will find a baby wrapped in pieces of cloth and lying in a manger."

Luke 2:11-12

"Away in a manger, no crib for a bed. The little Lord Jesus, lay down his sweet head. The stars in the sky look down where he lay. The little Lord Jesus, no crying he makes."

From the song "Away in a Manger"

*****

As a child, when you saw the manger scene with Jesus lying in the manger, the sheep, cattle, shepherds, and the angels and stars—you accepted this as a thing of grandeur, not thinking that this was a lowly environment for a baby to be born in.

Actually, I can remember looking at it in envy, wishing I could have been born in a manger. To this day, I still love barns.

Just think how dull our nativity scenes would be today if He had been born in a house (since they didn't have hospitals back then) or any regular type of environment! I don't think it would make for a very dramatic decoration to place in our homes during Christmas.

What was the significance of Jesus being born in a barn? The same lesson that He tried to get across to us during His lifetime on earth—living humbly with a sense of service and blessed assurance that we will be cared for by our heavenly father. What a different message than what had been taught in that day and continues to be taught today: I'm number one; strive to build up earthly treasures; social status implies power.

No, the message Christ brings with His birth requires us to alter our thinking from a proud, "I can do it myself" attitude to a more humble, "Through God, I can do all things," attitude. We need to have the attitude of service and self-sacrifice where you put other people's needs ahead of your own. You offer only your best at all times.

What a beautiful time of year Christmas can be. Unfortunately it has become so commercialized that unless we put a real effort forth to keep the real meaning and significance as part of it, it's easy to forget why we are celebrating.

It's easy to become so complacent with the comforts of life that we think if we don't have the best of things, we are suffering a hardship. I wonder if Mary and Joseph considered it a hardship to not be able to find an appropriate place to have their child or was their sense of God's presence so strong that they were able to accept their circumstances without fear—knowing that God would take care of their every need.

This is the attitude He wants us to have every day. If things don't happen the way you planned, accept it as God's plan for the way He wants it to be and just go with the flow rather than freaking out.

I have heard many a story where someone was stuck in a traffic jam or broke down causing them to miss a flight or meeting, which ended up saving their life. (Example: Sept. 11th) If we could learn to accept mishaps that happen to us as a gift from God, what a different outlook we would have on life. If we could just step back and look at inconveniences in the scheme of things, we would realize most things we get upset about are really insignificant.

Have you ever used the phrase "Were you born in a barn?" when referring to messes made by children or husbands? If you have, next time think about the one person that really was born in a barn. Realize how truly precious a gift we were given with His birth and how different the world would be without this Savior that had no crib for a bed. Rejoice this Christmas season in the many blessings you have. Know that you are loved unconditionally and understand that you are called to walk humbly with your Lord.

Prayer: *God, forgive us for all the times we have reacted to supposedly bad situations in life with anger and frustration. Give us Your peace to be able to accept even unfortunate circumstances as blessings. If the birth of Your son, born in a barn, can be made into the glorious story You have told, how much more have You planned for our lives? With this in mind, let Christmas happen every day of our lives. Amen*

Chapter 72
Anger/Cursing

"Reckless words pierce like a sword, but the tongue of the wise brings healing."

Proverbs 12:18

"A gentle answer turns away wrath, but a harsh word stirs up anger."

Proverbs 15:1

"But I tell you that anyone who is angry with his brother will be subject to judgment. Again, anyone who says to his brother, 'Raca,' is answerable to the Sanhedrin. But anyone who says, 'You fool!' will be in danger of the fire of Hell."

Matthew 5: 22

Jesus, referring to the Pharisees:

"You snakes! You brood of vipers! How will you escape being condemned to Hell?"

Matthew 23:33

"My dear brothers, take note of this: Everyone should be quick to listen, slow to speak and slow to become angry, for man's anger does not bring about the righteous life that God desires."

James 1: 19-20

*****

I have to confess, on occasion I use curse words. A frequently used one is "damn." I looked "damn" up in the dictionary and it means to condemn to

Hell. Why we get relief from condemning things to Hell and referring to disgusting body functions (the "sh" word) when we're angry, I'll never know.

I come from a family of cursers. My Dad was a sailor, therefore true to his trade, and "cussed like a sailor," and a lot of people I know curse. It's tempting to think that since so many people do it, it's okay. Matter of fact, I set out writing this story to prove that it's not that big of a deal thinking they are only words. But after studying the Bible, I realized that I couldn't justify this position.

The only reference Jesus made related to cursing was the one from Matthew 5:22 that says that we shouldn't even call someone a fool or "we are in danger of the fires of Hell." Does that mean I can't even call people an idiot that cut me off in traffic either? (Geez!) Come on, God—we need to get some relief somehow. Just a mean word muttered silently to our self here and there won't hurt—will it?

When God created us and gave us many emotions, anger was one of them. God himself has been angry on many occasions. The Israelites caused Him to be angry many times because they kept falling away from Him and sinning over and over again. It's amazing that even after seeing the many miracles God performed to free them—they still continued to sin and fall away. No wonder God got angry. There was many times that Moses had to convince God not to destroy them. You don't want to make God mad! Many other references to God's anger have to do with disobedience and sinfulness.

When we "damn" something we are condemning it to Hell. Are we trying to be God when we do this? No matter how loud we say it, it's not going to happen since we aren't God. When I use this word, I'm not consciously trying to, I'm just mad and it has become a habit to handle my anger by using this word.

Some of the things that make people curse is when someone makes them mad, when something they're doing doesn't go right, when something breaks, or if they make mistakes. I guess we're wishing the problem would go to Hell where it belongs. We might tell ourselves, well they're only words, but it's the loss of control and example we're setting that's damaging.

Until recently, I had been a Head Start teacher for four years, and before that a director/teacher at our church operated preschool for twelve years. Head Start is a federally funded preschool program for families that are at or below poverty level. The church operated school charged a monthly tuition fee.

It wasn't unusual for children from both social classes to use curse words when they were upset and, at times, just when they were telling a story. I even had a boy from India who couldn't speak English, but knew how to say the "sh" word very clearly. Another child used the "F" word quite freely throughout the day and didn't even realize it was an inappropriate word. Where did they learn these habits? As parents we need to realize the examples we are setting. Not only for our children, but also for unbelievers who are looking to us as role models. Habits learned as a child are very hard to break, but through God all things are possible.

Cursing amongst teenagers and in much of the music many of them listen to is often very offensive. To hear a parent curse at their child in a store while shopping; using belittling, filthy language, bothers me to the point that I just freeze, wondering what are they treating the child like at home if they are treating them like this in public? Also wondering what kind of person is this now damaged child, going to grow up to be like. I see a clone in making. Cycles are hard to break. If only I had the courage to say something that would make the parent realize what they are doing is causing so much damage. So far, I have not come up with a good solution as to how to react in these situations in a Christian way. If you have any ideas, please write.

Many times I can see God in a child's innocence. When speaking to a child or anyone, people should imagine they are speaking to God himself. If we did this we wouldn't be able to curse.

Stopping ourselves from cursing isn't just a matter of words; it's a matter of attitude. We have to be able to control our anger and thoughts to the point that we don't get so upset over what is usually a trivial event anyway, that way we don't feel the need to curse. This is easier said than done. For me it will be like learning to ride a bike all over again.

Jesus wasn't on earth when cars were here—does He realize how stressful driving can be? He wasn't here when there were computers that crashed and lost hundreds of hours of information that was put into them. He wasn't here for these things, but while He was here, He did prove over and over again that he has the patience of a saint—except for when it came to using the Temple for a den of thieves. He did lose his temper then, but the worst thing he could say in an effort to prove He had the authority to turn over the tables and drive them away with a whip was: *"Destroy this temple, and I will raise it again in three days."* (John 2:19) And He did refer to the Pharisees as a "snakes" and a "brood of vipers" when they were causing unnecessary demands on the people of the day. (Was "snake" the worst word He could think of?)

Fellow cursers, maybe we could try replacing curse words with funny words that would possibly turn a frustrating experience into a funny one. Instead of using a curse word when something breaks we could say, "Jeezy Weezy." Instead of calling someone the "A" (the body part) word when they follow too close or cut you off we could say, "You Snuggle Bum." But best of all, try not to sweat the small stuff and remain calm when you feel the world is ending because of a minor thing that is happening to you. It's going to take a lot of practice and an attitude change, but we can do it. God help us!

Prayer: *God, You know us well and You know sometimes we can REALLY get mad at things that happen to us throughout the day. Help us to control our anger and look at things in perspective of what's really important. In addition to the anger comes the cursing that has become a normal part of our life. You have told us how the tongue is like a rudder of a ship or a spark that starts a fire. Words can be very dangerous and hurtful. Help us to only say words that are pleasing Lord. You "Snuggle Bum!"*

Chapter 73
You Are Blessed

The Beatitudes:

"Now when he saw the crowds, he went up on a mountainside and sat down. His disciples came to him, and he began to teach them, saying:

Blessed are the poor in spirit, for theirs is the kingdom of Heaven.
Blessed are those who mourn, for they will be comforted.
Blessed are the meek, for they will inherit the earth.
Blessed are those who hunger and thirst for righteousness, for they will be filled.
Blessed are the merciful, for they will be shown mercy.
Blessed are the pure in heart, for they will see God.
Blessed are the peacemakers, for they will be called sons of God.
Blessed are those who are persecuted because of righteousness, for theirs is the kingdom of God.
Blessed are you when people insult you, persecute you and falsely say all kinds of evil against you because of me.'"

Matthew 5: 1-11

"In Christ, God has given us every spiritual blessing in the heavenly world. That is, in Christ, he chose us before the world was made so that we would be his holy people-people without blame before him."

Ephesians 1: 1-4

*****

We often hear people using the phrase "I am so blessed" because of circumstances that are happening in their life that are good. Before looking up the definition of "blessed" in the dictionary, I thought of it as meaning very fortunate or lucky.

The real meaning according to Webster's dictionary is, "Bless: *to make happy; to wish happiness; to consecrate.* Blessing: *A prayer imploring happiness upon; piece of good fortune.* I guess I wasn't too far off.

When someone sneezes, we say, "Bless you." I don't know why we wish someone good fortune just because they sneeze. I do remember learning as a child that when you sneeze you lose hundreds of brain cells. If this is true, I guess we're hoping they don't lose too many—especially if they didn't have many in the first place. (Just kidding.)

When someone does something very nice for us, we say (in a very sincere voice) "Bless you" or "May God Bless you." We honestly wish them happiness since they have done something to bring us happiness. Those who have done a great favor for us such as; a doctor who may have saved a loved ones life; a bystander who may have saved your life in an accident; or someone who was there for you in your direst need—to these we wish the greatest blessings.

In reading the Beatitudes, it has taken me many years to completely understand what Jesus meant when he blessed the "poor in spirit." To me this represented someone depressed or down on his or her luck. The more I have studied the Bible, I've come to realize the "poor in spirit" He's referring to is a spirit that realizes its unquenchable desire for God. Billy Graham's book, *The Secret of Happiness* tells how each of us has a body that desires food, drink, sex, and fellowship. But he points out *"we are so much more than a body—we are a living soul. The characteristics of the soul are personality, intelligence, conscience, and memory. The human soul longs for peace, contentment, and happiness. But most of all the soul has an appetite for God."*[20] That is why so many people spend their life trying everything they can do to please their body, but when all things are acquired, there's still a void—an unsettledness that tells them there's something more. Our soul is what makes us who we are. I was convinced of the fact that all living things have a soul when our pet cat died on my lap. The moment he died, he looked me straight in the eyes, let out a loud howl and collapsed. I could literally feel his soul leave his body.

We spend so much of our life feeding, dressing and perfecting our physical bodies and yet spend so little time on our spiritual soul. When we leave this earth our body will be left behind, but it's our soul that will either go on to eternity or to Hell.

For many who have gone through life wondering why they have never felt fulfilled, still empty—often realize on their deathbed—it's God they needed all along. That's why this first ("poor in spirit") and probably the hardest to understand beatitude is so important. If you can get it—the others will fall in place.

"Blessed are those who mourn." When we mourn He will be our strength. We know that this is not the end; there is a better place. Through mourning we are caring about other people, we are learning, stretching and growing in Christ.

"Blessed are the meek" is another one that may give you some trouble as it did for me. Does He mean that we should be shy and withdrawn, afraid to speak our mind? No, the meekness He's referring to can be compared to a wild horse that has been tamed. If the strength of that wild animal can be tamed to obey the command of a master, it is then able to do a great deal of work for a meaningful purpose. "Energy out of control is dangerous; energy under control is powerful."[21] (The Secret of Happiness," pg. 46)

"Blessed are those who hunger and thirst for righteousness." When you have a desire for and are in fellowship with Christ, you have a strong feeling of justice and love for all people. Just because you may have a good life—you are still not happy because there are still injustices done to other people. God creates in you a heart that wants to make all things right.

"Blessed are the merciful" is best expressed in Graham's book where he says, *"Christianity is, first, a coming to Christ—an inflowing of the Living water; second, it is a reaching toward others—an out flowing. It is to be shared in love, mercy and compassion with others."*[22] (pg. 83)

When you have mercy, you care about people. You aren't prejudice toward certain groups and you want to share Christ with them. In leading others to Christ, they must learn the message of the gospel; a message of being loved while we are yet sinners, the importance of being pure, the power of Christ's love. Since we have been shown mercy, we must be merciful toward others.

When we read, "Blessed are the pure in heart" we know this means to have clean thoughts and that we are to avoid sinful things. I think most of us would agree, this is easier said than done. Most of us fight sinful thoughts on a daily basis. This can only be accomplished by letting God take control of our lives; by letting Him into our hearts to help us keep impure thoughts out. You may think, "But they're only thoughts," but it's those thoughts that get out of control and get us into trouble. In the meantime, if we mess up, we need to ask for forgiveness and keep striving to be pure through strength in Christ.

Oh yes, and "Blessed are the peacemakers." Many people think of peace as being a pacifist who marches for peace, love, and happiness. When Jesus refers to peacemakers, He's referring to those who are at peace with God—those who aren't fighting God for control of their life and are following Him in love and service. Lack of peace; when tyrants take control, when people are mistreated, and where justice is not found, is seen where Christ is not known. Remember when He told the disciples? *"My peace I give you; not as the world giveth, give I unto you."* (John 14:27)

Lastly, "Blessed are you when people insult you and persecute you because of me." You may reason, "Well, that's not a problem for us in the United States. This is the land of the free." Since it is the land of the free, sometimes people take that as anything goes. Alcohol, sex, drugs, and cheating to get ahead, are all very acceptable in our society. At times you may be the "nerd" because you don't go along with what others are doing. By not doing wrong, you are making them look bad which causes dislike and ridicule. (Persecution)

Unbelievers are also suspicious of believers, always trying to "catch" them doing something wrong. They accuse your religion of being a game that only hypocrites play. Since Satan is loose in the world, even good things you do may be perceived as wrong. (Even by other fellow Christians) Yes, even in the land of the free we are still persecuted.

Wow, look at all these blessings we've been given! Notice this doesn't include the many material things we have. What a loving God we have that gives us such an abundance of blessings! Count your blessings each day and thank God for them.

Prayer: *God You have blessed us in so many ways. Thank You especially for the blessings You've given the down trodden and weary. In blessing us in these ways—You give us hope for a better future and a life spent with You without pain and loneliness. Continue to pour Your blessings on those that need them most, Lord.*

Chapter 74
Patches

"In the beginning you made the earth, and your hands made the skies. They will be destroyed, but you will remain. They will all wear out like clothes. And, like clothes, you will change them and throw them away."

Psalm 102:25-26

"Beware of the teachers of the law. They like to walk around wearing fancy clothes, and they love for people to greet them with respect in the marketplaces. They love to have the most important seats in the synagogues and at feasts. But they cheat widows and steal their houses and then try to make themselves look good by saying long prayers."

Luke 20:46-47

"It is not fancy hair, gold jewelry, or fine clothes that should make you beautiful. No, your beauty should come from within you—the beauty of a gentle and quiet spirit that will never be destroyed and is very precious to God."

1 Peter 3: 3-4

"Take nothing for your trip except a walking stick. Take no bread, no bag, and no money in your pockets. Wear sandals, but take only the clothes you are wearing."

Mark 6: 9

"Show mercy to some people who have doubts. Take others out of the fire, and save them. Show mercy mixed with fear to others, hating even their clothes which are dirty from sin."

Jude 23

Patches
Based on a true story

Patches was a little boy that lived in a small town. His family had little money and barely made enough to put food on the table. Most of their bills were usually behind in getting paid and his clothes weren't as nice as most of the other children's in the neighborhood.

In the small town that Patches lived there was a church that was in the center of town. Patches would see many people come and go in this church, including other children his age. It looked like a fun place to be and he finally got up the courage to go one Sunday by himself since his parents weren't church-going people. It was pretty scary going to a place that he wasn't familiar with and meeting new people, but he knew since it was a church it had to be a friendly place to go.

He felt a little more comfortable when he saw a friend from school who was in his grade so he knew where to go for Sunday school class. What a relief! When he walked into the class he met the teacher who greeted him friendly, but looked a little uncomfortable. He learned a story about Jesus and how loving and wonderful He is. He had heard about Jesus before, but had never heard Bible stories or studied about Him. As he was leaving the class, the teacher asked Patches to stay for a few minutes. She then told him that when you come to church you should wear your best clothes and asked Patches not to wear his worn out jeans with patches on them the next time. Did she not realize that these were his best clothes? Patches was very sad because he then realized he wasn't good enough to come to church. *Church must only be for rich people that have nice clothes,* he thought.

This story took place about forty years ago. It could have been any church. Many people have been raised to think as this Sunday school teacher did.

Patches is now an adult. He and his grown children are clients of the food pantry that operates in the basement of our church. His family has grown up not knowing the Jesus he heard about that day in Sunday school. I can't help but wonder if his life would have been different if that Sunday school teacher would have embraced him and accepted him as he was that day. What possibilities could have laid ahead for him if he had known a loving God?

In the past I was also of the mind that to come to church you had to wear your best clothes. In fact, it became almost as if it were a fashion show. Who had the nicest clothes or the latest fashion? What had started out many years ago as a tradition out of respect for God somehow turned into, are you worthy of coming to church if you have a nice enough outfit. I now know that God is more interested in our hearts, not our clothes. You can wear the nicest outfit in the world, but if your heart is not right with God, He is not impressed with you "respect" offered in a good outfit. Most churches have come a long way in the past forty years. I truly think the "Patches" of the world would be accepted in most churches today. The contemporary services that many churches offer have helped to change these attitudes.

So if you see someone at your church dressed casually, please don't judge him or her as not having respect for God. In fact, maybe if you come dressed more casual it will make the "Patches" feel less threatened and accepted. Nothing we wear makes us acceptable to God. It's what's in our hearts that is the pleasing sacrifice He desires. Let yours be pleasing to Him. Love your neighbor, regardless of their race, color, clothes, or financial status. In so doing, you are loving God Himself.

Prayer: *God forgive us when we have judged people by their appearances. You have taught us many times it's not what people look like, but what is in their hearts that is important. The "appearance" You desire is one that reveals a gentle and humble heart. Please help us to resist when Satan tells us otherwise.*

Chapter 75
The Light of the World

"The people walking in darkness have seen a great light; on those living in the land of the shadow of death a light has dawned. You have enlarged the nation and increased their joy."

Isaiah 9:2-3

"You are the light of the world. A city on a hill cannot be hidden. Neither do people light a lamp and put it under a bowl. Instead, they put it on its stand, and it gives light to everyone in the house. In the same way, let your light shine before men, that they may see your good deeds and praise your father in Heaven."

Matthew 5:14-16

"For you were once in darkness, but now you are light in the Lord. Live as children of light (for the fruit of the light consist in all goodness, righteousness and truth) and find out what pleases the Lord. Have nothing to do with fruitless deeds of darkness, but rather expose them. For it is shameful even to mention what the disobedient do in secret. But everything exposed by light becomes visible, for it is light that makes everything visible. This is why it is said, 'Wake up, O sleeper, rise from the dead, and Christ will shine on you.'"

Ephesians 5:8-14

*****

Have you ever noticed light shining through a window, particularly in the morning? As the ray of light beams through the house, every particle of dust in the air becomes very visible. (As well as what's on your furniture and floor.)

You can't help but think, "Wow, that means I must be inhaling all this dust." It almost seems as if the ray of light is making the dust, but in actuality it is simply making it visible to the naked eye.

This is one of those situations where you would rather not be able to see so clearly. Sometimes knowing too much can make you crazy. Such as in knowing there are so many germs everywhere and that even if you clean constantly—your house can never be free of all germs and dust.

Many places in the Bible refer to Christ as the "light of the world," then goes on to encourage us to be likewise. As with the light that shines in your house—exposing things you would rather not see; when you are the light of the world, your sins are completely exposed and you can only live in truth and goodness. There is no darkness or place to hide what we don't want others to know about. We become a beacon to others about righteous living.

God is described as a light so brilliant we have never seen one such as His. Those who have faced near death experiences, including my mother, have had the opportunity to see this light before they came back to this world. The light is usually seen as if they are at the end of a tunnel. The person is going toward it, looking forward to getting there, when suddenly they come back to human awareness. They are left with a sense of disappointment due to not reaching the light and not wanting to return to this world.

Nobody really understands this phenomenon, but it could be that God realized these people had some unfinished work in this world as they were headed toward Heaven. I know in my mother's case, she ended up helping to raise my brother's three small children. Without her it's hard to tell what their fate may have been.

In a very thought provoking book called *The Secret Place* by Dale A. Fife, the author claims to have had a spiritual experience similar to John's described in Revelations. At the beginning of his journey, he is taken up above the world (the third world), being able to look down on earth. He sees clusters of light dispersed at different places all over the earth. These lights represent God sending a multitude of white horses to descend on the earth to seemingly destroy it. But God holds them back and tells the angels to tell the church to wake up and pray.[23]

Another portrayal of light in the book is when the author meets Jesus face to face. His eyes are a piercing light that sees through the soul and makes you aware of your every sin. This is because He is so holy we aren't worthy of being in His presence until we acknowledge our sin and are repentant of every wrongdoing we have ever committed.[24]

Have you ever been in a completely dark place such as a cave? It is a very scary feeling. I can only imagine what it would be like to be blind. In a situation such as this, you realize the importance of light. Even the smallest flicker brings feelings of great joy.

One of the first things God did when He created the world was to create light as described in Genesis 1:2-5: *"Now the earth was formless and empty, darkness was over the surface of the deep, and the Spirit of God was hovering over the waters. And God said, 'Let there be light,' and there was light. God saw that the light was good, and he separated the light from darkness. God called the light 'day,' and the darkness he called 'night.'"*

In Alaska and other places in the northern hemisphere, they have light during some parts of the year for twenty-four hours a day. Can you imagine a day without darkness? Most of us would have difficulty sleeping. Darkness seems to connote a time to rest and helps us let go of the needs of the world for a while. It is also a time when many crimes are committed—with criminals taking the attitude—"If I can't be seen and I'm not caught; then it's okay."

When God talks about us living in the light, He wants our actions to be those that are worthy of being exposed to the light at all times—with nothing to hide or be ashamed of. We have all heard that favorite childhood song, "This Little Light of Mine, I'm Going to Let it Shine." How is your light shining today? Is it a spark, a flicker, a flame or a raging fire? Can others see your light or do you hide it under a bushel basket? Let your light shine so the world can see God's radiance reflected from you!

Prayer: *God, we are told to not look directly at the sun because its light will blind us. We know Your light makes the sun seem like a flicker. A light so brilliant that once we've seen It, we have new eyes and a new heart. Purify us with Your light so that others will see You shining within us. Yes Lord, I will let "this little light of mine" shine!"*

Chapter 76
Extravagance

"Do not be overawed when a man grows rich, when the splendor of his house increases; for he will take nothing with him when he dies, his splendor will not descend with him."

Psalms 49: 16-17

"Jesus sat down opposite the place where the offerings were put and watched the crowd putting their money into the temple treasury. Many rich people threw in large amounts. But a poor widow came and put in two very small copper coins, worth only a fraction of a penny.

Calling his disciples to him, Jesus said, 'I tell you the truth; this poor widow has put more into the treasury than all the others. They gave out of their wealth; but she out of her poverty, put in everything, all she had to live on.'"

Mark 12:41-44

"Jesus answered, 'If you want to be perfect, go, sell your possessions and give to the poor, and you will have treasure in Heaven. Then come, follow me.' When the young man heard this he went away sad because he had great wealth.

Then Jesus said to his disciples, 'I tell you the truth; it is hard for a rich man to enter the kingdom of Heaven. It is easier for a camel to go through the eye of a needle than for a rich man to enter the Kingdom of God.'"

Matthew 19:21-24

*****

Since I am a big country music fan, a trip my husband and I took to Nashville was very exciting for me. It was even more exciting because we were fortunate to stay at the Opryland Hotel. My husband was speaking at a conference there, so his employer paid for our room.

The lavishness of the hotel was something I had never experienced. You enter into a man-made tropical paradise with palm trees, beautiful plants, a man-made river with numerous waterfalls and fountains. This was all under a ten-acre atrium with shops and clubs to browse and relax in. I must admit it was nice to pretend like we were rich for a couple of days. One thing I didn't like was that the air conditioning was so cold that I had to go buy some long sleeve shirts and wore long pants most of the trip. (It was August)

Before doing my devotions one morning while we were there, I was drawn to an article in July's *Readers Digest* (2003) about Saudi Arabia. I was saddened to read that they seemingly are a corrupt nation. The scary part is how much we rely on them and they on us. We buy oil and provide them with security, while they buy weapons, construction services, communication systems and drilling rigs from us. In addition they keep as much as a trillion dollars in U.S. banks and stock markets. They also provide the world with surplus oil production that helps stabilize the international oil market. If that surplus is taken out of play or any of the other areas that we support are dramatically affected, it could lead to a global economy collapse. I'm not a political person, but this scares me. I would not want to be a politician because I know there is much more involved in decision making that we don't even know about. These decisions, right or wrong, affect the whole country and world. It seems that if you always did the honest thing, it might cause world chaos.

As I was freezing in the excessive air conditioning, I wondered, why do Americans have to go overboard with these excesses? Turning the air conditioning back at least five or ten degrees and not buying gas-guzzling cars could make a big difference in our need for energy and oil.

Another wasteful situation I noticed was how most restaurants give you much more food than you can possibly eat. Seeing the large amounts of food that was thrown away gave me images of hungry people that needed the excess food.

Although it was nice to pamper ourselves for a couple of days, I can see the danger of being rich and how easy it would be to fall into the world it creates. It becomes easier to forget about the poor and those in need when you are so comfortable. Like Jesus said, *"It is easier for a camel to go through the eye of a needle then for a rich man to enter the Kingdom of God."*

I have seen both sides. I visit an elderly friend in Kentucky every year that I became close friends with during a mission trip. We were able to build her a bathroom and give her indoor plumbing, which she had never had before. She has experienced more heartache than most of us will ever know. She lives in a "holler" with a running water creek as her driveway. You need a four-wheel drive vehicle or a truck to get to her house. When I visit, I always make sure I'll be there on a Sunday so I can take her to church, which she dearly loves, but very rarely gets to attend. She often goes for months without leaving her house since she has no means of transportation except family and friends.

One of the times when we went to her church, she searched her purse fervently for many minutes for money to put into the offering. This was difficult since she shakes uncontrollably. She got out all the change she could find and put it into the offering plate. This act touched me to tears. How closely it resembled the story of the widow that gave all she had.

This little old lady is one of the most spiritual people I know. It seems that people who have been through severe hardship are in many cases more spiritual. I feel close to God when I'm with her. Even though she doesn't have the luxuries many of us have, she is very satisfied with what she does have and is content with her life.

We all need to strive to be content with what we have. If we do have more than we need, we should share with those who don't. God also calls us to tithe a tenth of what we have to Him and His work. Even though it seems impossible, see if you can fit through the eye of that needle. You'll find that you get smaller the more you give to those in need.

Prayer: *God, help us to remember to store up treasures of Heaven and not of this world. Thank You for the food I will eat today, for a warm and safe home, a healthy family, and the money to pay our bills. Be with the rich to help them know they can play an important role in helping the needy in creative ways to make them productive citizens.*

Chapter 77
He Will Provide

"The Lord said to Moses, 'I have heard the grumbling of the Israelites. Tell them at twilight you will eat meat, and in the morning you will be filled with bread. Then you will know that I am the Lord your God.'

"That evening quail came and covered the camp, and in the morning there was a layer of dew around the camp. When the dew was gone, thin flakes like frost on the ground appeared on the desert floor."

Exodus 16:11-15

"And I will do whatever you ask in my name, so that the Son may bring glory to the Father. You may ask me for anything in my name, and I will do it."

John 14:13-14

"Look at the birds of the air; they do no sow or reap or store away in barns and yet your heavenly Father feeds them. Are you not much more valuable than they? Who of you by worrying can add a single hour to his life? And why do you worry about clothes? See how the lilies of the field grow. They do not labor or spin. Yet I tell you that not even Solomon in all his splendor was dressed like one of these. If that is how God clothes the grass of the field, which is here today and tomorrow is thrown into the fire, will he not much more clothe you, O you of little faith?"

Matthew 5:26-30

*****

As children, and then as we grow, we try to predict what our future will hold and what our place in life will be: What will be my occupation? Who will I marry? How many children will I have? Everyone's wish is to have a high paying job that they enjoy, marry their soul mate, and have children. (The amount depends on each person) Very few hit the mark in all these areas. In actuality, we're lucky to hit one. You may obtain one of these areas and then strive for the others throughout your life.

I married the man I thought was the man of my dreams. It has ended well, but we have traveled many rocky roads during our thirty some years of marriage.

We started our marriage with him making $6000 a year our first two years while he served in the Air Force and I worked odd jobs and finished college. (We got married during my junior year in college) Since we both love children and had already been dating for four years, we were anxious to start a family right away. First priority was for me to finish college, which I couldn't do until we got stationed at Davis-Monthan Air Force Base in Tucson, Arizona. Both plans became a reality when I graduated—five months pregnant with our daughter Cassie. Besides, we had to take advantage of having a free baby while in the Air Force.

This new member of our family brought us so much joy we couldn't wait to have more children. We originally wanted to have six. We achieved three in three and one-half years and after the third, we said in exhaustion, "That's enough!"

As far as homes and material things go, until recently, we haven't had real nice "stuff," but have always had a decent place to live and food to eat. Through the years Tim worked his way up to higher paying jobs and I was eventually able to use my teaching degree to start a preschool at my church once the children got old enough. Together we were able to meet the many expensive demands of raising three children and putting them through college.

We went through that very busy time in life with all three children involved in sports and many other kinds of functions, which can best be described as the "whirlwind years." We still keep very busy, but the stress level is less with no small children around. We are learning to get to know each other again as husband and wife rather than mom and dad of three children. What a good time in life this is!

Our story is one of starting out as what many would consider poor and then working our way up. Many couples today wait to do all the things we did at an early age until they have already obtained good financial status, a good home, nice cars, and the rest of the American dream first. This way they will be able to give their children everything they need.

Looking back, I have no regrets. Although we didn't have the best of things, we had a good life and a lot of love for each other. In fact, I think the first two children learned more life lessons than our last from not having as many material things. (We were making more money by the time he came along.) They remember stretching out one order of fries and one drink at McDonald's between three children (which was a real treat), they remember wearing almost all hand-me-downs, hand-made outfits, and yard sale clothes; they remember not going on vacations for several years because it was too difficult and expensive with three small children. Yes, we went through many tight times in our life, but looking back, I know God was there with us all along. Many times when I wondered how we would pay a bill or be able to afford something that we needed, little things have happened to make it possible. Like the time I went to visit my friend in Kentucky. I felt a strong need to go, but knew our money was tight at the time. (I had to rent a truck to get to her house) I went anyway thinking, "It will work out, I just have to go." As it turned out the rental company only charged me for one day's rent rather than for three. It would have been very tempting to let this slide, but my conscience wouldn't let it, so I called the rental company to bring it to their attention. They acknowledged the mistake and said, "Don't worry about it" and didn't charge me for the other two days.

Other things happened like when we needed to replace a very worn carpet before we sold our house. It turned out that there was a beautiful hardwood floor underneath so we didn't need to replace it. Other times money just showed up when I needed it most from forgotten sources. I especially began to see these things happen when I wasn't working but doing lots of volunteer work. I feel God was giving me these blessings as to say, "It's okay, keep doing my work instead."

As He provided for the Israelites in the desert for forty years, God will continue to provide for us, His chosen people. What makes you a chosen people? The chosen are those who respond to His call and come to Him in thanksgiving and praise.

What are you lacking today? Is it really a need or a convenience? Can you go on with your life in confidence that you will be cared for? Can you imagine completely depending on God for forty years for your every meal? Can you trust Him that much to provide for you? We like to think that we are responsible for what we have achieved and the things we have obtained. Yes, you worked for that food on the table, but God provided the means for it to grow. Yes, you work hard to provide for your family, but God gave you your healthy body in order to accomplish this. Yes, your creativity and determination has made you successful, but God gave you your mind and unique personality in order to be able to do what you do. Don't forget that, *"Freely you have received, freely give"* (Matthew 10: 8). Don't forget where your blessings have come from and in so doing don't forget to share them with others. Yes, God will provide!

Prayer: *God, thank You for; the earth, the rain, the seeds, the sun, our bodies, our minds, love, and Your Son. Help us to have enough faith in You that we know we will be cared for. We know You will provide for our every need. If You provide for the lilies of the field and the birds in the sky, You will surely provide for us. Just like the parent that gives their child much, You bestow unlimited blessings on us each day and fill our every need. Thank You for loving us so much!*

Chapter 78
Sin and Forgiveness

"Sin came into the world because of what one man did, and with sin came death. This is why everyone must die—because everyone sinned. Sin was in the world before the law of Moses, but sin is not counted against us as breaking a command when there is no law. But from the time of Adam to the time of Moses, everyone had to die, even those who had not sinned by breaking a command, as Adam had."

Romans 5: 12-14

"The law came to make sin worse. But when sin grew worse, God's grace increased. Sin once used death to rule us, but God gave people more of his grace so that grace could rule by making people right with him. And this brings life forever through Jesus Christ our Lord."

Roman 5:20-21

"Create in me a pure heart, O God, and renew a steadfast spirit within me. Do not cast me from your presence or take your Holy Spirit from me. Restore to me the joy of your salvation and grant me a willing spirit to sustain me."

Psalm 51: 10-12

"Now this was the sin of your sister Sodom: She and her daughters were arrogant, overfed and unconcerned; they did not help the poor and needy. They were haughty and did detestable things before me."

Ezekiel 16:49-50

Have you ever been chosen last for a sport or anything? Have you ever felt alone in a crowded room? Have you ever been left out by not being invited to a special occasion? Most of us have experienced these feelings at one time or another and we all have to agree—it hurts.

People's desire for love and acceptance can be as strong as the need for food and water. The only difference is that food and water feed the physical body, while love and acceptance feed the soul. You may know people who have had a terrible experience that affects them mentally, but in time if the situation isn't remedied or they don't come at peace with it, it begins to affect them physically as well.

Sin can affect us like this. A good mental picture of sin for me is a large group of people standing in a circle holding hands. When we sin, we are on the outside of the circle wanting to join in so badly it hurts. We feel like outcasts, rejected and uneasy inside. When we admit our sin and sincerely ask for forgiveness, we are asked to join in again and there is great celebration and dancing.

Recognizing your sin is the first step. I often think of people that were raised in a bad family situation where right and wrong were not taught. Is there hope for people such as these when they may not even recognize sin? Yes, because of God's grace and since He will use every means possible to lead the lost to Him, there is hope. You may wonder, "How could I help someone such a these?" Simply let the Spirit lead you. It may be by being an example of right living, possibly by being there to show love in a time of need, or by inviting someone to church or a church function.

Many non-believers have the misconception that people who go to church are already "holy." We prove daily that this assumption is wrong. We go because we are sinners and need to be reminded constantly of how to lead a Christ-like life. Romans 3: 23 tells us *"we are all sinners and fall short of the glory of God."*

There is a verse in a Brooks and Dunn song titled, "The Red Dirt Road" that is a good description of our struggle to get to Heaven. The verse says (describing the red dirt road, or our path to Heaven): "Where I drank my first beer, where I found Jesus. I found that the path to Heaven is filled with sinners and believers." I don't know one person that is without sin. Most of us sin every day. It may be a small infraction that we may not even be aware of; possibly by ignoring a need because it's too inconvenient to deal with at the time, or by hurting someone with an unkind word. Thank goodness God gives us many chances and blesses us with His grace.

Although we can't come near to being God, we need to strive to lead a Christ-like life. What would that consist of? Love and forgiveness. You cannot become whole until you are truly able to forgive. It may be a terrible injustice that was done to you or even abuse from someone you loved. Until you are able to forgive, you become the prisoner of this offense. This doesn't mean that the person that caused the offense shouldn't suffer the consequences for their action or that you should allow yourself to continue to be in the situation. Just that you are able to forgive and go on with you life.

Is there a sin that you are struggling with? Stop it now and ask for forgiveness. Don't feel like you can do it alone? Ask God to help you. Do you feel like it's too great of a sin to be forgiven? If you truly repent and are sincere, God is willing to forgive you ANYTHING and is waiting for you to start a new life with Him. He often chooses those that have been forgiven the most to do much of His work. Who knows what He may have in store for you.

Prayer: *Precious Lord, there are so many temptations and deceptions in the world. Help us to become strong through You so that we may recognize our sin, be able to ask for forgiveness, and be able to give forgiveness to those who have wronged us. As scripture says, "For if you forgive men when they sin against you, your heavenly Father will also forgive you." (Matthew 6:14) Yes God, "create in us a clean heart and renew a steadfast spirit within me."* (Psalm 51:10)

Chapter 79
I Love You This Much

"For God so loved the world that He gave His only son, that whoever believes in him shall not perish but have eternal life."

John 3:16

"Listen! I am coming soon! I will bring my reward with me, and I will repay each of you for what you have done. I am the Alpha and the Omega, the First and the Last, the Beginning and the End."

Revelation 22:12-13

"Jesus, the One who says these things are true, says, 'Yes, I am coming soon.' Amen. Come, Lord Jesus! The grace of the Lord Jesus be with all. Amen." (This is the last sentence in the Bible)

Revelation 22:20-21

*****

You may have noticed that for the final verses I've only chosen John 3:16 and the last few verses in the Bible. John 3:16 is so powerful it can stand on its own. It's the core of the entire Christian Bible. It's what the good news is all about. If we were a wise people, it would be the only verse we would need to know.

One way this verse has been portrayed that has touched my heart deeply is through the song "I Love You This Much" by Jimmy Wayne. What a powerful song! The first time I heard it was the first time he ever sang at the Grand Ole Opry. I was fortunate enough to have been there for this special event.

If you're not familiar with the song, it sums up God's love for us in a way that touches your soul. The video shown on GAC and CMT portrays it well:

It's about a young boy whose father is very hardhearted. When the mother and father get into an argument, the father ends up leaving. While he's leaving, the boy is quietly telling the father *"I love you this much"* as he stretches out his arms toward him, then asks, *"Do you love me too?"*

Years later, when the boy is an adult, the father dies—still not having had a relationship with the son. At the funeral, the grown son describes how he had always wanted his father's love. As he looks up from the casket, he sees the cross with Jesus hanging from it. Suddenly he realizes—he hadn't been alone and unloved all this time. In fact, God loved him so much that He let His only Son die for him. He notices that Jesus, like him, also has His arms outstretched as if to say, *"I love you this much, do you love me too?"*

That's exactly what Jesus is saying to all of us. It seems like such a simple thing, but most of us need to be hit over the head with a sledgehammer to realize how great His love for us truly is. Since the Father and Son are one, they both carried our sins and died for us. No more offering sacrifices to show our devotion, no more strict laws to follow to prove our loyalty. All He's ever wanted is a relationship with you—for you to acknowledge and love Him too. When you share this mutual love, laws are no longer needed because the love that pours out from Him to you is so great nothing bad can come from you. And now He's gone to Heaven to prepare a place for you and me so we can be with Him in eternity forever. No more suffering. No more loneliness. No more temptation.

How sad for those that go through life miserable and feeling unloved when the greatest love of all was right in front of them the whole time. Just waiting for them to acknowledge and accept it.

Have you accepted the love of Christ yet? Don't wait any longer! Let Him guide you on the path He has chosen for you. It leads to a place everlasting that is filled with love and mercy. There is NO sin so great that He won't forgive. Accept Him now—and accept love once and for all into your heart.

The beginning...

Make this prayer your own!

Study Guide/Self-Reflection

Chapter 1
The Promise
- Discuss promises you have made during your life. Have you always kept your promises?
- What are the consequences of not keeping your promises? Likewise, what is the result when you are known to always keep your promises?
- Have you ever regretted a promise you have made?
- Have you made any promises to God?
- What promises has God made to you?
- Have you ever broken a promise to God? Has God ever broken a promise to you?
- What the difference between a promise and a vow or is there any?

Chapter 2
Make Them Love You
- Have you ever tried to make someone love you? If yes, describe the tactics you used. Did they work?
- If there has been more than one person that you've tried to win over, did you use the same tactics with each or did you try different ones? How did you choose your tactics with each person?
- Have you ever felt God trying to win you over?
- What kind of tactics does God use to win our love?
- Do you feel unconditionally loved by God?
- Who are the people you love unconditionally? Is God included on this list?

Chapter 3
Sharing Joy
- What causes you the most joy, things you can buy or natural occurrences?
- Describe something you have purchased that has brought you joy.

- Describe a natural event that has brought you joy. Which was more meaningful?
- Have you ever experienced a joyous event alone? What do you want to do with joy once you've experienced it?
- How do you react when someone else is joyous? Are you happy for them or jealous?
- Do people tend to lose joy as they grow older?
- What makes God joyful?

Chapter 4
God's Voice
- Have you ever heard God's voice? If so, what did it sound like? If not, what do you think it would sound like?
- In what ways does God speak to us?
- Has God ever spoken to you before, during, or after you've done something wrong? Discuss how things would be different if He always did speak to people when they were doing wrong.
- Which voice would you best respond to? A soft whisper or one that was loud and thunderous?
- Do you think God only talks to you once you've reached a certain degree of holiness?
- Can you think of Bible stories where God has spoken to unlikely people? Did these people recognize His voice right away?
- There was a period of time in the Bible when God did not talk to anybody except for these people. (Clue: following Song of Soloman) Who were they and what were some of their names?

Chapter 5
Love Ya, No I Don't
- Have you ever said something that you regretted later? If so, did you realize your mistake immediately or later?
- When you say something you regret, can you take it back or fix it?
- Do you deliberately say mean things to hurt people? Have you ever accidentally said something to hurt someone?
- Are you able to forgive people for mean statements made to you or about you?
- Which is worse, to say something mean to someone's face or to say it behind their back?

- Can you think of anyone who never puts anyone down and only has good things to say about others?
- Which hurts worse, words or physical pain caused by another person?

Chapter 6
Let's Make a Deal
- Do you think God can be reasoned with?
- Would you have been able to remain as loyal to God as Job did when all the terrible things happened to him?
- Can you think of an incident where something good came out of a bad or tragic event?
- Have you ever made a deal with God? (Ex. If You do this, I'll do that) Explain.
- Has a bad experience ever happened to you and then you were able to look back years later and see where it actually helped you in some way?
- Do you think God has a plan for the way our lives should be? What would His plan for you be?
- What happens when you don't go along with God's plan?

Chapter 7
Does God Have a Sense of Humor?
- Who do you feel comfortable being goofy or silly around? Why?
- Why don't you feel you can be goofy or silly around just anyone?
- What makes you laugh?
- Why is humor important?
- Do you think God thinks humor is important? What are all the emotions He has given us?
- When is humor not appropriate?
- Name someone who makes you laugh and is fun to be around. Think of someone who doesn't laugh enough and say a prayer for them.

Chapter 8
Many Religions, Many Rooms
- How do you think God feels about all the different religions there are?
- Do you think God favors any one religion over another?
- If there were a litmus test for true religion, what would it be? (the basic ingredient)
- How would the world be different if we all had the same religion?

- If you have children, do you have a preference for them to marry someone with the same religion as your child? How would you feel if they were to marry someone from an extreme religion?
- Do you think there are different religions in Heaven?
- Is there hope for those religions that don't believe in Christ to go to Heaven?

Chapter 9
Sacrifices
- What was the purpose of sacrifices made in Bible days?
- What kinds of offerings were used and what were they to be offered for?
- When did God decide these types of offerings were no longer necessary?
- What type of sacrifice does God want from us today?
- What was the ultimate sacrifice? Who made this sacrifice?
- What comforts in life would you have the most difficulty giving up as a sacrifice?
- Do you give your best to God and others in all tasks you do throughout the day?

Chapter 10
Idols / Holy Places
- Describe some idols in society today. (People and things)
- What are your idols?
- Define an idol in Christian terms.
- Is it wrong to place too much value in a "holy" item?
- What makes something holy?
- Name some important Christian symbols? How can they become idols?
- What does God say about idols?
- What are some signs when someone has gone to far in worshipping an idol?

Chapter 11
Beauty and the Beast
- Tell what you think makes someone beautiful in your eyes. What makes someone beautiful in God's eyes?
- Describe someone you know who is a "beast."
- Can someone be beautiful but ugly at the same time and vise versa?
- Describe inner beauty. Do you know someone like this?
- Do you think everyone has "good" inside of them?

- Do you think everyone has "bad" inside of them?
- Do you know of anyone who has had a drastic happening in his/her life that has caused them to turned them into a beauty or a beast? Explain.

Chapter 12
Yeah, I'm Cool
- For those who are willing, describe a time in your life when you were trying to be "cool." Did it work?
- Define coolness.
- What's the advantage of being "cool?"
- Do people stop trying to be "cool" when they are older?
- Describe the type of person God would think is "cool."
- Are people that are "cool" secure or insecure people?
- Why is it "cool" to be a Christian? Why would some think it's not "cool" to be a Christian?
- Think of people you think are cool.

Chapter 13
Gifts and Talents
- What gift or gifts do you have? (Everyone has one.)
- Did this gift develop over time or was it as if you were born with it?
- What types of gifts does God give? (1 Corinthians 12: 4-11)
- Tell of a gift or talent that someone else has that you admire.
- How can gifts/talents be used in the wrong ways?
- What does God want us to use our gifts for?
- Are you happy with your gift or do you wish you had another one?
- Do you feel like you have discovered all your gifts yet?

Chapter 14
Misunderstood
- What situations cause people to be misunderstood?
- What problems does misunderstanding cause?
- How can misunderstandings be prevented?
- Describe a time when you misunderstood someone. Also a time when you were misunderstood.
- What steps can you take to understand people who are different than you?
- Do you want to understand people who are different than you?

- How does being misunderstood make you feel?
- Does God ever misunderstand you? Do you ever misunderstand God?

Chapter 15
Keep Them Safe
- What are your biggest safety concerns for yourself?
- What are safety concerns for your family?
- What are some measures you take to keep your family safe?
- Do you think there is such a thing as guardian angels?
- Describe they types of things people do that make themselves and other people unsafe.
- When do you feel the most safe?
- When do you feel the least safe?
- Describe a time when you were in danger. What got you out of the situation? Did you pray?

Chapter 16
Graduation
- Describe the different types of graduations.
- What was your favorite graduation? Describe your feelings on that day.
- How do graduations change us or mark milestones in our lives?
- Is it ever too late to stop learning?
- How do your children's graduations affect you?
- What attributes best prepare our children for the world?
- What is the best Christian attribute to have as you go into the world?
- Why is it so hard when children leave home?

Chapter 17
You're Not Dotting Your I's and Crossing Your T's
- If God were to speak to you, what would He say? (One sentence.)
- What are your feelings in regards to speaking in tongues? Have you ever witnessed this before? Look up some verses about this: Isaiah 36:11, Acts 19: 1-7, 1 Corinthians 12:27-31
- Do you think your relationship with Christ is as good as it can be? If not, what can you do to improve it?
- If you're not "dotting your I's and crossing your T's," what do you think that means in your Christian life?

- What does Paul say about speaking in tongues and interpreting it? (1 Corinthians 14:26-28)
- How would your church react if someone were to start speaking in tongues during worship?
- What does it mean when someone says a church is Spirit-filled? Do you believe your church is Spirit-filled?

Chapter 18
One of These Days
- Have you ever met someone who made it apparent that they disliked you from the first acquaintance? Describe. Did you understand the reasoning for them disliking you?
- How do you react if someone is unloving or hateful toward you?
- How does God want us to react?
- How do you treat people you do not like? What are reasons to dislike someone?
- Can those who don't know you, recognize that you are a Christian by your actions?
- How did Jesus react to those who spit on, tortured, and killed Him?
- Can we even come close to Christ-likeness when it comes to situations like this?
- Have you ever become friends with someone after many years of a not so friendly relationship? If yes, Explain.

Chapter 19
Are You Ripe Yet?
- What years do you think are the most difficult for growing up?
- Can you think of a child that is mature for his/her age? An adult who is immature for their age? If so, why do you think they are this way?
- What do we need to do to be prepared for Christ's return? Do you feel you are ready?
- Is your first impression of people determined by what they look like or by their personality or mannerisms?
- What qualities would God look for in a "ripe" person?
- Do you think God allows us to become "ripe" in our own time?
- Read and compare what Jesus says about Judgment Day and then one of the descriptions of how the good and bad will be "harvested" in Matthew 25:31-46 and Revelation 14:14-20.

Chapter 20
Goodbyes
- Describe some of your most difficult goodbyes.
- What can you do to prevent any regrets if your last goodbye to a loved one is the final one due to a death?
- Do you think you will see all those who have gone before you again someday? If so, who would you look forward to seeing?
- Compare how those who witnessed Jesus' crucifixion and His ascension would have felt so differently in regard to saying goodbye in both instances.
- When could a goodbye be a good thing?
- Why do goodbyes to loved ones hurt so badly?
- Why are goodbyes more sentimental and more difficult the older we get?

Chapter 21
Does Meek Man Weak?
- What does meek mean?
- Can you think of some meek people? Describe them.
- Does God want everyone to be meek?
- If more people were meek, how would the world be different?
- Do you think of meekness as more of a woman's trait than a man's trait?
- Was Jesus meek?
- What differences would you have to make in your life to become a meek person?
- How does Jesus say the meek will be blessed in the Beatitudes? (Matthew 5:1-12)

Chapter 22
Please Be Patient
- Do you know anyone who God is "finished" with yet?
- Do you have patience with people when they aren't "finished" yet? (They mess up, make mistakes.)
- Is there a point when you draw the line after too many mistakes have been made?
- What is usually the result when a parent is very controlling of a child and doesn't allow for mistakes?
- Does God allow for us to make mistakes? How many?
- What usually are the results of mistakes made?
- Who are the people who love you unconditionally? Who do you love unconditionally?

Chapter 23
Simple Things
- What causes our lives to be so complicated and demanding?
- What could we do to make our lives less complicated (more simple)?
- Name some things you enjoy doing that require money to participate.
- Name some things you enjoy doing that are free.
- Which activities from the two questions above give you the best memories?
- What happens if we don't take time to enjoy life and relax in God's beautiful world?
- How do you think Jesus would react to the busy lifestyles, schedules and very technological society we have today if He were to return? What would He say to us?
- Are there "things" you are willing to give up in your life in an effort to make it more simple? What are they?

Chapter 24
Depression
- What are some causes of depression?
- For those who are willing, if you have ever been depressed can you describe the feelings you had during that time?
- Are you a weak person if you have suffered depression?
- Can people be possessed by demons that tell them they are bad and hopeless?
- What are ways of overcoming depression? Can you do it on your own?
- Do you think God wants us to seek medical treatment for depression or should we be able to pray ourselves out of it?
- If you are or have been depressed, do you think that leaves you with a stigma of "not being mentally right?"
- What are some ways you can help a depressed person?

Chapter 25
The Big Picture
- What is meant by the phrase "Watch what you wish for, you might get it?"
- Do you think God answers all prayers with a yes?
- Can you describe a time when you wanted something very badly (job, relationship, item, etc.) but you didn't get it?
- How do you react when you don't get what you want?
- Do you think God cares if we get rich while we are here on earth?

- Do you think God has a plan for us all?
- What could your purpose be?

Chapter 26
Handicapped
- Discuss types of handicaps. Which handicap would you consider the most difficult to have?
- How do you react when you see or meet a handicapped person? Do you feel uncomfortable? (Be honest.)
- What is your handicap? (We all have one.)
- Think of people who have overcome handicaps with a positive attitude. How do you think they were able to do this?
- How would you react if you suddenly lost your sight, ability to walk, or hearing?
- How have we done as a nation in addressing the needs of the handicapped? Is your church handicap friendly?
- What types of jobs can handicapped people do? Would you hire someone with a handicap?

Chapter 27
Angels Among Us
- Tell what you know about angels.
- Can you become an angel when you die?
- What types of jobs does God give to angels?
- Have you ever had an angel in your life?
- Have you ever been an angel to someone else?
- Although artist portray angels as beautiful and with wings, read some of the descriptions of angels from Acts and Revelation: Acts 13:6, Revelation 9:14-17, Revelation 10:1-2, Revelation 12: 7-9. Is this different than what you had imagined?
- Try to think of the Bible stories you know concerning angels. Try to find them and read them to the class.

Chapter 28
Wrestling with God
- What do you think is the significance of the story of Jacob wrestling with God? (Genesis 32: 24-29)

- Have you ever "wrestled" with God? Explain.
- Is it okay to wrestle with God? Does He want us to?
- Does God want us to accept His word without question or would He rather we experiment with it to make sense of it?
- What types of issues do most of us wrestle with throughout our lives?
- If we don't agree on an issue with a friend or loved one, how can we resolve it in a Christian way?
- If you could ask God one question, what would it be?

Chapter 29

Let Go, Let God

- Who is one person you trust completely?
- How does someone earn trust?
- Although it can take a lifetime to build up trust, how long does it take to lose it?
- What behaviors do people have that make us mistrust them?
- Why is it so hard to trust God?
- Is it hard to trust a God you cannot see or touch?
- What is the advantage of letting God control our lives? The disadvantage?

Chapter 30

Help! I've Got a Plank In My Eye And a Foot In My Mouth

- Why is it so easy to judge and criticize others?
- Why is it so hard to see our own imperfections/sins?

Matthew 7:1-3 tells us that we will be "judged according to the measure with which we judge others." If that's the case, will God judge you harshly or mildly?

- Have you ever refused to help someone because of the attitude, "They made their bed, now let them lie in it?"
- Does someone have to prove themselves to you in order for you to help them?
- Have you ever had to ask for help before? If so, how did it make you feel? Did you have to plead?
- Will God ever condemn you for helping someone that could have done more to help himself or herself? Will He condemn you for not helping someone who was truly in need?

Chapter 31
Amazing Grace
- Have you ever been forgiven for either a small or large infraction? If yes, how did it feel to be forgiven?
- Have you forgiven others for small or large infractions done to you? If yes, how did that make you feel?
- Have you ever not forgiven someone for an offense done to you? Have you ever not been forgiven for an offense you did to someone else? How does that make you feel?
- How many chances does God give us to mess up?
- Does the prisoner on death row deserve grace? If so, does this mean he shouldn't receive the consequences of his sin?
- Which is harder, to accept grace or to give it?
- When is grace "Amazing Grace?"
- If you feel comfortable doing so, sing *Amazing Grace* together.

Chapter 32
Pride
- What are some things you are proud of? (The good kind of pride.)
- Describe two types of pride. (Good vs. bad.)
- What negative attributes might you acquire from pride? Define pride.
- When you accomplish a great task, is it all because of your own efforts?
- How can pride ruin relationships?
- How can pride be good?
- Are you able to say you're sorry if you've hurt someone?
- How does God often teach those who are too proud a lesson?
- What does God think about too much knowledge? (1 Corinthians 8:1-3)

Chapter 33
Music
- What would the world be like without music?
- What types of music do you like?
- What types of music do you dislike?
- What things in nature can make a musical sound?
- From what book in the Bible are many songs in church hymnals taken from?
- Read some.

- What types of instruments were used to make music in Bible times?
- What types of instruments are used to make music in churches today?
- Is there one type of worship music that is better than another? (Traditional/contemporary)
- What types of lyrics do people relate to the best?
- If you feel so moved, sing the song "Pass it On" together as a group.

Chapter 34
Is There Hope?
- What gives you hope?
- What would happen if we didn't have hope?
- What can cause someone to lose hope?
- What kind of things do you hope for?
- How does God give us hope?
- Do you think the people that live in third-world war-torn countries have hope?
- How can we be active in helping people to not lose hope?
- Have you ever lost all hope? What was the result?

Chapter 35
Changed Hearts
- What events can change people's hearts for either good or bad?
- Why is it that some people simply need a tap on the shoulder to change for the good, while others need to hit rock bottom?
- What caused Saul's/Paul's change of heart? (Acts 9) How did he change?
- When someone accepts Christ for the first time, in what ways do they begin to change?
- When someone is changed in Christ, what is the main ingredient that is noticeable in his or her behavior?
- What is our role as Christians in helping to change people's hearts?
- How does Christ change hearts?

Chapter 36
Nakedness/Wisdom
- Explain what the connection is between nakedness and wisdom in this story.
- Do you think of nakedness as a bad thing?
- Is it wrong for women or men to wear clothing that exposes much of their bodies? Why or why not?
- Is there a difference between seeing a naked baby and a naked adult?

- At what point is nakedness inappropriate?
- What do you think people from Muslim countries think of how the women dress in the United States?
- Why is it so important to them that women cover their bodies to the extent of not even showing their faces? Is this a cultural law or a religious law?
- If you "accidentally" went to a nudist colony :) how would it make you feel?

Chapter 37
Birth
- Can you think of any other pain that you may experience that results in something as beautiful as a child?
- God told Eve that after she ate the fruit from "The Tree of Knowledge of Good & Evil" that now she would have great pain during childbirth. Can you imagine what it would be like if we had no pain during childbirth? Would people have more babies?
- Do you think God is okay with us controlling how many children we have with birth control?
- If you have children, what were your thoughts when you saw that beautiful gift from God for the first time?
- Does it give you comfort knowing Jesus went through the same birthing process as we did?
- Do you believe God had a plan for you at conception?
- If someone is unable to conceive, what other options do they have to become parents?

Chapter 38
Weeds/Farming
- After Adam and Eve eat the fruit, Eve is punished with pain at childbirth. How does God punish Adam? (Genesis 3:17-19)
- Do weeds have a purpose?
- In what ways has farming changed since Bible days?
- Would you want to be a farmer? Why or why not?
- How will we get our food if farming becomes a thing of the past one day?
- What tasks or hobbies do you do that give you satisfaction from the work of your hands?
- Describe the process involved in getting food from the farm to your table? (All the people and processes involved)

Chapter 39

If You're Happy (Or Sad) and You Know it Clasp Your Hands

- When do you pray?
- Are you more likely to pray in desperation or thankfulness?
- Is God ever too busy to hear your prayers?
- Does your bedtime ritual with your children include prayer? Tell how children's prayers are special.
- Do you think God favors heartfelt prayers over rote prayers?
- Do you sometimes have a hard time concentrating when you pray?
- Do you have a private place to go to when you pray? Describe
- What do you think God thinks of long drawn out prayers spoken in public?

Chapter 40

Who Needs God?

- Do you know families that have never gone to church?
- Do you think religion would be scary or strange to someone who has never experienced it?
- What do you think of Joseph Girzone's story of Christ returning to Heaven?
- What is your fear for those who are close to you that don't know God?
- Is there anyway we can convince someone that they need God?
- Why would God be scary to someone who doesn't know Him?
- When do you need God the most?
- When do you think you need Him least?

Chapter 41

This Is Love?

- If you are brave, tell about your first love?
- How does love for a spouse change over the years?
- What's the most dramatic thing you have ever done for love?
- What are the different ways people show love?
- What can you do to keep love alive?
- Do you think God has a soul mate picked out for each of us?
- What is the sweetest act someone has done for you out of love?
- Describe some things you do to show love to your family on a daily basis.

Chapter 42

Chaos Happens

- Describe a time when you've had chaos in your life?
- How did you survive?
- Did anything positive come from the experience?
- What was the most extreme action God has taken when chaos got out of control? Explain.
- Are we responsible for the chaos we have in our lives?
- When we read the newspaper and watch the news, at times it seems like chaos is getting out of control again. What is the cause of so much chaos in society today?
- Compare Satan's role in chaos verses God's role.
- What are some actions we can take to prevent chaos in our lives?

Chapter 43

Thirst/Desire

- Describe something you are passionate about?
- In what ways are you driven by this passion?
- Have you ever had the same passion toward Christ?
- Do you think knowing God's word is important? Why or why not?
- Have you ever become complacent in your relationship with Christ?
- Compare the difference in attitude between someone new to Christ and someone who has gone to church all their life?
- Compare your relationship between Christ and your spouse? In what ways are they different and the same?

Chapter 44

Prejudice

- List all the prejudices you can think of in the world.
- When did prejudice begin?
- What were some prejudices in Bible times?
- What are some prejudices of today?
- What measures does the government take to control prejudice? Do they work?
- Where does prejudice begin?
- Does God favor any race, religion, sex, etc. over another?

- If everyone was exactly the same would there still be prejudice?
- How can we get rid of prejudice? Is it possible?

Chapter 45

A Dogs Life/ Lessons Learned

- What is the benefit of having pets?
- What is it about a pet that makes us love them so much?
- What characteristics do pets have that can resemble human behaviors?
- In what ways are some pet behaviors better than human behaviors? In what ways worse?
- How does it affect you when you see a pet mistreated?
- What lessons can we learn from animal behaviors?
- Do you think God intended for us to make animals the pets we have made them today?
- Can pets take on their owner's personalities?

Chapter 46

Real Religion

- Use the word "religious" in several sentences. Does it project a positive or negative meaning?
- What's the difference between being religious and being a Christian?
- What are some bad things "religious" people have done in history and continue to do today?
- What is the type of religion that God wants?
- How do you think God feels toward the "religious" who act in unloving ways as opposed to those who are unbelievers who act in unloving ways?
- Which do you think is more important to God, our knowledge of the Bible or our acts and deeds?
- In what ways has man messed up what God has planned for His church?

Chapter 47

Warm Fuzzies

- What makes you feel better when you are down?
- What acts of kindness can we do to help pick up others when they are down?
- What basic human desire do we all long for?
- What happens when we don't feel loved and accepted?
- What happens when we do feel loved and accepted?

- What types of "warm fuzzies" does God give us?
- How can we give God "warm fuzzies?"
- Write a "warm fuzzy" for each person in your class. Each person should end up with the number of "warm fuzzies" as there are people in your class. Take these home and read only one day.

Chapter 48

Does God Change?

- Compare the differences and similarities of the God of the Old Testament and the God of the New Testament?
- Think of all the instances you can where God has changed His mind in the Bible? Describe. Did someone convince Him?
- What are some of the methods God has tried to keep His people from straying?
- What was the most dramatic thing God has done to get our attention as to how we should act?
- What types of disciplines do we use as parents to keep our children on track?
- Does any one type of discipline work for all children?
- Compare the ways God has disciplined us as compared to how we discipline our children.

Chapter 49

Know You By Name

- How does it make you feel when someone doesn't remember your name or spells it incorrectly?
- How does it make you feel when you can't remember someone's name or spell it incorrectly?
- What is the significance of a name?
- Our culture usually changes the woman's last name and takes on the husband's. What are the advantages and disadvantages of this practice?
- Discuss how other countries customs on how husband and wife names are passed down or change according to marriage.
- What is the significance of nicknames?
- What are some of the names for God?
- Does God know you by name? What other names might He give you?

Chapter 50
Suffering
- Discuss any suffering you may have experienced or witnessed.
- Can anything good come out of suffering?
- Have you ever prayed for God to take someone rather than let them continue suffering? If so, was this a hard prayer to pray?
- Does God want us to suffer?
- What suffering does God know is worse than any other?
- Why do you think God allowed Jesus to suffer the terrible death He did?
- You hear how people torture other people, especially during war. Can you in any way fathom how one human being is able to do this to another?
- After someone survives great suffering in what ways are they likely to change?

Chapter 51
What the World Needs Now
- What is the result if a parent shows favoritism toward one child over another?
- What is the result when a child is denied love especially during the first two years?
- Define love.
- Are there people in your life who are hard to love?
- Is it possible to love all people all of the time?
- When you see through the eyes of love how do you see: the grouchy elderly neighbor, your spouse when they come home from work in a bad mood, the neighborhood child that picked on your child, a friend that disagrees with you, the teenager dressed in all black with piercings all over his body?
- Close by reading 1 Corinthians 13:4-7 together. Ask for God's help to show love to everyone you meet today.

Chapter 52
Rules, Rules, Rules
- Each person recall one of the Ten Commandments until you've listed them all. (Without looking)
- Which commandments are the hardest to keep?
- Which commandments are easy to keep?
- Can you describe some irrational rules or laws that you've encountered?
- Can you think of some laws we have that aren't strict enough?

- What happens when you have many laws and rules but no allowance for love and compassion?
- What is the greatest commandment of all?
- What do you do when there is a conflict between God's law and man's law? Name some.

Chapter 53
Servanthood
- Can you think of someone who performs a servant role? If yes, do they do this grudgingly or with grace?
- What types of servant roles do you perform? Do you do these gracefully or grudgingly?
- Why was Jesus' servanthood model so hard for the disciples and everyone else to understand?
- There have been many people who have done good things for people. Why does Mother Teresa stand out amongst these?
- What can you do when you hear of or experience injustice or suffering?
- As a nation, do you think the United States does a good job in reaching out to those in need? Name some organizations that help many people.
- Do you prefer to be the servant or the person being served? (Be honest)

Chapter 54
Love Hurts
- Most of us have experienced lost love. Can you think of any other emotional pain that hurts as badly?
- Another pain that hurts deeply is for a parent to witness their child hurt as a result of rejection or physically by another child. What's the best way for parents to help their children through these situations?
- When you are hurting emotionally or physically, what gives you comfort?
- Has anyone ever had feelings for you that you didn't share in return or vice versa? How do you handle these situations?
- How do you think God feels when so many people reject Him daily?
- Another pain caused by love is the death of a loved one. How can we get through difficult times such as these?
- Does God truly understand our pain? Explain.

Chapter 55

Seasons of Life

- What "season" of life do you think you are in now? (In order: spring, summer, fall, winter.)
- As you look back, which season has been your favorite so far? Which was your least favorite?
- What are some of your best memories from your childhood years?
- What are some of you worst memories from your teenage years?
- Do you have any fears about your next season in life?
- How have your priorities changed from one season to the next?
- The *Footprints* poem describes how God has walked along side of us and has carried us at times during our lives. Can you give examples of both during your life?

Chapter 56

Hindsight

- What are some nudges you may get that may be encouraging you to make a change in your life?
- Do you fight change or go along with the flow?
- Think of some major decisions you have made that changed your life? Explain.
- Can you think of someone in your life's path that has had a "hardened" heart that has caused you to make a change? If yes, do you think God may have played a part in that situation?
- Have you ever faced a circumstance that has hurt you so badly that you felt you couldn't go on with life? If so, how do you see that situation now with more mature eyes?
- Are there any decisions you have made in life that you wish you could change?
- What are some of the best decisions you have made?
- Have you made the decision to have Christ as a part of your life?

Chapter 57

Creation

- What is the last thing you created? Explain what steps were involved in the process?
- What is your favorite thing that you have created?
- Do you have or have you had a job that brings you great satisfaction?

- Are you more likely to read directions when putting something together or do you try to do it on your own and look at the directions as a last resort?
- Name some of the coolest things that you think God has created.
- What is your responsibility for God's creation?
- Have you ever given someone something that was valuable to you and then they didn't take care of it? How did that make you feel?
- Is there anything that man has created that compares to what God has created?

Chapter 58
Stagnation
- If you are a longtime Christian, do you think you have become stagnant or are you still fresh in your Christian walk?
- Describe how a Christian who has become stagnant would act.
- How can we keep our Christian life fresh?
- Why is it so easy to forget about those in need when we are so comfortable?
- Why is it easier to lead the same, easy, routine life rather than to make some changes and reach out to others?
- What are some ways Satan encourages us to become stagnant?
- Find some passages that talk about Christ's living water. Read them out loud and discuss them. (John 4: 4-14, John 7: 38-39, Revelation 21: 6-8)

Chapter 59
Like A Child
- What does Jesus mean when He says "Anyone who will not receive the Kingdom of God like a little child will never enter it?"
- What does Jesus mean when He says "I praise you Father because you have hidden these things from the wise and learned and revealed them to little children?"
- Discuss some actions or things children have said in their innocence that has made you laugh.
- What attributes do children lose as they lose their innocence?
- What do you find amazing about babies, children, and teenagers?
- Can you think of a game you played as a child that you like to play again?
- Do you think all the high technology games created for children today has hampered their creativity?

Chapter 60
Contentment
- Name some areas in your life that you are very content with.
- Name some areas in your life that you would like to change.
- Name areas you have changed in your life out of discontentment. Did these turn out to be good changes?
- Are you ever satisfied with what you have or is there always something else you want?
- What causes discontentment?
- What causes contentment?
- Can people be content when they have very few comforts (material things) in life?
- Why is it that people that have many material things are sometimes still not content?

Chapter 61
The Church
- Did you go to church as a child? Do you still attend the same church?
- What makes a church, the building or the people? Explain.
- What are the benefits of belonging to a church?
- Why do people feel so strongly about their church and the decisions made concerning it?
- How should a church deal with a family that acts like they own the church?
- What are some ways to get people within the church more involved rather than just coming for an hour on Sunday?
- Many churches are concerned about the number of members they have. What are some ways churches try to attract new members? In what ways would God's numbers be different that man's numbers in regards to membership in a church?
- What happens if a church never changes and never waivers from the same old same old?

Chapter 62
The Tower of Babel
- Have you ever been in a group of people who don't speak the same language as you do? If so, how did this make you feel?

- Can you speak another language? If so, how long did it take you to learn the different language? How long does it take a child to learn to talk?
- If you are helping someone with little education, a low paying job, owes a lot of bills, doesn't speak English well, and has medical problems, and has no food, what is the best way you can help them?
- In what ways are people all over the world the same? What do we all desire?
- What happens when any group of people become proud and arrogant?
- What language does God speak?
- Is lack of communication a language problem or a listening problem?
- How can people in the United States make those who come here from other countries feel welcomed without losing our own culture and values?

Chapter 63
I Hope You Dance
- Describe how you express joy.
- In what ways can dancing either alone or with a group, compare to our Christian faith?
- In dancing, one person leads and the other follows. Are you the leader or the follower both in dancing and in life? Could you switch roles if it were necessary?
- When groups of people don't work together well and don't agree on major issues, what is the result?
- In Lee Ann Womack's song "I Hope You Dance," a verse goes " I hope you still feel small when you stand beside the ocean." What do you think she means by this?
- In Womack's song she is talking to her child saying "I hope you dance." What does dancing mean in this instance?
- If dancing is one expression of joy, what do you think would make God dance?
- Are you willing to let God lead you in the dance of life?

Chapter 64
Peace vs. War
- If you are a "good Christian" are you supposed to be opposed to war?
- What is true peace?
- What should our response to injustice and oppression be? A. I'm glad it's not me. B. Let them figure it out themselves. C. Let's stand beside and defend them to help them straighten this out. D. Let's bomb and kill all the oppressors to put an end to this.

- What makes our country so great?
- What are some mistakes we've made as a nation?
- Could all countries be as successful as the U.S. if they had freedom, equality and justice like us?
- What causes the downfall of many countries?
- Say a pray for the many soldiers in harms way. What greater love is there than one that will lay down his life for his brother?

Chapter 65

Have You Heard?

- Would you be willing to leave your job and family to follow someone you just met as the disciple did?
- If the original twelve disciple were able to spread Christianity throughout the world, how much more are million of Christians today able to accomplish?
- Could you stand strong enough in your faith to be persecuted for it?
- Why are there still so many that don't know Christ today?
- How is it easy to get a false sense of security thinking that we don't need Christ?
- Do you feel uncomfortable talking to others about Christ? What are the consequences of doing so at work, at a party, when with a group of friends?
- Why has society gotten a "Godphobia" attitude? (Ex. Happy Holiday now replaces Merry Christmas, Christmas now to be called winter break or Christmas tree to be called a holiday tree, no praying in public places, no Ten Commandments in public places, Easter egg roll now spring egg roll)
- How do you think God feels about situations such as those mentioned above? Do you think our founding fathers meant for separation of church and state to go so far?

Chapter 66

Guilt

- Describe how guilt makes you feel?
- Why do many people try to blame their sin on someone else? What name did they give this in the Bible?
- What happens if you never accept the consequences of your sin?
- Is guilt good or bad? Explain how it can be good. Explain how it can be bad.
- What would happen if people didn't feel guilty for wrongs they've committed? Is it possible to not feel guilt?

- Do you feel better once you've confessed to a wrong you've done?
- What happens when you can't get rid of guilt?
- Why do you think God gave us guilt as an emotion? What part of the Trinity moves us to feel guilt? (Father, Son, or Holy Spirit.)
- Can God forgive all sins?

Chapter 67
Chasing God
- Do you think God is hard to find? Why or why not?
- Why is the game of Hide and Seek so intriguing to all ages?
- How do we "find" God?
- Why does it feel like we can't "feel" God at times?
- According to Rick Warren in "The Purpose Driven Life" what does God want us to do when we can't feel Him?
- Since God is such an abstract for many people, how can we prove that He is real?
- When you do find God, what do you do with Him?

Chapter 68
No Fear
- What are some of your fears?
- What does the Bible tell us the only thing we should fear is? (Matthew 10:29)
- Why are some people able to be bold and courageous during times of fear? Give some examples from Bible times and today.
- In general, is fear a good emotion to have? What happens if we have too much fear or not enough fear?
- When God calls people to a task, do they always say yes? What are some examples of what He might do if they say no?
- What are some reasons why we don't want to do God's work?
- Why does Satan like it when we are fearful?
- Have you had any "giants" in your life lately? Explain.

Chapter 69
Father, Son, Holy Spirit
- In your own words describe the Trinity.
- If any one of the three were missing, what would be the result?

- Do you think of different parts of the Trinity when you are praying or are they all one to you?
- Which part of the Trinity gives us power and strength in times of need?
- Which part of the Trinity shows us how to love and care for others?
- Which part of the Trinity provides many good things for us and convicts us when we do wrong?
- Which part of the Trinity forgives us when we do wrong?
- What is meant when it is said that someone is "full of the Spirit?"
- Once you are full of the Spirit is it there to stay or does it come and go according to your openness to it?

Chapter 70
Temptation
- Name some temptations you are willing to talk about.
- Describe the stages from temptation to sin shown in James 1: 13-15.
- Why do you think it was important for Jesus to be tempted in the desert for forty days before He begins His ministry? (Matthew 4: 1-11)
- What significance does this have in regard to the temptations we face each day?
- How did Jesus resist temptation? How can we resist temptation?
- Do you think God holds those who don't know His word as responsible for sin as those who do know His word?
- List some of Satan's tricks in tempting us.
- Is there any temptation we can't withstand? (Read 1 Corinthians 10:13 again.) Discuss.

Chapter 71
No Crib for a Bed
- What was the significance of Jesus being born in a barn?
- Does Christmas have special meaning to you or has it become so commercialized and routine that it has turned into an endless list of tasks that need to be accomplished?
- What can we do to put real meaning back into Christmas?
- How do you think Mary & Joseph felt about their baby being born in a barn?
- How would the lessons that Jesus' taught while here on earth have had different meaning if He had been born in royal circumstances as people of that day expected He would be?

- Tell about your most meaningful Christmas. Your least meaningful.
- The years between Jesus' birth and when he began His ministry are not recorded in the Bible, with the exception of Him talking with the teachers at the synagogue when he was twelve. What do you think those years of being the child Jesus and son of a carpenter would have been like?

Chapter 72

Anger/Cursing

- Do you curse on occasion? Be honest.
- Is talking to someone in a mean, demeaning way as bad as cursing?
- Recall some Bible stories when God has gotten angry. What did He do with His anger?
- Describe the one instance that we are aware of that Jesus got angry. What made Him angry? What did He do that indicates He was pretty angry?
- Is being angry a sin?
- Is what we do with anger what makes it a sin?
- What are some ways you deal with anger?
- Can anger be used for a good purpose?
- Do you know of anyone who never gets angry? Is it possible to never get angry?

Chapter 73

You Are Blessed

- Tell ways in which you are blessed.
- When you bless other people, what are you implying?
- What does the phrase "Blessed are the poor in spirit" mean?
- In the beatitudes Jesus wished nine different types of blessings on people. What are the results of those blessings? (Matthew 5: 1-10)
- Why do many people still feel a void after they have acquired many things?
- According to Billy Graham, what are the characteristics of the soul?
- What are the characteristics of each of these types of people? The meek, merciful, those who hunger and thirst for righteousness.

Chapter 74

Patches

- What are your feelings on the proper appearance for church?
- Does wearing nice clothes make you closer to God? Does it show respect to God?

- What makes you beautiful according to 1 Peter 3:3-4?
- What do you think could have been the possibilities for Patches had he grown up in a loving, Christian environment?
- What attitude should every teacher of the word have toward anyone who comes to him/her to learn about God?
- Can any one person cause a life changing effect on another person by either positive or negative actions?
- Does your church consist mostly of high or middle class persons? Are lower class families welcomed in your church?
- What can your church do to be more welcoming to lower income families to its membership?

Chapter 75

The Light of the World

- Can you explain why Jesus is referred to as "The Light of the World" in many instances in the Bible?
- Could you imagine if we always had either day or night twenty-four hours a day without a change? Which would be worse?
- If your light is "shining" how do you act? If you hide it under a "bushel basket" what are you behaviors?
- Have you ever been in total darkness for any length of time? How did it affect you? How did it feel when you got the first glimpse of light?
- How would we be different if our sins were exposed for the world to see them twenty-four hours a day? Would our behaviors change?
- List some of the beautiful things we have in the world/universe that are made by or made visible due to light?
- Why do many crimes take place at night?
- Tell the importance of night and day?

Chapter 76

Extravagance

- Do you like to have a little (or maybe a lot) of extravagance in your life? Describe ways you like to treat yourself.
- What is the danger of being rich?
- Are rich people happier than poor people?
- What are some advantages of not being wealthy?

- If you could come up with a plan to lift the poor up and out of their poverty without giving handouts but a hand up, how would you do it?
- See if you class could come up with a plan as a group. Give suggestions to your mission team.
- If you were extremely rich and anything you wanted was yours, how would you spend your money? At what point do you not need any more "things?"
- Are the poor responsible for their situation? What are some causes of poverty?

Chapter 77
He Will Provide
- What are some ways God has provided for you?
- In what ways has your life improved over the years?
- Do you take credit for your successes or are you aware that God may have played a role in where you are today?
- What are the lessons learned when you start your adult life out with little money and then work your way up the social ladder?
- What are the disadvantages of having had everything handed to you with very little effort on your part?
- What are the advantages waiting to start your married life only after you've obtained a good paying job and financial security? Does having little money at the beginning of a marriage have any advantages?
- Which situation from above is better to raise a child in?
- If you totally lost everything, could you trust God to provide for you?

Chapter 78
Sin and Forgiveness
- What does it mean in Romans 5: 20-21 when it says that "The law came to make sin worse?"
- What were the sins of Sodom? (Ezekiel 16: 49-50)
- When you sin, how does it make you feel?
- Do you try to rationalize your sin? Explain.
- Do you know anyone that is without sin or even close to it?
- What happens to you when you are not able to forgive?
- When someone is forgiven, does that mean that they don't need to suffer the consequences of their sin?
- Describe how it feels to be forgiven?

Chapter 79

I Love You This Much

- Is anyone ever truly alone in this world?
- Explain in your own words what you think the phrase "Ask, and God will give to you. Search, and you will find. Knock, and the door will open for you" mean?
- When parents that should love us reject us, is there hope for a normal life?
- How can a parent become so hard hearted?
- What was the full extent of God's love for us?
- Are we as capable of loving as much as God?
- Have you ever felt God's arms wrapped around you? If not, sit by yourself, open your heart to Him, and bask in His embrace right now. It will be the best hug of your life! (Do this at home if you are in class.)
- Tell how you can share God's love today, tomorrow, and every day the rest of your life?

Footnotes

Chapter 8

[1] Mark Water, *World Religions Made Simple,* pg, 5. (AMG Publishers, Chatanooga, Tenn., 2002) Used by permission.

[2] Water, *Origin of Islam,* pg. 37

[3] Water, pg. 35

Chapter 9

[4] *The Student Bible,* New International Version, *The Reason for* Sacrifice, pg. 111.

[5] Ibid

Chapter 13

[6] Merit Student Encyclopedia, Crowell-Collier Educational Corp., (1967,1968).

[7] Rick Warren, *The Purpose Driven Life,* (Zondervan, 2002) pg. 32.

Chapter 28

[8] Warren, pg. 95

Chapter 35

[9] Information pamphlet given at the Ryman Theatre.

Chapter 39

[10] Warren, pg. 87

Chapter 40

[11] Joseph Girzone, *The Shepherd,* (Collier Books, 1992) pg. 73.

[12] Karen Kingsbury, *Gideon's Gift,* (Warner Books, 2002).

Chapter 45
[13] *Life Lessons Learned from Dogs* Spring 2002 High School Materials, (Standard Publishing, 2002) Used by permission.

Chapter 46
[14] Dale Fife, *The Secret Place,* (Whitaker House Publishing, 2001), pg. 173

Chapter 53
[15] Jose Luis Gonzalez-Balado, *Mother Teresa, In my Own Words,* (Gramercy Books, 1997), Introduction
[16] Gonzalez-Balado, pg. 99

Chapter 65
[17]Corrie Ten Boom, *Each New Day,* (Fleming H. Revell, 1977) pg. 83

Chapter 67
[18]Warren, pg. 109
[19] Ibid

Chapter 73
[20]Billy Graham, *The Secret of Happiness,* (W. Publishing Group), pg. 18
[21]Graham, pg. 46
[22] Graham pg. 83

Chapter 75
[23]Fife, pg. 33
[24]Fife, pg. 133

Dictionary references come from *New Webster's Expanded Dictionary,* (Paradise Press, Inc., 2002 Edition)